PRAISE FOR

SECRETS of the LADIES MISSION SOCIETY

"Laurie Dick's poignant and very human story revealed in *Secrets of the Ladies Mission Society* is worth that special celebration that comes only with fine characters, a teasing, almost transparent story, and delicate, yet exuberant writing. Anyone who has ever been exposed to a small community will find themselves home again—in spirit, if not in flashes of good and pleasing memory. This is the kind of happy experience that readers cherish."

—TERRY KAY, BESTSELLING AUTHOR OF TO DANCE WITH THE WHITE DOG AND THE BOOK OF MARIE

"The deadliest and most enthralling secrets are the ones concealed (grinning and silent!) behind soft-spoken Southern mannerisms and polite smiles. This is a fine story about such secrets. I greatly recommend it."

—AUGUSTA TROBAUGH, AUTHOR OF SOPHIE AND THE RISING SUN AND THE TEA-OLIVE BIRD WATCHING SOCIETY

"Laurie Rothrock Dick's wonderful first novel, *Secrets of the Ladies Mission Society*, sheds a soft but penetrating light not only on individual lives but on the inner workings of a culture. At times ironic and hysterically funny, at others brutal and sere, she throws off the stereotype of our conventional wisdom concerning the South and replaces this with the complexity of the heart-felt truth. I loved this book. You will too."

—DEBORAH JOHNSON, AUTHOR OF THE SECRET OF MAGIC AND THE AIR BETWEEN US

D1506360

SECRETS of the
LADIES MISSION SOCIETY

SECRETS of the LADIES MISSION SOCIETY

A Novel

LAURIE ROTHROCK DICK

TURNER

Turner Publishing Company
424 Church Street • Suite 2240 • Nashville, Tennessee 37219
445 Park Avenue • 9th Floor • New York, New York 10022

www.turnerpublishing.com

Secrets of the Ladies Mission Society, A Novel

Cover image: azur13/Bigstock.com
Cover design: Nellys Liang
Book design: Kym Whitley

Library of Congress Cataloging-in-Publication Data

Dick, Laurie Rothrock.
  Secrets of the Ladies Mission Society : a novel / Laurie Rothrock Dick.
     pages cm
  ISBN 978-1-63026-496-3 (pbk. : alk. paper)
  1. Women--Fiction. I. Title.
  PS3604.I2826S43 2015
  813'.6--dc23
                                    2015000333

ISBN: 978-1-6302-6496-3 (paperback), 978-1-6816-2046-6 (hardback)

Printed in the United States of America
14 15 16 17 18 19 0 9 8 7 6 5 4 3 2 1

For my wonderful family, husband Bill, and children, David and Dana.
A special thanks to my agent, Harvey Klinger, whose belief gave added courage.

SECRETS of the
LADIES MISSION SOCIETY

{ONE}

SHE AWOKE TO THE TOUCH OF A SLIGHT breeze, like a hand caressing her cheek. White sheers at the open window quivered with luminosity. The garden—he would be out in the garden in the early morning light. She lifted her head slightly to look beyond the window. Yes, there he was, spade in hand, wearing his favorite hat, weathered and stained. The aroma of the rich loam of the earth carried on the fresh morning air. He leaned lovingly over the land. She could see his eyes—nearly as dark as the rich brown dirt over which he bent—and feel the touch of his hand, gently stroking, inserting the seed. And then, as if he could sense she was watching, he sat back on his heels and looked her way. His smile, that wonderful smile, enveloped her, lifting her skyward into the sun-flooded sky.

"Come away, Adie," his smile said. "It's spring. Join me in the garden. Don't you see the pecan trees budding?"

It was an old theme, one they often used for time to turn the earth. It came from her mother who used to tell her that spring hadn't really come 'til the pecan trees bud. An indigo bunting sat on one of the pecan tree limbs just outside her window, chirping *sweet sweet, cheer-cheer.*

"Oh, Lester," she whispered, stretching a hand toward the window.

"Well now, we are awake and Eula has fixed you a good breakfast."

"No." Adie's voice broke as Eula, in an apron that seemed too small for her ample frame, waddled into the room, carrying a tray. "No, go away," she said, her voice stronger, as she looked up into Eula's broad copper-colored face, baring the elongated, puffy scar on her left cheek.

But it was no good; the garden and its verdant greenery disappeared, taking Lester with it. In its place was the wasted brown earth, barren and seedless. She looked down at the hand that had reached out to Lester. The flesh was mottled and stretched like a thin film over its bones.

"Miss Adie, don't you go getting the snuffles on me." Eula set the tray on a bedside table and reached for a washcloth in the basin.

"Don't," she pleaded as Eula gently wiped her face. "Please don't."

"Now, Miss Adie, this be your favorite time of year. While you was sleeping, I opened the window for you to see the pecans putting out. And listen to that bird chirping its heart out . . . how pretty, blue with black-streaked wings."

"An indigo bunting," she informed.

"Yes, that's right." Eula smiled, surprised as ever at what Adie could remember in her confused state. "Jest couldn't bring it to mind. Now, come on, Miss Adie," she pleaded. "You has to keep up your strength. Look what I gone to cook for you."

She turned an expressionless face toward the maid. "Take it away. I don't want any."

"Now, Miss Adie, you got to eat. Get your strength going.

Doc wouldn't want you going on so."

"No," she agreed, "he would not. "He would want to be right here with me and you, or out there." She turned her face toward the window again. "Working the land he loved."

"Heaven got plenty of garden. God got him spading away. He so deserving . . ." Eula turned her back and blinked away the tears she felt threatening to overflow as she poured Miss Adie's tea. She cleared her throat. "Look at this, your favorite. Eggs scrambled just right with bits of ham and fresh baked bread with orange marmalade."

"You eat it." She shooed her hand toward the table and Eula's offer and snatched at the edges of the quilted coverlet she made years ago as a present for Doc, pulling it up until it nearly covered her face.

"Now, Miss Adie . . ."

"Don't Miss Adie me," she said with a sharpness in her voice Eula had never heard.

The shock of it made Eula's face fall toward her chest as if someone slapped her and she was avoiding a second blow. It brought too clearly to Eula's mind the violence of her past.

The gesture brought remorse to Miss Adie's voice. "Eula, please forgive . . . don't know what got into me."

"Oh, it be all right. Grief is a stranger to our real self. It make folk do all kind of thing they never do. I done already forgot it. Now, jest to make sure you don't mean a thing by it, please take one bite or two of this breakfast I worked so hard over."

"All right then," she agreed, struggling to lift herself, "but only a teensy bit."

Eula helped her by bolstering the pillows behind Miss Adie's birdlike frame. She pulled a chair close to the bedside and lifted a fork toward her thin lips. "Now, ain't that fine?"

she asked, watching Miss Adie's bony neck take a swallow. It was a neck so thin, she could almost see the food making its way down her throat.

Eula lifted another forkful toward her mouth, but Miss Adie waved her hand in the air toward the bedside table and Eula's breakfast offer. "No more," she said, sliding down underneath the quilt.

"But, you got to keep up your strength."

"Why?"

Seeking a reply, Eula looked toward the window and the silhouette of the pecan trees in bud. Spring was popping out while Miss Adie wasted away with her ailments and missing Doc.

Lawd, she prayed silently, *help me. All her life been given to nursing the needs of others; she a town fixture even if the town ladies think they better. She and Doc birthed most and their children, tended to their sicknesses, listened to their problems. She be a living history.*

A shaft of sunlight flooding through the windows lay across the bookcases shoved against the far wall. Doc and Miss Adie sure did read a lot, she thought, and not jest their daily devotionals. Eula's heart leapt. Why, there was the answer. A history of the town; no one knew it more better than Miss Adie. Thank you, Lawd, she breathed, a plan plumping itself up like one of the crusts on her deep-dish pies.

"A book," she said, stroking the parched skin of Miss Adie's arm. "That's why."

"Book? What book?" Miss Adie frowned up into Eula's face.

"Yours. About the town and . . ." she added, suddenly inspired, "the ladies."

"The ladies?" Miss Adie repeated. A wrinkle rippled across the furrows in her forehead. "Watched them grow, marry, have children, and all the other," she added, mysteriously.

"The other?" Eula asked, keeping the conversation going as she lifted another forkful of food toward Miss Adie's lips.

Miss Adie looked toward the dresser mirror facing her bed as if she alone could see there a history unfolding across the years. "A long time," she said, Eula's question forgotten.

"No one knows this town's history better than you. Put it all down on paper."

"But . . ."

"You write it down." Eula ignored her frown and any further protests. "I do the rest—something for the town and for the ladies."

Adie picked at a loose thread on the patchwork quilt covering her. In the colorful circles that she had sewn so long ago, she could see their faces, their histories and those of the town.

"A history?" she repeated, looking up at Eula.

"No one knows it better."

"Yes," she said. "No one. But," Miss Adie hesitated, looking up at Eula with a question in her eyes, "the ladies? Eula, it seems I haven't seen them in a long time. Not, since Doc . . ."

"No, you haven't," Eula agreed, nodding her head. "But," she said as if in apology to mollify Miss Adie, "their lives so busy."

Not that busy, Eula thought, more selfish than anything. Miss Adie watched them come and go over the years with their various distresses. A necessity is what Miss Adie was to them, and now that their beloved Doc was gone, she receded into their backgrounds like a chipped and broken piece of crockery shoved to the back of a forgotten cabinet.

"Always wanted to write a book," Miss Adie said, surprising Eula.

"Then you should." Hiding her excitement, Eula busied

herself, plumping up Miss Adie's pillow. "If it's a book you longed to write then I thinks there's no better time," she said, not adding that time was wasting away just like her birdlike body.

"You really think so?" Miss Adie turned her head toward Eula gathering up her breakfast tray.

"Yes'mum, I do."

"A book—a book for the ladies—but I haven't seen most of them . . . a long time," she repeated.

"You will," Eula said, the hint of a chuckle in her voice as she picked up the breakfast tray off the bedside table. "Yes," she mumbled, walking down the hallway toward the kitchen, a smile on her lips. "They be beating a path to your door, landing on the doorstep like crows in a cornfield."

She put the dishes in the sink and watched the hot suds rising. "I has flat out stumbled into a hornet's nest," she chastised herself. How was she going to manage Miss Adie's scribbling, much less get it into a book? There was a renewed vigor in Miss Adie's voice and some added color to her pasty complexion. But what did she mean by "the other?"

"Surely," Eula said, scrubbing a pot, "Miss Adie don't suspect about my mama and my daddy. We done worked too hard for her to find out, now, Lawd."

{TWO}

ELOISE PARSONS COMPLETED THE SLIDE SHOW on the Korean orphans with her plea for clothing to be dropped off at The Baptist Church. Wynene Chalmers, the pastor's wife, suppressed a long-held yawn. Teatime at the Ladies Mission Society, a social and philanthropic organization whose membership was composed of Simpsonville's elite families, signaled the ending of another meeting, one of her required appearances as wife of their minister. Wynene helped Eloise pack away the screen and projector as the rest of the ladies bustled around the refreshment table like a bunch of cackling chickens headed for their seed.

Verabelle Studstill's "not natural" muttering caught her attention as did rapt expressions on the rest of the ladies' faces as they took their plates, sinking their bodies into love seats and chairs that looked as overstuffed as most of the women in the room.

"Simply not natural," Verabelle continued, biting into an egg salad sandwich and wiping her lips discreetly with a linen napkin, "her being so secretive all these years, looking at you with those eyes like she could read your mind. She thinks she's better than us just because she made a lucky marriage. Her family is still mill folk. My grandmother told me," she said, dropping a heaping spoonful of sugar into her teacup and stirring, "that Miss Adie was sort of plain, bookish ... shy. What the good doctor saw in her nobody knew. She certainly wasn't one of the town's best cooks or housekeepers. Granny recalled that the cleanest place in their house was Doc's office and he kept that himself till Eula came along. And opinionated! If Grand Callie called Miss Julie a spendthrift, Miss Adie replied that Julie did have good taste. She always had a knack for putting herself out with the ladies." She lifted a slice of raspberry cake from Eloise's offered plate. "I do declare it's a sin, Eloise, you don't let on what all's in this cake. So moist. Girls, I believe she will take the ingredients to the grave." A titter ran agreeably around the room. "What's the good in a family recipe if you don't have anyone to inherit it?"

Eloise stiffened. Her face flushed. Wynene pursed her lips and placed a hand on Eloise's shoulder. Verabelle knew fully well that Eloise lost her only child, a son, to a hunting accident. Eloise, who rarely spoke his name, turned a closed-off library in her house into a memorial with pictures of her son. Over their teacups, the ladies gave each other questioning glances indicating they did not approve of the slight. It was a vicious comment, even for Verabelle's brand of sarcasm.

Ignoring the silence, Verabelle grinned, her teeth stained with raspberry. "A Vinson's still a Vinson, no matter who she married."

"She was never unkind," Eloise defended, "and heartbroken now that she has lost her beloved Doc. She was always at his side. Did she teach any of you Sunday School?"

"Jim says she knows the Bible practically word for word," Wynene added, hoping to put an end to Verabelle's gossip.

"Her garden has gone to seed," Norma Mae Adkins interjected. "When Doc was alive, it used to be one of the best. Looked like an artist's palette. It was a pleasure just to drive past it. For all her lack as a cook and housekeeper, Miss Adie had a green thumb. She won nearly every county prize in Alabama for her acorn squash and Roses Eternal."

"Now, she sits there with that Eula, writing," Verabelle continued, ignoring their words of defense. She looked around the room, keeping her audience waiting as she slathered a piece of prune bread with rose-petal jam. Having regained their attention, she took a bite, chewed it slowly, and then continued. "Some kind of book, according to Fedora, the maid. You know Fedora. She cleans and cooks for that elderly couple, the Langleys, a few doors down from Miss Adie. Well, Fedora saw Eula out sweeping the walk the other day and she walked over to ask how Miss Adie was faring. Says Eula put her head to the side, kind of jaunty like, and gave her a big happy grin. 'She be a mite bit perkier,' says she, 'since Miss Adie started in on her book about the town.' On my way to the grocery, I happened upon Fedora one day walking back to the quarters and stopped my car to offer her a ride. She happened to mention how peachy pleased Eula seemed about Miss Adie's book.

"Ladies, I tell you it's not human to be as close-mouthed as Miss Adie has been all these years, what with her helping Doc and privy to the town's secrets. She's old, ancient, and her memory is still pretty good after the strokes. Writing day after day, pages; I've seen them."

Plates rattled, half-eaten pastries forgotten as a chorus of voices exclaimed, "You have? Catch any words?"

"A few names."

"Whose?" they chorused, teacups chattering like poorly

fit teeth in the elderly they visited in the town's nursing home.

Opal Hopkins set her cup on a nearby table, hiding her shaking hands, now tightly clasped in her lap. A wave of near nausea swept over her.

"Yours," Verabelle turned to Eloise.

Eloise shuddered. Tea sloshed onto her best paisley-print dress. "How clumsy; excuse me," she apologized, disappearing into the kitchen.

Wynene stiffened in her chair. "Verabelle, perhaps you should put aside your tea. A fair share of caffeine for the day seems to have made your tongue more active than usual."

Now, Opal thought glancing appreciatively toward Wynene and taking a deep breath, the conversation will take another direction.

Verabelle gave Wynene a sardonic grin. She had an audience and pastor's wife or not, Wynene wasn't about to stop her run down the tracks, horns blaring. "There was a long list of names, in fact," she continued, looking from face to face, enjoying their rapt attention.

Opal rigidly composed her expression as Verabelle's eyes lit briefly on hers before she continued. "Must have been nearly every soul in Simpsonville," Verabelle concluded. Setting down her finally empty plate, a double chin draped scarf-like across her neck, drooping toward her pendulous chest as she swallowed a belch. "Thomas Wolfe wrote his book and he never could come home again. She knows she won't. What's the harm, she thinks. Not that any of us has anything to hide," she added, giving Wynene a capricious grin.

"Why, Lord, no!" exclaimed Hattie Turpin.

"Certainly not," Sarah Ellen concurred. Her Great-Uncle Barclay shot the bank president before he foreclosed on the family farm. It had taken years to live down that scandal.

Everyone in town knew about it, but why dredge up dirty well water?

"Course not." Norma Mae brushed crumbs off her dress as she reached for her purse on the floor beside the sofa. "Lovely tea, Eloise," she said to their hostess, who had just re-entered the room, taking a seat beside Wynene, who gave her an apologetic, sympathetic smile. "Must be going. Ted wants his supper early."

"Yes, lovely," they all affirmed, retrieving handbags, hats, and gloves, their goodbyes humming at the open door like bees exiting a hive.

"Call you," Norma Mae hollered to Eloise as she pulled away from the curb.

Verabelle, a sneer on her overly generous lips, spun her car away from Eloise's curb. "That should get them going," she said, chortling to the pecan tree–shaded streets.

"And what harm is there in suggesting I have actually seen a few names? Bunch of hens."

And just like those hens, they would be out pecking away and in the time it took to play a hand of bridge, the mystery of Miss Adie's book would be solved. It all started with a random visit—one suggested by Richard Studstill.

"Haven't paid a call on Miss Adie in a while," he commented to his wife one morning before he left for his annual board meeting at the bank.

Verabelle couldn't visit the bedridden without taking something. So, she slaved away in the kitchen baking the family recipe, Heavenly Reward, its ingredients carefully guarded over the years. As a child, her mother and grandmother herded her out of the kitchen when they baked the moistly delicious cake. She could recall the anticipation as she fidgeted impatiently outside the closed kitchen door, trying to peer through the keyhole. It was similar to the anxiety she felt on Christmas mornings when she wasn't allowed into the living room laden with Santa's gifts until she completed a breakfast that, mixed with her excitement, often left her feeling nauseous. She had to wait until her wedding day when the recipe was presented to her on an expensive piece of linen textured stationery embossed with the family crest.

Driving down the street toward Miss Adie's, she passed its wooden fence, paint peeling, bordering Doc's long-neglected garden. Eula was too busy tending to Miss Adie to plow and plant. The big oak still stood shading the screened-in side porch where Doc and Miss Adie had often sat on nice evenings. But the once-trimmed green yard had gone to red clover as if suffering with rash, and untamed ivy climbed up the side of the garage. The fountain Doc built near the screened porch was stagnant and crumbling.

Carrying the cake up the brick walkway to the front yard, she nearly tripped over a loose stone. When she rang the bells dangling from the rusty iron post on the porch, a black face appeared behind the screen door—Eula.

"Why, Miss Verabelle."

The screen squeaked open. A swirl of dust rode in on a shaft of sunlight.

"Hello, Eula, how's Miss Adie today?" she asked, walking through a slant of sunlight into the living room that smelled of stale potpourri.

"Jest the same. Some days better than others."

A bell sounded.

"That be Miss Adie's," Eula explained, taking Verabelle's cake. "She wanting to see you, I'm sure."

"Who's there?" the frail figure braced by a dark headboard, demanded in a surprisingly strong voice as they rounded the corner of the bedroom.

"Miss Verabelle," Eula announced. "Look what she done brought you." She put the cake on a side table and set about puffing up pink cotton pillows, raising bones clothed in a blue gown.

It had been such a long time since she had seen the old lady, Verabelle felt a wave of sympathy shudder through her body. Something akin to tears blurred her eyes, evoking a misty memory of a rather plump figure wearing a straw hat and gardening gloves: Miss Adie hoeing away in her fenced side yard garden. She used to look up with a bright smile and wave as Verabelle beeped her car horn upon passing. And beside her on the weekends and in the early evenings was Doc. Miss Adie, from the wrong side of the tracks, was never really part of the town's social scene, but was accepted because she was the beloved wife of Doc—a privilege that elevated her social status. She had also been his nurse. That's how she met him. When he was a young man studying in Atlanta, she was in nursing school. She had never been particularly pretty, but there was always a twinkle in her eyes and a soft glow to her creamy complexion. Doc, with his good looks, could have had any woman he wanted in Simpsonville, or for that matter in Atlanta, but he chose Miss Adie, and they had been a devoted couple. Now, here she was after all these years, a wasted figure lying in her bed with her devoted Eula tending to her every need. Turning her back and swiping quickly at her eyes, Verabelle pulled a chair with a faded needlepoint seat closer to the emaciated figure.

"How are you, Miss Adie?" she yelled, sending her voice across an invisible chasm.

"Bring me my glasses, Eula." The shriveled figure pointed a gnarled finger toward the bedside table. Bifocal-clad eyes like two milky marbles searched the face before her through the glasses Eula adjusted on her face. "Changed, but, the eyes . . . Verabelle!" she said in surprise. "Good to see you. How are Dick and the children?"

"Fine. All the ladies send their love, too."

"The ladies." Miss Adie had looked toward her dresser mirror as if she could see something in it Verabelle couldn't. "Still meet first Tuesday of every month?"

Eula raised an eyebrow in surprise. A smile lit up her face.

Verabelle nodded, amazed that she remembered. She studied Miss Adie's eyes, like a doll's penetrating, unblinking stare, and, like a doll's, not asking anything of her.

"You remember," she blurted out.

"Remember?" Miss Adie's sunken cheeks swelled, parting cracked lips over stained, nibbled-down teeth. "I remember whole generations of your family, people you never met, child."

Verabelle watched wrinkles ride over Miss Adie's face like a never-ending wave.

Remembered and outlived them all.

"Generations," Miss Adie added. "I recall your birthing. Your ma had a right tough time; must have labored forty-eight hours. You wouldn't come, you'd turned wrong; had to twist you round." She laughed, her chest heaving with the effort. "But then out you popped, screaming, your face crimson and black with bruises. Your pa wouldn't hardly look at you for fear you would look beaten all your life."

"She never forget the past," Eula said under her breath, shaking her head in amazement as she shuffled a pile of papers on the nightstand. Snapping the papers like a cleaver on the stand's wood, she pulled out a nightstand drawer and stacked them neatly inside. "She might not remember at first," she said in a half-whisper, "but she know their family history."

"Do declare, what's all that?" Verabelle asked.

"Something Miss Adie's working on," Eula said, sliding the drawer shut.

"Would you like some lemonade, dear?" Miss Adie asked. "Eula." She gestured toward the maid.

Eula hustled out of the room, taking the aroma of biscuit dough with her.

"Glad you came," Miss Adie said. "Town always good."

"So that's it, your thank you's?"

"What? Oh, you mean those papers? No, dear," she added with a sly snicker in her voice. "That's my book."

Verabelle sniffled. "Your book?"

"Always meant to write one; never had time." Her all-knowing eyes peered into Verabelle's. "Lester and I busy with doctoring and all."

"You have a publisher?"

"A publisher? Child, you must think I'm that woman ... what's her name who wrote that book ... oh, you know about the War of Northern Aggression?"

"*Gone With the Wind,*" you mean?" Verabelle informed, sighing with relief, "by Margaret Mitchell? Then, it's only for your pleasure," she stated, but their conversation was interrupted by Eula bringing in two diamond-faceted glasses and a plate of cookies.

"Eula's macaroons. No one makes them better, don't you think?"

"No one," she agreed, taking the lemonade and a cookie in a linen napkin with the faint scent of mothballs.

Miss Adie pursed her lips, seeking the crooked straw Eula held in her lemonade. A blue vein on her neck pulsed, ticking off time as emaciated cheeks drew in, lifting a pencil-thin length of fluid. Waving away the glass, she fell back on the pillow, her eyelids closed. Purple webbing covered the lids.

Eula shook her head, her face turned down in pity. As Verabelle rose to go, Miss Adie's eyes rolled open. "Don't go just yet," she spoke as if in caution.

Verabelle settled back in the chair, feeling as if she had been called down by the school principal.

"I'll be in the kitchen if you needs me," Eula said, leaving Miss Adie's glass on the nightstand.

"Plenty of time," Miss Adie informed, looking through Verabelle as if she was invisible. "A legacy for the town. Should have been written long ago—secrets kept too long."

"What's that?" Verabelle patted her lips with the delicate linen, trying to hide her anxiety.

"The book." Miss Adie's eyes fastened on Verabelle disapprovingly as if she were a child caught napping in class. "Thought I might get a printer to run it off; just enough for you ladies. A mistake," she added.

"A mistake?" Verabelle swallowed hard. A ragged edge of macaroon wedged in her throat. "Aah. Eh. Eh!" she choked, causing Miss Adie to frantically ring her bell for Eula, who came bustling into the room.

"Oh, it's you, Miss Verabelle," she said, worry lines dissolving as she thumped her on the back. "Drink some lemonade."

She took a quick swallow, smiling foolishly before Eula left to finish up supper. "A mistake?" she croaked as if the word was foreign.

"My book. Give you ladies something to chew on after I'm gone to join Lester. Now, dear, no need to look so troubled. All of us have to go sometime, and I never intended to live this long. "Tell me, what did you bring? Your Heavenly Reward? My, this is an occasion. Tried to copy it once for

Lester but left out some special ingredient. Even Lester said, 'not as good as yours.'"

"Maybe you didn't use enough eggs," Verabelle suggested, standing up to leave, then hesitating at the bedroom door. "The book?"

"The book," Miss Adie echoed, her body like a bleached white tombstone rising against the dark mahogany headboard, its wood as rich as a mound of freshly dug earth. "I've had my fun, don't you see."

"Won't be here to savor the results," Verabelle slung the words like a clump of dirt.

"Past all that." Oblivious to the slight, Miss Adie slid down, disappearing into the counterpane. "Town's history roll on long after. No one disappointed. Take care, dear. "Come back soon."

Spices wafted into the living room from the kitchen. Verabelle's stomach rumbled. She checked her watch—past time for her cocktail hour.

"Miss Adie sure did enjoy your visit," Eula said, walking her to the door. "It been a good day." She shook her head. "Never know what might get her mind going. Your visit perked her up. She usually pretty quiet. She never complain, but she do get mighty lonesome."

Lonesome was something Verabelle understood too well.

THREE

THE ONLY LIGHTS ON AT ELEVEN O'CLOCK IN
Simpsonville were streetlights and two lights in Pastor James
Chalmers' house: the kitchen where Wynene, the pastor's
wife, stood in her flour-flecked apron and the study where
Reverend Jim was reworking Sunday's sermon. It was a familiar sight to the occasional passerby: the faithful pastor in
his study and his dutiful wife in the kitchen preparing a dish
for someone in need. An owl hooted outside the open kitchen
window. The early evening breeze ruffled the curtains behind
her, bringing the faint scent of honeysuckle and Confederate
jasmine that perfumed the night.

Sprinkling more flour on the cutting board, Wynene
thought about the upset at the Mission Society. What was
Verabelle up to this time? She just couldn't keep from stirring
up trouble.

"I'm so tired of this charade," she said, rolling out a large
rectangle of dough. The Society was just one more boring
duty as a pastor's wife, but one she couldn't avoid. And what
could Miss Adie possibly be writing about? She thought of
the fateful day Doc had passed away. She had looked over the
crowd gathered to honor him. Miss Adie had been ailing for

some time and the lack of her presence at the graveside added further poignancy to the devoted couple's only separation.

Miss Adie had kept Wynene's secret. Unmarred was the image of the faithful, adoring pastor's wife. And standing there, looking at Jim, the handsome profile, his blond hair blowing in the slight breeze sweeping over the gravestones, she felt, even after all the disappointment in their marriage, a lingering fondness. He changed little over the years. A slight paunch in his middle and patches of gray at his temples only made him look more distinguished, as did the glasses he now wore over his azure eyes. And he wore his frock well. His elocution was the same as the young valedictorian at high school graduation. Sermons and eulogies were poetically heartfelt. Jim's way with words was what had, after all, won her. If only he retained some of that passion for the bedroom, Dan would never have resumed a presence in her life. Jim was Mr. It in high school: president of their senior class, football quarterback, several Senior Superlatives in their yearbook. Every girl in her class had a crush on him, but he'd picked her, a rather shy, bookish girl, to go with him to Senior Prom. They went to separate colleges, but became reacquainted when she came home for a Christmas vacation. She was seeing someone else, but Jim had been so ardent and their history together was such a strong one that he soon convinced her to marry him. As soon as their marriage vows were exchanged and he entered seminary, all his passion went into his congregation and heavenly reward except for infrequent, quickly executed couplings. If Jim had been Catholic, he would have been a priest—her life with him was as barren as their marriage. There were no children to soften the hard edges.

"Duty calls," she said, lifting the dough and placing it in the pie tin, crimping the edges.

Wynene stared into the night where a thousand insects sounded out their passion in castanet strum. The streetlight reflected through the giant magnolias in her side yard cast shadowy leafy patterns across the lawn.

"Oh, Dan," she murmured. If they were together on such a night . . . "Soon, very soon," she promised, sending her desire across the night sky, reminiscing on their fateful encounter.

It had been a routine trip to Montgomery to visit an ailing sister and do some shopping. Wynene stopped in front of a window display with mannequins clothed in the latest sixties fashion, short skirts and pillbox hats. A man's reflection striding past flickered in the glass front, superimposing itself across one of the mannequins.

"Wynene?" The reflection stopped and was coming toward her.

He seemed to be walking toward her in slow motion like something out of a dream. Time seemed suspended. She hadn't seen him in years, and except for a little added weight, he looked unchanged.

"Dan? Dan Scott?"

"I never thought," he said, his eyes looking into hers.

He was standing so close, she could have reached out and touched his face, traced his jaw line. The same flecks of gold in the amber eyes; eyes that seemed to take in the whole of her; eyes that reflected back the face he stood studying.

"Never thought," he continued, "that I would see you again."

She felt lit up like a darkened room locked for years suddenly opened, flooding with light.

"It's me," Wynene said, feeling suddenly more herself than she had been in a long time.

Dan laughed a laugh that echoed across the years whenever

she thought of him. It was a rollicking masculine laugh that always brought a smile to her lips. A laugh that one could taste—it bubbled up from the very essence of his being, spreading the generous mouth across his teeth. She answered it with a laugh of her own as if she were a child delighted with some unexpected gift.

"Have you had lunch?" he asked.

Wynene shook her head and found herself walking down the street arm in arm with him, leaving behind the mannequin of the woman she had become in the shop window. Over their lunch in an intimate café, they swapped histories of the years that separated them. In high school, they often passed each other silently in the hallway on the way to classes where he was always chatting with one of the "popular" girls, more attractive and outgoing than she ever hoped to be. When they shared an English class together, he insisted on sitting behind her.

"What pretty hair," he complimented in a half-whisper, reaching out discreetly so the teacher wouldn't see him stroking his fingers through her long hair.

She could still recall the tingle that rippled through her body, a sensation that made her feel as if his fingers were caressing her skin. Wynene was surprised when he started waiting outside the classroom to walk her to the next class and amazed when he asked her to attend his Senior Prom when she was a junior. That date turned into many, but Jim soon became his competition. On weekend or holiday visits home, Dan called wanting to see her, but by that time, she and Jim were fully committed. Dan, a year older, attended a small college upstate and was now a professor of English at one of the local colleges. A marriage of seventeen years yielded no children and little joy, ending finally in divorce.

"I was at loose ends after you broke up with me to marry someone else," he said, stirring cream into his coffee. "Laurel became a poor substitute. Loneliness can sometimes drive one to make strange compromises. I thought perhaps with time our marriage would improve, things would get better, but it only drew out what should never have occurred in the first place. And you?"

Looking down at the napkin folded in her lap, Wynene fidgeted with its embroidered edge.

"It never should have happened," she stated bluntly. "We are two separate people in a marriage with blurred edges."

"No commonalities."

"None at all except for a belief in a God."

Dan's knee touched one of hers underneath the table. An accident or was it intentional, she wondered, but she didn't withdraw her leg. How was it possible that his knee touching hers after all these years could carry such intimacy? Dan placed his hand, palm up, across the table toward her, a small inviting gesture, and she placed one of her own in his. His fingers laced around hers.

"I've never forgotten you," he said, a longing tenderness written on his face.

"Oh, Dan, after such a long time?"

"We still have plenty of time. Would you like that?"

Wynene threw her head back and laughed with unadulterated joy.

"If there is a God, and I believe there is," she responded, her hold on his hand tightening, "He has chosen to bless me."

"There is a God. There most definitely is," he said, wrapping his legs around hers underneath the table. "He has blessed us both."

And that is how Miss Adie, in town with Doc for a physicians convention and meeting a group of ladies at another table, found them, staring into each other's eyes like two smitten teenagers on a date, their hands tightly clasped across the table in the first phase of what would become a long affair. But Miss Adie never mentioned seeing the two of them together. The first time Wynene saw her after her lunch with Dan was that winter, when she reluctantly went to see Doc at Jim's insistence with a high fever and flu-like symptoms. She was apprehensive about what Miss Adie might say, but Adie was her usual professional and friendly self, never inquiring about the man with Wynene in Montgomery. Indeed, except for social events that included both husband and wife, the town had long ago excluded Miss Adie from Simpsonville's social gatherings, and Wynene rarely saw her. The pious ladies considered her beneath their pedigree, a woman from the wrong side of the tracks who made a lucky marriage. If it hadn't been for the beloved doctor's pedigree, she would never have been included in Simpsonville's social gatherings. When she was, it was seldom. She seemed content assisting in his busy practice, perfecting her exquisite quilting often on display at church bazaar sales and working side by side with Doc to nurture the massive garden of vegetables and flowers planted beside their home. Often, Wynene envied the anonymity the town afforded Miss Adie.

"Pity those two couldn't have children of their own," was the general consensus of the Ladies Mission Society when speaking of Doc and Miss Adie.

Over the years, Doc's voice began to sound worn and frayed at the edges like a piece of cloth that had outworn its use and Miss Adie's walk became less brisk. Doc insisted she hire a maid to help with kitchen duty. He and Miss Adie went down into the quarters one weekend where they gave free medical care and returned home with Eula, a big black woman whose voice and laugh competed with her size. Eula became somewhat of a curiosity as none of the ladies had encountered her in the quarters when they went to pick up their help. There was talk she came from out of town and moved in with one of the local blacks who died or walked out on her. But Eula's personal life remained as private as Simpsonville's homes in the summer, their shutters closed against the scorching neon sunlight, holding secrets within, as cloistered as the human heart.

With the passing years, Doc's appearance in the garden with his beloved Adie became less frequent. Two other doctors attracted by the town's serenity and proximity to Montgomery and the Gulf Coast allowed him to further reduce his office hours. Eula began to drive the devoted couple to church each Sunday, where the now gray-haired, elderly Doc and Miss Adie, holding hands, took halting steps to their favorite front pew. It was rumored that Doc was losing his mind, although he still was able to take short evening walks with Eula beside him. As if the couple made a prearranged exchange, Miss Adie's mind remained alert, but her body began to deteriorate. Finally, both were forced to give up the practice and the garden, its vegetation and multiple flowers now sprouting weeds. Eula's presence in the guest room allowed the couple to remain at home. Miss Adie continued to quilt for the church bazaar, handing over her artistry to Eula, who delivered it to the church, where the couple's visits became less frequent. Doc could be seen seated in a front porch rocker with Eula keeping watch while she sat, stringing beans for the couple's supper, ears alert for the sound of a bell pealing from Miss Adie's bedroom through the open window behind her. Then came the fateful day in June when Doc disappeared from the porch and the lives of the town he had faithfully served over the years. And now, it was said that Miss Adie's mind was becoming a bit addled.

"A book?" Wynene questioned, staring at the sink's back-splash as she washed up her cooking utensils while the cake baked in the oven. "What kind of book?" Was Miss Adie, suffering from the stroke that left her bedridden, attempting to get back at a town that had rejected her?

{FOUR}

THIS CAN'T BE HAPPENING, OPAL THOUGHT, driving down the tree-lined street past houses where windows with double sashes were open to welcome an infrequent breeze. Miss Adie writing a book? Was it an exposé of the town? She recalled the first time she had seen Simpsonville as Mrs. Hank Hopkins, a new bride.

On the way, she watched the miles eat up her past as she and Hank passed kudzu-covered shanties and signs advertising God's Way Baptist Church, Pigs for Sale, and Indian River Fruit. It had been April. Plastic pink bunnies sat beside Easter egg trees in front yards where neon-colored eggs were attached to tree branches. When they approached the town's city limits, she looked out the window at a quaint, quiet town of tree-sheltered streets dotted with churches and sidewalks built high off the street like a western town without the horse hitching posts. There wasn't even a movie theater, and only one grocery. Opal found herself smiling as she relaxed further into the car's vinyl-covered seat cushions, consoled by the realization that she had achieved anonymity and the status of being the high school principal's wife. Her ma would be proud. It had been easier than she imagined to slip into the persona of a young girl with a lofty pedigree. The name St. John had preceded her.

"Not *the* St. Johns?" was the frequent comment, "formerly of Atlanta and Charleston, S.C.?" "Why, my grandfather often spoke . . . a fine family." "There was a Colonel St. John served at Chickamauga," a history buff informed her. "You must join the Fine Arts Club." Before she could say, "Nice to meet you," she became the member of every organization Simpsonville had to offer, and Hank was offered an honorary membership in the country club that consisted of a small golf course, a swimming pool, tennis court, and a restaurant serving fresh seafood shipped in from nearby Florida. The only swimming she had done was in a muddy pond near the trailer park. And a bonus were the white sands and emerald waters of Ft. Walton, Florida, a mere hour away.

Then the unexpected happened. At a picnic at the country club to welcome them, Opal met Doc and his wife, Adie.

"I believe we have met before, my dear," the slight dark-haired lady said, her eyes crinkling behind her glasses as she put out her hand.

They were standing off to one side of the pool while Hank and Doc were engaged in conversation with other town occupants near a table laden with fresh shrimp and finger food.

"Met?" Opal repeated, staring into the older woman's face.

A spring breeze bearing the scent of Confederate jasmine chilled the air. A mockingbird began its imitative song. There *was* something familiar about this woman's face. And then she knew: a woman in white coming toward her from the trailer door, taking her hand in hers. Pa slumped on the trailer doorstep. So many years ago, but the sorrow of that day and the girl she thought she left behind never left her. The country club pool disappeared and Opal St. John was once again a little girl named Kylie Mae.

Studying a shaft of sunlight across the tiny white shoots of crocus at the foot of the tree stump, Kylie Mae sat waiting. It had been hours, and still the nurse hadn't come out to announce the birth of a baby brother or sister.

"Just another damn mouth to feed," Sydney complained.

Taking a swill of his beer, they sat at supper the night her ma told her, smiling, "Kylie Mae, you goin' to be a big sister."

And her ma started growing a tummy to match her daddy Sydney's. She still carried the heavy slop jars from the pigpen behind the trailer and rolled out the breakfast biscuits before she left early in the morning to work in the rich ladies' kitchens. At day's end, she would come across the fields at a slower gait to cook supper, piling their broken china with poke sallet and deer meat from Sydney's kills. After supper, Kylie Mae stood at the sink helping her ma wash dishes while she listened to her describe the coming days when "a gift from God almighty hisself" would arrive in their home. Then she would help Kylie Mae with her homework at the kitchen table where Sydney sat, beer foam on his chin, complaining about his long day working in the mill.

Her thoughts were disturbed by another cry, sooner and sharper than the others she'd heard before, that sent squirrels scampering across the pine needles. Kylie Mae began to perspire even though it was only early spring and still not that hot. She begged to stay with her ma, but she told her no.

"When the gift is heah, baby. Then."

Kylie Mae's bare toes traced a figure eight in the dirt. Maybe when the gift came, her ma would come to the PTA.

"But, Ma, why?" she would complain after she told her she couldn't come. "Miss Turner wants to meet you."

"Baby, I jest can't. Your pa will be there," she said, a pinched smile on her lips.

Kylie Mae had frowned at the thought of her pa walking into the classroom, his breath reeking of beer, wearing a crumpled shirt, his belly bulging over his jeans. Her ma always smelled fresh and clean like the clothes she hung on the clothesline to dry. Kylie Mae focused on the black loam of the earth at her feet. Would the baby's skin be like her daddy's, ruddy as the dull reddish banks of clay that lined the far side of the creek running behind the trailer? Maybe it would be like her own, the color of river stones glowing in the sun, like the skin of the rich girls at school after they returned from spring-break beach trips. The door of the trailer opened. The nurse stood at the top step. She was looking away into the trees as if she was seeking something. Couldn't she see Kylie Mae sitting not far away from the open door? The nurse's mouth moved, but no sound came out. Then she closed her eyes. When she opened them, she was looking toward Kylie Mae.

She stood up. The nurse was coming toward her. Something about her . . . The birds quieted; the air was very still. Her daddy Hal stood at the top step of the trailer, a beer in his hand. His face looked flattened out. He sat down heavily as if an unseen hand pushed him down.

"Ma," she said into the motionless face of the nurse standing before her.

She didn't actually hear the words the nurse said to her. All she felt was the nurse's hand taking one of Kylie Mae's and squeezing it tight. She was wearing a starched white uniform and was probably about the age of her ma. The blue eyes behind the nurse's glasses glistened.

Kylie Mae vs. Opal St. John studied the eyes smiling into hers at poolside. She felt she was looking into a mirror, one that reflected back the face of her mother. And then she knew the familiarity in this woman's face. The woman at the pool; the recollection of the woman in white; the woman holding her hand in hers was the nurse who tended to her mother in her dying moments.

Her pa stayed drunk through the funeral when her ma was buried with Kylie Mae's stillborn brother. She felt as if her life, too, had vanished into the earth with her mother. With no one to help and Pa deep in his drink after coming home from work, she was forced to take on her mother's chores around the trailer. There was no one to share her homework or her life. She buried herself in her studies, watching with envy the girls at school making friends while she remained reclusive. Every night, her pa sat in his undershirt and jeans guzzling beer after beer, taunting her.

"Whar's my supper? Stupid chickens lay eggs faster you cook that ham and greens. Don't give me that look, sister," he warned. "What you need is a good fanny tanning. Yore ma done spoiled you with all that book learnin'. What you expect to do with it? Ain't no place for you to go."

She would set the bowl of hog jowls and greens on the table turning her face away from the smell of his sweat and beer-drenched breath as he ordered: "More pot likker. This turnip green liquid ain't enough for my cornbread, and whar's that cornbread, girl?"

At night, she lay in her bed looking through a broken windowpane at the twinkle of a star, imagining it was her ma looking down on her, keeping watch. Her pa's snores from the other room rumbled through the trailer. He was right. There was no place for her to go. The only future waiting for her was tending to her pa and working in some stranger's kitchen.

When she turned sixteen and she could drive, her pa

started sending her to the One Stop in his battered truck to pick up canned and paper goods and the few other supplies they needed. Kylie Mae looked forward to these trips, because other than the woods and school, she had no other place to go. She loved to roll the windows down on good days to let the wind blow through her hair and across her face. Her ma had always leaned over her bed to kiss her goodnight. She liked to pretend the wind touching her cheek was a kiss from her ma brushing lightly across her cheek. Ma would be proud of her high marks at school. Just the past week, Miss Rollins, the school counselor, had called her into her office. Kylie Mae sat stiffly in front of her, shuffling her scuffed loafers beneath her chair, wondering why she was there.

"I want you to apply for a college scholarship," Miss Rollins said, smiling. "Your grades certainly merit it."

"College takes money and . . . " she protested.

"A scholarship will go a long way," Miss Rollins continued. "It will pay for your books and board. I am prepared to recommend you. There will be a scholastic test to take, but I can guarantee that will present no problems for someone with your aptitudes. Your grades have been consistently high. I expect great things from you in the future."

Kylie Mae squirmed in the chair. Her entire body felt warmed as if the sun itself was glowing over and in her. No one since her ma died had been this proud of her.

"Thank you," she managed through quivering lips.

She wished as she neared home that there was someone to share the happy glow with, but her pa would never understand. Although she knew her ma, wherever she was, was proud of her, she ached to actually have her there in front of her. She parked the battered truck at the curb in front of the One Stop.

"Lookit thar," a man in jeans tight as skin and dirt-encrusted boots said to his stubble-chinned companion standing next to him in the doorway. "Ooo-whee, baby!"

She brushed past them, blushing, as if they had undone the flies on their faded, torn jeans.

"Don't mind them," the store owner said, ringing up her purchases. "No bettah than dogs. I'll watch you out."

Hurrying to the truck, she placed the supplies in the back and spun away. Selecting a radio station, she began to sing: "My heart is free-ee. Buzzing like a bee-ee after hon-nee."

Turning off the main road, she tooted her horn at an old woman who sat rigidly watching in a rocker from the wraparound porch of a dingy white frame house. The old woman, her bland face expressionless, didn't wave. Farther down, she passed a shanty and two black women hanging out wash on a line that bobbed in the wind. Seeing them put a pain in her heart. It reminded her of her ma. In a field, men were burning leaves. She took a deep whiff of the earth-rich odor. A smoky haze covered a pine tree and pecan grove as if an invisible fire smoldered in the heart of red clay. Jumping out of the truck, she grabbed the supplies.

"What took you so long?" her pa growled, looking up from the kitchen table. A cigarette was stuck to his lower lip like it had been glued there. Empty beer cans were strewn, squished in the middle, on the floor. "What you hiding?" he questioned, jumping up, knocking his chair over.

He bent her head back. She recalled the red webbing covering the whites of his eyes as if an itty-bitty spider had tracked across them. "You look too happy," he scolded. "What you been up to?"

"Nothing, Pa," she protested. "Let me go."

"You been with someun," he accused, his breath sour.

"Not true," Kylie Mae yelled as his hand tightened on her hair. "Pa. Stop it, Pa," she pleaded. "I brought you everything you ordered."

"You ain't no good," he said, releasing her and plopping back on the chair.

He popped the lids of two beers, guzzling and crushing them with one large fist before he tossed them with the others. His Adam's apple bobbed up and down like a turkey's as he swigged another beer.

"This place's a mess," he snarled, his mouth drawn to the right. "That's something yore old lady didn't tech you."

"Ma has nothing to do with this," she said, her eyes misting.

She had never seen him *this* drunk. Taking the bags to the sink, she placed the paper products and the new knife he ordered to cut up his deer kills on the counter while she put the milk in the refrigerator. She opened a drawer to put away the knife. There was a rumble of thunder—a storm brewing. She could smell the ozone in the air. She had forgotten to roll up the windows in the truck.

Poolside, Opal jumped, spilling her drink. "Oh," she apologized to Miss Adie, "how clumsy of me. I'm sorry." She managed to keep her voice steady. "It's a pleasure to meet the doctor's wife. He's very well thought of, but we've never met before."

Miss Adie cocked her head to one side. Eyes behind the thick glasses squinted as they did a quick scan of Opal's features. Did she see a thin pigtailed girl, her body rigid with fear, waiting? "Perhaps the mistake is mine, my dear," she finally said. "For a second there … but no, the young lady I knew … Well, that's another story. Yes, Lester's a very good, caring doctor. We met years ago when I was furthering my nursing training in Atlanta and he was in residency."

"What brought you to Simpsonville?" Opal skillfully diverted the conversation toward Miss Adie and away from herself as they walked toward their husbands.

"Lester was raised here, just like your Hank. City life wasn't his style. There's something charming about a small town, don't you think? When we aren't busy in our practice, there's time to work in the garden. You'll find it peaceful here."

The soft warble of birds nesting for the evening in a nearby tree branch was a hushed song, a plaintive cry of hope quieting the unrest in Opal's soul. She had convinced Miss Adie she wasn't the girl she'd met in that other life. Kylie Mae Applegate's life faded further into the distance.

Passing the last of her neighbors' houses and the tree-lined streets of her Simpsonville life, Opal pulled into her driveway. Hank was already home.

"Hello," his voice called from the den. "Have a nice meeting?"

"The usual," she said, tossing her purse into a chair and walking into the comfort of his embrace as he stood to greet her.

Holding her at arm's length, he frowned. "Something wrong?"

"Just bored with the day and glad to be home."

"Mom," Mattie, eleven, came bounding down the stairs, her ponytail swishing. "Carol is having a sleepover this Saturday. It's her birthday. Say yesss," she hissed between her braces.

Opal smiled into her daughter's pleading face; her large brown eyes even bigger than usual from the anticipation. She looked so much like the grandmother she had never known: the same dimpled chin and widow's peak hairline. If only . . .

"What does your father say?" she asked, looking up at Hank.

"He said," Mattie hunched her shoulders and rolled her eyes in a gesture of exasperation, "to ask you."

"Then, yesss." Opal mimicked her daughter. "But I have to talk to her mother first."

"Oh, Mom!"

"You know the rules. No written invitation, then a telephone call."

"All right, all right." Mattie shrugged her shoulders and bounded back up the stairs, shaking her head, a whispery, "Adults," floating like an epithet on the air.

Hank chuckled. "Wait until she becomes a teenager," he said, smiling.

"What's with Miss Priss?" Paul asked, turning the corner. "She nearly knocked me down on her way to the telephone. Have you seen her room, Mom? Every pajama she has is slung on her bed. What's the deal?"

Opal looked at her son. Only fourteen, he was nearly as tall as his father with the same sandy hair and greenish blue eyes, and even at his early age, had a similar personality— steady, sensible, and focused.

"She's excited about a sleepover," Hank explained, grinning. "Off to your tennis match at the club?"

"Dad ... thought you and Mom were coming?"

"Oh, Hank, don't tease. Of course we are. Give me enough time to change and get Mattie going and off that telephone."

The tennis match . . . she forgot it was tonight, but watching her son's athletic prowess on the court would keep her mind off the rumors circulating about Miss Adie's book.

Lucky, she thought. No, blessed: a husband who loves me deeply and two beautiful children. She wouldn't let anybody or anything destroy what she succeeded in working so hard to create.

{FIVE}

ELOISE OPENED THE COOKBOOK GINGERLY. THE pages were curled and splattered. Many bore nearly illegible writing—*good; excellent; add more eggs*—notations from her mother and generations before. Tabs were turned down and the cover of the nearly 100-year-old cookbook was missing, but the ingredients were still decipherable and the existence of former cooks, her ancestors, evident in fingerprint smears, flour smudges, or pastry residue. Eloise considered typing the pages and neatly binding them, but somehow it would have diminished the charm. She gently flipped a page.

Southern Belle Cake:
Ten eggs, separated
Two cups each, sugar and flour
Lemon and orange juice. Half a cup of each.

Miss Adie always favored the cake, with its orange filling and frosting mixed with sweetened whipped cream, sprinkled with grated orange peel. It was wickedly rich—ten eggs. Carefully separating the egg yolks from the whites, she thought about how concealed they were behind their delicate shells, a fragility reminiscent of life itself and the secrets hidden in each person's soul.

"*Who cooks for you-cooks for you?*" an owl hooted outside the window.

Jake loved the cake. He often appeared in the room, particularly if the hour was late and she was alone. If she turned now her son would be sitting at the table patiently waiting to run a spoon around the rim of her mixing bowl to lick up what was left of the frosting. It was a treat that started when he was a child.

"Look, Mom," he would call, a chuckle in his voice, and Eloise would turn to see an orangey mustache on his upper lip.

It was his favorite of all her cakes. Kitchen visits, she called them, times when he would talk about his day, about climbing trees, running through the woods, the books he was reading, what he wanted to be when he grew up.

"A cook," Jake announced one day, so she let him tie on an apron and help with the cake.

"But it's a secret," she told him.

"A secret?"

"No one outside the family knows how to make this cake. It's a centuries-old recipe handed down from one generation to another."

"A secret," he repeated, looking up at her, his large green eyes full of glee.

A mischievous and studious child, Jake often preferred a good book and walks alone through the woods to the company of other children.

"That boy needs to hang out with other boys," Walt complained about their son when Jake started school. "Get involved. He's too solitary."

So, Eloise enrolled him in Scouts and offered to be the den mother. Walt was delighted when Jake began to take a real interest in obtaining badges, particularly the ones that required anything to do with nature and books, and he made friends. His solitary nature became more outgoing. All of his teachers commented on his genial nature and superior grades.

"He's very well liked," many commented. "Wish I had a classroom of Jakes."

His father, a hunter, gave him, against her wishes, a rifle when he was 13.

"Time the boy learned to shoot," Walt stated.

When Jake was presented the rifle that Christmas, he frowned. She could feel his hesitation, but then he turned with a bright smile, thanking his father profusely. His first hunting trip with his father turned into a huge disappointment.

"Can't aim the fool thing," Walt complained to Eloise. "Had that turkey in plain sight and he flubbed the shot."

"Walt, he's . . . sensitive."

"Sensitive, hell. What does that have to do with his aim?"

"Perhaps he can't kill."

"I'm not asking him to shoot a human being, for God's sake, Eloise. It's nothing but a damn wild turkey."

On their next forays into the woods after game, Walt returned, his chest pumped up with pride. "Bagged two turkeys," he exclaimed, slapping his son's back. "And damn near got himself a buck."

Jake became ill that night and couldn't come down to supper.

"Flu's going around," his father said, pushing his mashed potatoes around the plate. "Just a bug. He'll get over it."

But Jake had excuses for his father when he asked him to the next hunts—an important test or a meeting at the school for one of the many clubs he joined.

"Sure it's not some girl?" his father asked, looking hopeful.

"Well . . . " Jake fudged.

His father's lips pursed into a restrained grin and his eyes warmed. "Go have your fun, son. Is she a looker?"

"Dad," Jake complained, his face flushing.

And his father left him alone. "He's hunting, all right," he told Eloise one evening, "but it's a different kind of game. That's my boy."

But Eloise heard nothing from her friends about seeing Jake around town with some girl and he skipped his Junior Prom, spending it moping in his room.

"Damn girl. Must have turned him down," his father rationalized. "Told him they are a dime a dozen. Pretty damn picky, though; the boy's got looks. All to your credit," he added, slipping his arm around her waist.

The memory of his touch brought a yearning Eloise hadn't felt in a long time. She poured the cake mix into the pans and wiped her hands on a kitchen towel. Plopping down into a kitchen chair, she stared out the window. Another spring— budding leaf, flowering branch. She couldn't believe that it was a mere five years ago when Walt suffered a sudden massive heart attack. He had just finished eating dinner when the pain started in.

"My arm," he complained, leaning forward.

"What's wrong, Dad?"

"Indigestion." Walt rose to get out of the chair, then sat down abruptly, the chair rocking with the sudden motion.

"Walt?" Eloise rose from her seat.

He turned to look at her, a surprised look on his face, and toppled to the side, falling heavily on the floor. It sounded like a tree falling.

"Dad!" Jake jumped up, his eyes wide. "Dad! Call an ambulance," he screamed at his mother as he turned his father over and began the mouth-to-mouth resuscitation he learned in Scouting.

Everything after that seemed to play out in slow motion: the ambulance, Doc and Miss Adie at the hospital, the funeral. "It was massive," Doc reassured her and Jake. "You did your best, son." He placed a hand on Jake's arm. "Probably gone before he hit the floor."

Eloise moved through the following days, weeks, and months in a daze. And, Jake—he took solace in long walks in the woods, disappearing for hours.

"My fault," he told her one night at the supper table.

"What?"

"Dad . . . his heart attack."

"Oh, no, honey, you mustn't blame yourself."

She got up from the table and went over to him. Standing behind him with her arms around his neck, she consoled, "You did your best. Doc told you so."

"You don't understand," he said forlornly. "I'm sorry, Mom." And he left the table and the house.

She knew that he was seeking solace in the woods. It was a place where he spent more and more time.

When he came home from school, he dropped his books in his room and headed out the back door. His father's absence was felt even more keenly when Jake was to graduate with high honors. Several colleges offered scholarships.

"Taking anyone to the Senior Prom?" she asked, hopeful.

"Don't know," was his bland reply and then he added, "What difference would it make?"

"Oh, Jake," she placated. "Your father wants you to be happy, to go on with your life. He would be so proud of

you . . . was so proud of you. Look to the future. Have you
been working on your valedictorian speech?"

"Sure," he answered blandly. "Think I'll take a walk before supper."

"Oh, well, perhaps it will give you some inspiration," Eloise called after him.

Even though she was hungry, she put their supper on
warm in the oven and sat down, feeling lonelier than ever, to
work on his graduation invitations. Perhaps it wouldn't hurt
to talk to Doc about Jake's depression and his feeling that he
was responsible for his father's passing. It had been nearly a
year now. She was halfway through the invitations when she
noticed that it was growing darker and Jake still hadn't returned. The gnawing hunger in her stomach turned to pangs
of fear. Her hands shook as she dialed the telephone.

"Doc." Just saying his name brought some relief.

"Eloise."

The warmth of his voice brought sudden tears to her eyes.
"It's Jake," she said, her hands shaking. "He went walking in
the woods hours ago and he hasn't come back."

"Was he with anyone?" Doc asked.

"No. He was alone."

"Was he hunting?"

"No. He just walks. Oh, Doc ..." her voice broke.

"Now, now, Eloise, you know these young people," he
placated. "Adie and I'll be right there."

But when they arrived, the sheriff was with them. Miss
Adie sat beside her on the sofa, her arm around her as the
sheriff related how a group of hunters had come across an
accident. A young man, they thought. Must have tripped and
his gun went off.

Eloise jumped to her feet. "We must go to the hospital. It might be Jake."

In subdued tones they told her there was no need, and Jake wasn't at the hospital. Adie spent the night with her and called relatives and friends who put the word out to the town. Doc ruled it an accident even though he knew Jake never hunted. Jake's high school dedicated the school yearbook to his memory and a moving address was made at the graduation he didn't get to attend. His cap and gown still hung in his closet with the rest of his clothes. Eloise didn't have the heart to remove them. It was something he earned in the most sterling way. In the first stages of her grief she railed at God for allowing the deaths of her husband and her son, and then, she started in on Jake for taking away his presence when she so badly needed it. Time eased the pain, but not the sensation that a limb had been cut from her body. And a growing suspicion about Jake's death began to grow like a cancer in her mind. She took that suspicion to Doc, who, in Miss Adie's presence, confirmed what she already suspected about her son.

"When things like this happen," Doc told her, "the person who inflicts the ultimate loss on him or herself is not thinking of anyone but themselves. They can't help it. Their pain is so great; it has consumed them. It's their way of cutting it out. He was an anguished young man. It doesn't mean he didn't love you, Eloise. He still does. And, if he could, he would be right here to tell you what a mistake it was and how sorry he is. God knows the human heart far better than any of us."

"God didn't stop it," she railed in rebuke.

"We don't understand why God doesn't stop tragedies," Doc said, "but He hasn't deserted you."

"Jake is with Him, now," Miss Adie added.

"He was different," Eloise divulged in a deflated tone.

"So are we all," Doc said. "Some changes we can control; some we can't."

"Then you knew?" Eloise questioned in surprise. "I don't think Walt suspected. Maybe I was wrong. Did Jake tell you?"

"Desperate to get help, he confided in me on a routine health exam. He wanted to be like the other boys. I told him to accept himself, that it was not his fault and that he had many wonderful attributes. If I had known about the outcome, I would have suggested counseling. I'm sorry I couldn't have advised him better. He was such a fine young person."

It took a long time, but peace finally came. Even though Jake's physical presence was denied her, a simple act like baking this cake brought him into the room. No one could take away her memories. But now, according to Verabelle, Miss Adie, bordering on senility, was reputedly writing a book about the town. It was inconceivable that someone as kind as Miss Adie would slander the life of her son, but would she in her current state of dementia reveal what she knew about Jake? Surely the town didn't suspect. She shuddered. She would not have the town gossiping about her beautiful son, tarnishing the goodness of his life. Thank God, Wynene put an end to Verabelle's snide remarks at the Ladies Mission Society. She would take her cake to Miss Adie. Perhaps her visit would clear up the mystery of the rumored book.

{SIX}

NORMA MAE SAT DOWN ON A POOL CHAISE lounge to slather the backs of her two girls, Lu Ann and Patty Sue, with suntan lotion. She chose a shaded spot underneath the club overhang to unload their swimming bags and towels.

"Quit fidgeting," she scolded thirteen-year-old Patty Sue. "The sun's not going anywhere and neither are you till you're coated."

"Oh, Mom," Patty Sue whined. "That's enough."

"Okay, next," she commanded Lu Ann, who without objection, sat down at the end of the vinyl chaise. "Now, you know the rules," she said, rubbing the lotion into the back of the nine-year-old. "Patty Sue, I haven't given you permission to leave yet. Come back and sit."

Patty Sue raised her eyebrows in exasperation and plopped down in a chair opposite her mother and sister. "No dunking or running around the pool," she mimicked her mother, cocking her head and screwing her lips to one side, "and stay together."

"Okay, go enjoy," Norma Mae said, ignoring Patty Sue's sarcasm. "I'll order lunch in another hour."

"Why don't you put on a suit and come?" Lu Ann whined.

"Just had my hair done," she said, stretching out on the lounge. "Stay near your sister."

"But you never come in anymore," Lu Ann said, frowning.

"Young lady, go." She waved her hand toward the water.

She watched her girls' slender bodies, so like exclamation marks, walk toward the water and splash in. Once, she had been lithe and thin. She stared at her legs stretched out on the lounge: bulge, lost muscle tone, and a spare tire or two developing around her midriff. Taking morning showers before breakfast, she avoided stepping on the scale. Instead, she pushed it underneath a makeup stool to keep it out of sight. She weighed more now than she did when pregnant with the girls. Ted became an infrequent lover. But could she blame him? She couldn't recall exactly the last time they had sex. Was it a month ago, or two or three? Their marriage had instead dissolved into a pleasant conversation, and that was infrequently. She was always busy with the girls and her various clubs, the Ladies Mission Society, her bridge group . . .

A muscular young man, no, a boy still in his teens most likely, strode by. Taut thigh muscles and stomach, strong arms: an Adonis. He moved like a lithe panther past the young women seated at a poolside table. One dropped her French fries on her paper plate, splattering catsup down her chin as her friends giggled; another on a lounge chair pushed her sunglasses down to get a better look. A shapely young woman on the diving board arched her breasts forward and did a double somersault designed to get his attention. Surfacing, she swam with an elegant stroke toward him. *Caution*, Norma Mae wanted to shout, *beware*, as if the young man was truly a predator and they the prey. She could almost smell the pheromones being released into the air. The guard, for he was just that—it was marked on the side of the skimpy suit that covered his manhood—kept his eyes directed toward the tower and the ladder he would climb to his perch. But he *had* noticed the attention, the changes in the prey. A snicker of a smile lay across his lips. Norma Mae watched along with every other woman under eighty as taut muscular legs practically leapt up the ladder. Once seated, he casually combed his fingers through his blond hair and sat back to observe his admirers. Oh, to be young again. She felt an urge she hadn't in a long, long time; a warming between her thighs, a pulsating heat not produced by the sun. At her age! She looked around the pool. Every female's eyes were riveted on the lifeguard. Now was the time to drown!

She knew that the young, or not so young, would gladly have that mouth pressed against theirs as that Adonis attempted to resuscitate his victim. How delicious it would be to open your eyes into his mesmerizing, paralyzing gaze— Years, oh, it had been so many years ago. How dare he come prancing into her life again, these memories, that blond hair and tantalizing touch, climbing the ladder to the forefront of her thoughts.

Norma Mae was but seven years older than Patty Sue during a summer visit to their cousin, Kat, in Atlanta. They spent the entire week at the community pool hanging out with Kat's friends and her boyfriend, Larry. They had just selected their pool chaises on the first day of their visit when Norma Mae noticed him. Muscular and blond with high cheekbones, his lean body poised on the diving board. Norma Mae felt that all her life, he had been waiting, his supple body dividing the pages of her life like a bookmark.

"Who is that?" she asked Kat.

"Bart Richards. He's the head lifeguard."

She watched as the board sprang up and down as this Bart Richards arced into the air in an elegant sweep. Before she gave it a second thought, she jumped into the water. When she surfaced, shaking out the water in her hair and eyes, light was reflected back at her from the slightly slanted blue eyes of Bart Richards.

"Hello," he said, a stroke away.

"Hi," her voice squeaked.

The sun was hot, but she found she was shaking, if not externally, internally.

"You're new around here, aren't you?" he asked, gliding beside her.

"That's my cousin." Norma Mae pointed toward Kat, who was watching her with a raised eyebrow.

"Oh, Kat." He raised a hand and waved. "She goes to my high school. I'm a senior," he informed.

With a lazy aristocratic air, sleekly wet, he pulled himself out of the pool. Then he reached down toward her. His hand closed firmly around hers. She found herself standing in front of this boy, her eyes riveted on his as water dripped down their bodies.

"And you?"

"Me?"

His eyes had a laugh in them. "What year are you in school?"

"Oh, that." She took the towel he lifted off a chair. "I'm a junior at Simpsonville High."

"I'm going to the State University next fall," he stated, shaking water from blond hair gleaming with sun. "I want to be a vet."

"Oh, I love animals," she said, inanely, feeling suddenly shy.

She had never been shy.

"Hungry?" he asked.

This god actually ate! She followed him to the snack bar, where he ordered two hamburgers and Cokes.

"You're allowed to eat?" Norma Mae asked as they took a seat at a poolside table.

"I'm actually off right now. See the guy up there." He waved. A brunet in yellow trunks, grinning somewhat knowingly, waved back.

The hands that lifted his burger were slender with long tapered fingers.

"Careful, he's a worker," her cousin told her on their walk home, prefacing the warning with a giggled, "You had every girl there insane with envy."

They went swimming together every day after that as soon as his guard duty was over. One day he asked her to stand in the water near the shallow end with her legs apart.

"Why? she questioned, suddenly wary, remembering her cousin's warning.

"I'm practicing a new sidestroke," he told her.

When she obeyed, he maneuvered his body underwater. Norma Mae looked down to see his blond hair streaming between her outstretched legs. As he passed between them, his fingertips lightly stroked her flesh sending a shocked shudder up her body. After one pass, he did a flip and returned, this time fluttering his hands up and down her legs. Each time, his caress inched closer and closer. Once, he swam nearly on the bottom of the pool, face up, surfacing his head just beneath her groin. A fingertip pulled at the fabric of her suit. When his fingers went beneath the suit, she didn't stop him. Every nerve in her body tingled with his sleek watery touch. She knew if he continued, the pool water would begin to boil around them. She was weak-kneed and shivering when he pulled her out of the water.

"Cold?" he asked wrapping a towel around her shoulders.

She looked around for Kat, but she was gone.

"I'll walk you home," he offered.

Only they hadn't gone directly to Kat's. He directed her toward a vacant wooded lot. Lifting the towel from her shoulders, he placed it on the ground over warm pine-scented needles where they lay, their arms and legs wrapped so tightly around each other's naked bodies, nothing could slip between them. Coaxing secrets out of her he already knew, he kissed her mouth, her breasts, and then sitting back on his knees, lowered his head, blowing whispered breaths of air across her—whispers designed to make her shudder with pleasure. Then kneeling before her, he put his blond head between her knees. Placing his tongue on her, he licked, stroking her, nearly bringing her, before he lowered his body and entered her, slipping gently further and further into her in a swimming motion until he burst apart her virginity. As he continued to dive past her momentary twinge of pain, Norma Mae felt her body rising, rising into his and past him into the trees that weaved with a dazzling light that made her eyes glisten with tears. His body shuddered as a scream of exquisite joy escaped her parted lips and she laughed with thankful pleasure.

"I love you," she said to the now-motionless body lying heavily on her.

He sat up, found her bathing suit and his. "Time to go," he said, tossing her suit toward her. "Your cousin and aunt will be looking for you."

And she never saw or heard from him again. Then one day she discovered that he had left a part of himself with her.

She sat up. Where were Patty Sue and Lu Ann? She spotted Lu Ann in the shallow end of the big pool, but where was Patty Sue? The pool had become more crowded since their arrival. Surely she hadn't gotten too far away from her sister. Perhaps she had hit the refreshment bar inside. The lifeguard wasn't in his ivory tower, either. Where ...? He was sitting on the side of the pool talking to a girl. Patty Sue? It couldn't be, not with all the older girls drooling for attention. She jumped off the chaise lounge.

"Patty Sue," she called, nearly charging across the space that divided them.

The girl beside the lifeguard turned her head, her eyes narrowed. Patty Sue. It was Patty Sue. What on earth?

"Mom," Patty Sue stood up. This is ..."

"I don't give a rat's ass who this is, young lady," Norma Mae heard herself say in a loud tone. "What are you doing?"

"Doing?" Patty Sue's face turned sunburn red. "Mom, what . . . ?" Patty Sue looked around the pool, her face getting rosier.

"Get your sister and your things," Norma Mae commanded. "Don't look at me that way, young lady. Go."

"Sorry, Chase," Patty Sue apologized with slumped shoulders as she walked away.

"We'll talk later," Chase called after her. "Mrs. Adkins," he offered her his hand. "I'm Chase Hatteras."

Norma Mae ignored his attempt to shake hands. "Don't ever bother one of my girls. Do you hear?" she said in a commanding tone. "Strut your stuff with someone else's, not one of mine."

"I don't understand," he was saying as she turned away.

Then and only then did she notice that every eye was on her as she gathered up the girls' shoes and her beach bag.

Patty Sue and Lu Ann were in the backseat of the car when she opened the car door. Patty Sue kept her gaze on something unseen outside the window on the way home. Lu Ann was sobbing quietly.

"Stop that right now," Norma Mae commanded.

"But Mom, you're mean today," Lu Ann stated. "We were having fun; everybody was staring."

"Your sister started this," she replied.

"Started what?" Patty Sue hollered. "I'll never go back to the pool again."

"Don't think me stupid, young lady," Norma Mae said. "I saw the way you two were sitting there so cozy-wozy."

"So what? If I want to take swimming classes with the rest of my friends, so what?"

"That was about swimming classes?" Norma Mae's voice softened.

"What else?" Patty Sue sank further into her seat. "Mom, what's wrong with you?"

Ted was already at home when she and the girls pulled into the driveway. His cases as a lawyer must have finished early today. Her daughters leapt from the car and charged into the house and up the stairs. Lu Ann was still snuffling.

"Get those wet suits off," Norma Mae shouted up the stairs, "and hung in the bath to dry."

Marching into the kitchen, she set her beach bag on a counter and reached into a cabinet for a glass. Thirsty, she was so thirsty. Filling it at the sink, she slumped into a kitchen chair.

"What's going on?" Ted asked, walking into the kitchen. "Anything wrong?"

She looked up at him as if he was a stranger in his own home. Another's image was still implanted in her mind. Like a billboard from the past, an advertisement for the epitome of youthful vitality, he stood poised on a diving board, lean and muscular. As if blinded by the sun, she blinked. The face looking down at her had a double chin and a too-round face above a square block of a body.

Getting up to refill her glass, she turned her back on him. "Oh . . . nothing, really." She downed the water in one long drought.

"Nothing? Lu Ann was crying. Some kids at the pool start something?"

"No, it's just a misunderstanding. What would you like for supper?" She opened the refrigerator. The coolness of its interior fanned her face. "How about chicken, broiled or fried?"

"Norma Mae," he said, his voice frayed.

"Yes, Ted." She took the chicken out of the refrigerator and set it in the sink to clean.

He shrugged his shoulders. "Nothing, just nothing."

"Ted," she called after him, as he headed for the den and the evening news. TV had long ago replaced their conversations. "Ted, broiled or fried?"

"Who cares," he responded, guffawing flatly. But she thought she heard him mumble. "As if ... that easy."

Left alone in the kitchen with no sound except the running water to clean the chicken, she reflected with grave remorse on her actions at the pool. She created a scene that would probably be the subject of every gossipmonger in the town, and even worse, she embarrassed her girls. Somehow, she would make up this day to them. For now, she would cook supper, wash dishes, and then ponder about Miss Adie and this supposed book she was writing.

That fearful night she came to Doc was so long ago. Surely Miss Adie wouldn't remember. It was a night she, however, never forgot and never would. Wiping a kitchen towel across her moist eyes, she salt and peppered the chicken and reached for the flour.

{SEVEN}

"CLARE CALLED," WYNENE SAID TO JIM'S BACK as he sat at his desk working on Sunday's sermon.

"What's that, dear?" Jim turned in his swivel chair. The desk was cluttered with books. Crumpled pieces of paper lay at his feet. His glasses had slipped slightly down on his nose. He wore such a distracted expression on his face that Wynene could almost picture the way he might look when he was older. She knew that his thoughts were still embedded in the writing of a sermon.

"Clare, my sister. In Montgomery," she added to remind him.

"Oh, yes. Yes, of course." He pushed his glasses securely back up on his nose. "How is she?"

"She's somewhat better, but lonely and wants me to come for a visit this weekend."

"This weekend? Wynene, have you forgotten the children's festival? Surely you don't want to miss it. They have worked so hard."

"No one will notice my absence. All their Sunday School instructors will be there. And, Jim, Clare needs me. I'm all she has."

"Yes, of course." He sighed. "When are you coming back?"

"I'll leave early Friday and be back Sunday evening."

He turned back to the sermon he was working on. "All right," he said, reluctance in his voice as he shuffled papers.

With a mixture of joy tinged with a twinge of guilt, she nearly ran up the stairs to pack. She felt like a child playing hooky. Her sister knew about Dan and agreed to cover for her, but the agreement came with a warning:

"I don't approve," she said. "If you feel you are wasting your life with Jim, why not just leave him? Affairs rarely work out, anyway. Jim will divorce you if he finds out. And, Wynene, what about the town? You will have every gossip-monger feeding on the corpse of your reputation. Think what that will do to Jim and his status as a minister. The church could fire him."

"That is why I am still his wife," she said.

"Then separate or divorce."

It sounded so easy. Wynene's joy with Dan was conflicted. She honestly didn't want to hurt Jim, and the love that had originally brought them together was, if not completely a flame, still an ember. Affection is what she felt, affection and admiration for the genuine emotions he displayed when one of his flock suffered. She had seen tears fill his eyes at the death of a child or the suffering caused by an incurable disease. Many times, she found him in his office on his knees praying about a loss or for a cure for a member of his congregation. At funerals, he always ended with the words, "And love above all is the thing that lasts." Jim spoke eloquently of spiritual love. He was a good man. Dan was also a good man. The difference lay in their sensual nature. Jim loved her spiritually; Dan loved her physically and spiritually. If she could reverse her fate, she would have married Dan. She didn't know what the future held, but she couldn't deny the intense sexual emotions that Dan aroused. She felt a heat build between her thighs thinking about his touch as she pulled her suitcase out of the closet and began packing for her early-morning drive.

She awoke to a breath of air blown across her cheek; a brush of lips across her cheek. A sigh passed her lips. She reached out for his embrace.

"Don't forget to call."

Jim's voice, not Dan's. She was still at home.

"What time is it?" Wynene asked, sleepily, turning to look at her alarm clock. She didn't hear it go off.

"Six, decided to go in early. Do some catch-up work," Jim said. "Be careful and tell Clare I send my love."

She swung her legs out of bed. Dawn paled the sky. Better to get up half an hour early. She could make better time on the road. She walked into the kitchen to get a cup of coffee from the pot Jim had already set on the stove.

"Wynene," Jim called from the front door.

"Forget something?" she asked, walking into the hallway.

"Nothing." His eyes had a questioning expression. "Just that ... well, I will miss you."

The door closed. Through the living room sheers, she watched him back the car out of the garage onto the street. A twinge of regret made her stomach turn sour. Dan . . . he was waiting. When she was with him, everything would be all right.

She met him on the outskirts of Montgomery at the car wash where they always met. His smile, that wonderful broad smile she remembered all these years, brought a laugh of happiness to her lips. How could she have possibly felt any remorse? His smile told her she had come home, not left it.

Wynene followed him toward some unknown destination. When he turned into a subdivision, she wondered if he was finally taking her to his home. They went down a long drive and into a garage that closed behind them.

"Your home?" she asked, stepping out of the car.

"No, a friend's. He's away on a business trip."

"You didn't tell him, did you?" she asked tersely.

He grabbed her in his arms, kissed her neck, then her chin, and finally her lips. She felt a heat build between her thighs. "Not to worry," Dan said. "He actually believes I have a friend interested …"

"In what?" Her voice sounded harsh as she pulled away from him.

"Wynene," he half-scolded, pulling her into his arms again. "He wants to sell the house. Before he lists with an agent, I told him I knew of a couple who might be interested. Relax. No one knows about you, about us." He unlocked the door off the garage. "I thought a house," he explained as she stepped onto a wooden foyer, "would be more comfortable than the motels. Believe me, if I thought the neighbors wouldn't notice, I would take you home." He grabbed her in his arms and kissed her again. "You belong in my home. Come home to me," he breathed in her ear.

"Oh, Dan, I want to."

"Then do it. Don't I make you happy?"

"More than happy, I'm afraid. I've told you that, but there are others to consider."

"You're afraid of hurting him, of petty gossip, but have you thought of the damage you are doing to me, to us? You aren't happy in that town anymore. He doesn't satisfy you. Don't you love or trust me enough?"

"You know I do," she reassured him as she followed him,

hand in hand, up a winding staircase. The house was spacious and beautifully appointed. The view toward the backyard through a bay window revealed tall oaks and a wide expanse of lawn. She followed him into a bedroom with a stacked stone fireplace. Dan had already pulled aside the beige bedspread on a king-size bed. A scented candle was burning on the dresser and a large vase of red roses sat on a side table.

"Oh, Dan," she exclaimed. "It's lovely."

"Not as lovely as you," he said, facing her and reaching behind her to undo the zipper on her dress that dropped obediently at her feet. He traced the outline of her lips with the tip of a finger, breathed in her ear. "Wynene, I have always loved you."

He drew her into his chest until she felt she could simply walk into him and through him, as if a door long closed was now open. His tongue thrust over hers, thrust by thrust, until a deep moan escaped her lips. Her legs folded beneath her. Only his arms held her up. Wynene's hands moved to the zipper of his slacks. They moved quickly to undress each other, a pleasure unto itself. She and Jim had never been this intimate with each other. His occasional couplings with her were nearly always when he awakened her in the middle of the night when they couldn't see each other's bodies. Now, she looked down the full of Dan, at his desire for her, the hair at his groin, on his chest. She reached down to touch him. He pulled her toward him. As she faced him, he slid a hand down her buttocks, caressing them and then gliding down her thighs and between them. The hardness of him rose between them as he backed her toward the bed and gently laid her on her back, spreading her legs apart over the edge of the bed. She looked up at him, at the flush of desire on his face. When he entered her, erotic waves of electricity rippled up her spine. She raised her legs in the air to take in the whole of him. She could feel him quivering inside her, gliding in and out. She arched her back as he sent her higher and higher and further away from herself, rising into the air, floating toward the ceiling. Their breaths came quicker and quicker until a simultaneous roar like two animals in heat erupted from their lips.

"I love you, love you," she said, rolling over on top of him where he now lay on the bed.

The wetness of their love felt like a salve over a wound. Their lovemaking brought such pleasure, such release, both physically and spiritually. He kissed her forehead as she lay with her head on his chest listening to the rapid beat of his heart.

"Leave him," Dan whispered, his arms tightening around her. "This is where you belong, where you have always belonged."

{EIGHT}

CICADA STRUM, THE SOUND OF SIZZLING summer heat, sounded nearly like a snake's rattle before it struck, thought Eula, out in the early evening sweeping the front walkway. Seems they had started their chatter earlier this year. She turned an ear toward the living room window listening for a possible bell summons from Miss Adie. Lawd, it was getting harder keeping the walkway swept for the sudden appearance of one of the ladies from the Mission Society. After years of never showing their faces, they were flocking like a bunch of peacocks, their feathers fanned and flashy, in their best going-to-church clothes, to Miss Adie's bedside. The refrigerator was crowded with their baking. Eula had taken to freezing what she could.

It was the book that drew them. The book and trying to discover what lay in its pages. In a small town like Simpsonville, anything different was news. One would think the ladies had secrets to hide. Doc would understand. He knew the human heart as well as the body better than anyone she had ever known. "Doc," Eula said to the dazzling blue of the sky and the huge limbs of the massive oak that spread some shaded relief over the front walk. She looked toward what used to be the small fountain of a waterfall he fashioned years ago on the side of the yard. For days, he had labored away, stacking huge slabs of colored stone to make a cozy spot for him and Miss Adie to sit and listen to the trickle and splash of water into the trough below. It was still shaded by the oaks on the side of the house, but the stone crumbled years ago—jest another reminder of the absence in their lives of a man she, Miss Adie, and the town adored.

And the garden: its seed long gone—its earth, parched, unfertile. Lawd, that man and Miss Adie had worked so hard to plant and grow massive rows of the best tomatoes in the town, not to mention the other vegetables. Miss Adie, when she wasn't busy working with Doc to patch the wounds, external and internal, of the town, slaved away in the kitchen putting up jar after jar of the garden's yield. Now, she lay in her bed, crippled mentally and physically, crumbling jest like the fountain, drying up along with the garden. Lately though, the book had perked her up. That mind, so full of spirit and life, would never be the same and the man she loved would never return to till the earth or tend the body, but one took from life its sticks and stones and badgered on. For all its hurts and wants, life, Eula believed, was God's gift. If she hadn't, she too would have crumbled like the fountain's brick.

Her mama told her over and over, "Life is no birthday party with sprinkles and candles on a cake. It do have its pleasures, though, for all its work, and God, though He seem sometime out of reach, still has you by the hand." Eula stopped sweeping to stare up through the branches of the oak at a cloud. Sometimes, if she looked, her mama's face was there to tell her, "Take courage." Courage is something Eula had to work hard at, but she wasn't lacking. She thought about her father, his sudden visits and the pleasure it brought: her mama's face all smiles; her daddy, all hugs. Even as a little girl, she knew her mama and daddy loved each other even if he didn't stay for long. Sometimes, in the middle of the night when her father was there, she woke to hear her mama call out in a deepened voice as if she had been surprised by something. One night, Eula called out, fearfully, "Mama?" And her daddy answered, "Go back to sleep, baby. Mama's all right." And, later, still awake, she heard them murmuring to each other in voices that sounded like a lullaby, a low sweet sound that put her back to sleep. The next morning, her daddy was gone.

"Daddy, where Daddy?" Eula would ask her mama over her Cream of Wheat and orange juice.

"He gone, baby, but he be coming back," her mama told her, her voice and body all soft and relaxed looking.

And she was right. It was always like Christmas morning when she heard his familiar call, "Lyla, where are you and my baby?" And there he would be with her mama, their arms wrapped so tightly around each other, they looked like one person instead of two.

Even when her daddy didn't come, Eula was content to just have her mama alone to herself. She tried not to think about the terrible day her mama woke with a pain in her side. It was a day when Eula, then five, had her mama all to herself. When she walked into the kitchen, her mama wasn't there fixing her breakfast. She heard a moan from her bedroom and walked in to find her all crumpled with her knees pulled up to her chest. Perspiration covered her forehead and her sheet was soaked. She was panting through clenched teeth.

"Baby, go on quick down the road. Get Lila Mae," she begged, her voice like a whisper.

She was scared to walk down the road. Her mama always told her to never go without her, but Eula found herself running.

"Lawd, what is it?" Lila Mae said when she saw Eula dash onto her porch.

"My mama," Eula bent over, panting, her voice shaking. "She's bad sick."

Lila Mae grabbed her hand and they raced back to Eula's house. When they entered the house, Eula thought her mama must have gone to sleep, because the noise had stopped. She ran into her mama's bedroom where she still lay crumpled up, but she was still and her face had a set expression on it like a doll's, a very pretty doll.

"Mama." She pulled at the sleeve of her gown. "Lila Mae is here."

"Child," Lila Mae said, her voice low as if she was afraid she would wake her mama, "you go get yourself some water and stay in the kitchen. I'll be out soon."

When Lila Mae finally walked out of her mama's bedroom, she closed the door behind her and said, "Child, let's go onto the porch."

"No." Eula stomped her feet. "I want my mama."

Lila Mae's eyes looked up at the ceiling. She sucked in her breath. "Your mama isn't here," she said.

"Yes, she is. She is." She got out of her chair and started toward her mama's room. Lila Mae grabbed her by the arm, but she kicked out at her, screaming, "Leave me alone. I want my mama. Mama," she called toward the bedroom. "Mama."

But there had been no answer, and Lila Mae grabbed her around her waist and half-dragged her, kicking, onto the porch where she was plopped down in a rocker. Standing over her with her hands on each side of the rocker to prevent her exit, Lila Mae leaned over her and in a whispery voice, as if she was telling her a secret that she was afraid her mother would hear, said, "Your mama has gone to live with God in heaven. That don't mean she took away her love. She was sick and God made her well."

"Then she'll be back?" Eula asked in a quivery voice.

"No, child, but all your life, she watch over you."

Something wet started falling on Eula's arm and she realized that Lila Mae was crying. Eula put her hand on one of Lila Mae's and patted it, a gesture that made Lila Mae cry harder. Eula tried real hard to think on what Lila Mae told her. Her mama was still back there in her bedroom, but she was in heaven, too. If God took away her sick, why was he keeping her?

"God's mean," she said, "to keep my mama."

"Don't worry, child," Lila Mae said through her tears, "You won't be alone. I'm taking you home."

"This my home," Eula had told her. "Daddy won't know where to go."

"Your daddy is on his way," Lila Mae said.

And he did come that night. She was in the kitchen where Lila Mae made a porridge, but she couldn't eat. As soon as she heard the car door close, she raced out the door into his waiting arms.

"My baby, my baby," he said in a voice with all the happy gone.

She sank her head into his chest and he sat down in one of the front porch rockers and rocked her to sleep. When she woke up the next morning, she was at Lila Mae's and her daddy was gone.

At first, he came every week to see her, but after a year, his visits were less frequent and finally she saw him only right before Christmas. Then he was all snuggles and gifts. What she liked the best were the snuggles.

"My girl," he started calling her as she got older.

On one visit as they sat on Lila Mae's porch talking, she complained, "Daddy, I don't look like my mama."

"You have my eyes," he said, "but you are still a pretty girl, because she's responsible for the rest."

"Why don't you come the way you used to? Is it 'cause Mama lives in heaven now?"

He studied her face, his eyes soft-looking, sort of dreamy, as if he could see her mama in his mind. "Eula," he finally said, "your daddy has a wife."

"A wife?" Her voice sounded harsh to herself. "Don't you still love my mama?"

"I'll always love your mother. No one can replace some-one else, although God knows I have tried." He placed his hand on his chest where his heart was. "She lives here, but a man gets lonely, Eula. Someday, you will understand that. I needed someone here on earth to love, too. You would like her."

"No, I won't and I don't now, Daddy. Does that mean you don't love me either?"

"Eula." He frowned and reached out for her, but she stepped away. "You are my girl and always will be. Of course I love you. No one can take that away."

"Yes, they can," she said, getting up. "I can."

She dashed into the house, slamming the door, and went to her room, locking the door behind her. She could hear him talking to Lila Mae in the next room, hear the hurt in his voice, and Lila Mae calling to her in a scolding voice telling her to come out, but she didn't. She threw herself on the bed, hugging her pillow to her chest, until she heard the engine of his car start up. He was gone by the time she reached the front door. The next Christmas, his gifts came by mail, but she didn't open them or any of the others he sent.

A bell sounded through the open window, bringing her back to the trickling fountain and the rhythm of the cicada strum. That would be Miss Adie, she thought, watching the cloud with her mama's face dissolve in the blueness of the sky. She always regretted closing a door to her daddy, but life with all its twists and turns still had plans for him in her life. Her mama and God must have worked it all out, although the roads she took prior to their next meeting cost a lot of miles.

{NINE}

"ANOTHER MEETING?" VERABELLE COM-plained, staring down the long dining room table at her husband. "What is it this time?"

Dick put down his napkin. His look of disdain rippled down the length of the antique mahogany table toward her. The table seemed to represent the distance that developed between them over the years. This is where she usually saw him or briefly in the kitchen where he hurriedly drank his cup of coffee, washing down a piece of toast while standing at the kitchen counter. She often complained, "Can't you sit down for breakfast with me just once?" His response this time at the dining room table was of the same composition.

"You have that tone in your voice," he accused.

"What?" she asked in a sarcastic-laced voice, slathering butter on another biscuit.

"Let's not play games, Verabelle. I have a job, a very important job. It keeps you in this house, clothed and fed. Amply fed, I might add. How many biscuits does that make? Thought you were going to lose weight. You know tonight is my bank board meeting."

"It's always your night for some meeting. Work and meetings, that and golf, that's all you do. You never do anything with me anymore."

"I don't have time for this," he said, looking at his watch and pushing back his chair.

His rapid footsteps receded down the hallway. She heard a closet open and close.

"When will you be home?" she called.

"Whenever the meeting ends," he replied, entering the dining room again and planting a hurried kiss on her cheek. "Don't wait up, and save the rest for later. Thanks for supper."

The front door opened and closed. She heard his car back out of the garage and the rattle of the garage door as it came down, locking her in. His empty chair faced her down the long table. Gathering up his dishes, she took them into the kitchen and dumped his leftovers into a bowl. When she opened the refrigerator, a rush of cool air greeted her.

"Leftovers," she said to herself. "That is what I have become, a leftover."

She opened the china cabinet and took out a cocktail glass. Going to the guest bedroom, she rooted around in the back of a closet for a shoebox containing her secreted bottle of Scotch. Returning to the kitchen, she poured into the glass the comfort it would give her to survive another lonely evening. Two ice cubes and a slice of lemon completed the cocktail. Richard's hours away from home lengthened with board, deacon, and Civitan meetings. She often had to put away his dinners to reheat for whenever he returned home. Lonely, she found solace in a bottle. Her cocktail hour often became hours.

"If only I could have sustained my pregnancies," she said savoring the smooth taste of the Scotch. Taking the glass into the living room, she plopped down on the sofa. "Why," she asked, staring into the glass prisms, "did all of them have to end in miscarriages and a hysterectomy?"

She attended dozens of baby showers over the years, giving away parcels of gifts that should have been coming her way. Many times, she could barely drive home from them for the tears flowing down her face. It wasn't fair. She and Richard considered adoption, but with her luck, Verabelle was frightened they would end up with a deformed or maladjusted child, and then there were Richard's hours away from home in meetings to consider. Still, a child's presence would have given her comfort. Of course, they could have adopted and hired more maids to help, but as time went by, she smothered her loneliness in something far less complicated. It took little time to make a cocktail and there were no dirty diapers to change or a wailing child to disturb her sleep. Being childless, she justified, did have some compensation. She swirled the glass in the air to further chill it. Smothering her loneliness in a cocktail was easier than raising a child.

"Must be careful," she said to the glass in her hand. "One, just one, that can't hurt," she agreed, recalling when her five o'clock cocktail hours suddenly became three o'clocks, and not one cocktail, but several.

In the past, she even started having a quickie on the sly before she and Richard attended parties or dinners out with bank clients or visiting officials, and she kept plenty of strong mouthwash in an empty perfume spray bottle to hide the aroma on her breath. The more she drank, the more her system adjusted and the heavier she became. Although she knew Richard remained faithful, their lovemaking decreased. She often found herself weeping into her cocktails, feeling deserted and friendless. The only real pleasure in life came from the tingle of a cocktail as it trickled down her throat, warming her stomach and soothing her nerves.

Sitting at a Mission Society meeting, bridge club, or church function, she looked forward to the time she could drive into her own driveway and return to the other life she led, a secret one that became increasingly more real. And the liquor loosened her tongue. While losing her own life, she became more interested in the intrigues of the lives around her. After finding her one night draped across the bed in a drunken stupor, Richard gave her an ultimatum.

"You either get sober or I'm going to send you to Birmingham to an institution to dry you out."

He ordered her to the car and drove her to Doc's, where he and Miss Adie were sympathetic. Doc handed her a prescription for medicine to be taken twice a day with the warning: "If you drink when you take these, you will become sick to your stomach."

And he made future appointments to keep track of her progress.

She stayed sober for some time, but Dick's banking skills increased and he often had out-of-town speaking engagements that left her lonelier than ever. Throwing away the pills, she once again sought solace in the bottle. None of the ladies suspected her little secret except for that one time when she dumped a little too much champagne into a bridal punch, and instead of crème de menthe on an ice cream dessert served at a luncheon, she ladled on Baileys with such a heavy hand, the dessert became more liquor than ice cream.

When Doc passed away, the only people who knew about her little secret were Dick and Miss Adie. Dick, of course, would be too embarrassed to admit his wife had a relationship with a bottle, and Miss Adie, well, she was Miss Adie. In fact, she never heard Miss Adie gossip, but then she never did see her except on Doc's arm at church or out in the garden. Now, Doc was gone and Miss Adie, an old woman, lay wasting away in her bed and writing a book! Eula had acted excited about the book. Miss Adie's comment, "Secrets kept too long," added more suspicion to its contents. "Secrets kept too long . . . whatever did she mean? The words made Verabelle shudder. In Miss Adie's addled state of mind ... no, it was inconceivable, but a wasted mind with spells of lucidity, who knew what she might do or say? And Eula? No one knew very much about Eula—only that Doc and Miss Adie took her in and she had been living with them for years, cooking and tending to them as they aged. Eula knew something. Of that Verabelle was certain.

She slowly swallowed the last of her Scotch and headed back to the bedroom for just a "teensy bit more." She would take a long bubble bath, brush her teeth, and gargle away the evidence. Long before Dick came home, she would be asleep in the bed they shared only for sleep. For just a moment, she entertained thoughts of what they used to share, but she willed away the memories that brought only regret. Sleep, however, did have its compensation. Then she didn't have to think, only dreams entertained her mind, and even those were quickly disappearing.

{TEN}

"WHY MISS OPAL," EULA GREETED, "HAVEN'T seen you in sech a long time." She swung the screen door open.

Opal, fascinated as ever at how Eula acquired it, tried not to stare at the puffy scar on her cheek. It looked particularly purple today on Eula's golden brown skin. "How is Miss Adie?" she asked, removing her gloves and stuffing them in her purse.

"'Bout the same, some days better than others. She be specially glad to see you."

"But will she know me?" Opal asked, handing off to Eula her offering, her rich and creamy Deep Dark Secret cake.

"Goodness," Eula exclaimed, skirting the question and taking the cake. "What a treat. This be 'bout the most chocolate dessert I has ever seen. It should perk up Miss Adie's appetite for shore. It's already got me going."

Opal followed her into the kitchen and reached for the refrigerator's handle to open it for Eula.

"Oh, no," Eula said as if in warning. "Don't bother. I take care of it later. 'Sides, Miss Adie bound to have heard the doorbell. She be eager to see who's there."

Opal suppressed a smile. Eula wasn't fooling her. Others had been here before her and like her they had come not strictly from a benevolent state. They were as curiosity-driven as she about Miss Adie and the rumored book. She followed Eula obediently down the hallway and into Miss Adie's bedroom. The ruined body in the bed surprised her. She still held an image in her head of the nearly hyper woman who helped nurse half the town at her husband's side and still had time to till the garden's earth, planting and pruning its massive produce. In the past, Opal often found herself feeling a bit shaky whenever a health issue forced her to Miss Adie and Doc's home office. Particularly emotional were the two times she delivered her children. She burst into tears when Miss Adie placed her first into her waiting arms.

Miss Adie's words on that day reverberated in her ears. "Now, now, dear," she said in a reassuring voice as she passed a cool cloth over Opal's forehead. "He's a perfectly formed child."

"Congratulations," Doc added, a smile crinkling the deep brown eyes above his mask.

Kylie Mae Applegate longed to have her mother standing there. She felt as if Miss Adie's voice had a tone of prevailing suspicion toward the young mother who lay on the table. Did the image of another woman, dying in childbirth, linger in her mind?

"My mother," she cried, touching the silken skin of her firstborn, cradled in her arms. "She died ..." Her mouth clamped shut. Horrified at her stupidity, she stared up into Miss Adie's eyes.

"Yes, dear," Miss Adie said, her voice a sympathetic whisper. "I know."

Those words *I know* lingered in Opal's mind through the following years. Thankfully, there was little occasion to encounter Miss Adie except in her husband's office. According to the town ladies, if she hadn't been married to Doc, Miss Adie would never have been part of any of Simpsonville's social scene. Except for the fact she was Doc's nurse, she was seen only on rare occasions that included Doc. All the town ladies wondered why she and Doc didn't have children of their own because Miss Adie's loving feelings toward children was evident when they were brought to Doc with an illness. She seemed more animated when she saw a child. Many of the ladies had been patients of Doc and Miss Adie when they were children or they had taken their own to them during times of illness. There was a twinkle in Miss Adie's eyes and a softness in her voice as she helped minister to their needs, but her personal life before her appearance in Simpsonville remained private, a closed door to all but Doc and her heart.

Like my own heart, Opal thought, recalling the young nurse who came down the trailer steps toward her the day she lost her mother. She alone knows, Opal thought, forcing a smile on her face as she walked toward the bed and its wasted occupant who vaguely resembled the woman who took her in her arms on that fateful day.

Miss Adie frowned.

"Look who's calling on you," Eula said, her hand on Opal's arm, gesturing her forward to a chair beside the bed. "Might be one of her bad days," she whispered.

Opal took the seat and looked down at Miss Adie's hands, pitted like spoiled fruit.

"Perhaps . . . " Opal looked up at Eula as she half-rose from the chair.

"You," Miss Adie said, pointing, "I know you."

"Of course you do." Eula had a laugh in her voice. "Miss Opal. She brought you something special."

"Then why didn't she give it to me?" Miss Adie frowned up at Eula.

"It put away in the fridge; a special dessert for later."

"Thank you, child," Miss Adie said, searching Opal's face as if it were a road map taking her somewhere. "You're the one," she said, fanning the air with a withered hand between Opal and herself. "Just a child. I had to tell you. No one else."

Eula and Opal exchanged glances. Eula's was puzzled; Opal's edgy.

"A bad day," Eula said, but not low enough.

"Yes," Miss Adie agreed, "a very bad day. So good to see you, dear," she said, her withered lips cracking a smile. "How nice of you to come. It's been a long time. All grown up," she added, "a pretty child, still pretty. I like your hat."

"I really should . . . " Opal rose from the chair.

"Don't go just yet," Miss Adie admonished, "seems you just got here. Tell me about yourself."

"About myself?" Opal clutched her hands in her lap.

"How did you manage?"

Opal looked into Miss Adie's eyes. The milky blue reflected back the image of the child she used to be, helpless, bereft of her mother; her father, trailer trash. The sorrow she felt that day was in the caring eyes looking down at her. She crumpled into the nurse's waiting arms. Kylie Mae Applegate had been nothing, had nothing, and out of that nothing, she built a life, a wonderful life. As if she were that child again, she wanted to tell this woman what a success she made of her life. Only the two of them knew from what a meager existence she came. However much she loved them, she took for granted Hank, her children, the good life she built in this town. She pulled her chair closer.

"I met a wonderful man," she related. "Hank Hopkins."

"Oh," Miss Adie placed her hands together in prayer fashion pointed toward the ceiling. "What a nice boy; used to deliver the newspaper."

"He's the town principal now," she reminded the diminished mind, "and we have two children, Paul and Mattie."

"Children? Oh, my." A wistful expression rippled across her face. "Do they look like you?"

"I think Paul resembles his father and Mattie, I believe, looks a lot like I used to when I was a child."

"A beautiful girl, then. God is good," Miss Adie said, looking at the window and out toward the wasted garden. She smiled as if she saw something there neither Opal nor Eula could.

"Doc would be pleased," Miss Adie said, turning back toward Opal and reaching out for her hand.

Opal took it into her own, amazed at how fragile it looked: the veins puffy and the fingers nearly bare bone with a layer of thin skin over them.

"You got on then," Miss Adie smiled up into Opal's face. "You managed."

"I've been lucky," Kylie Mae Applegate told Miss Adie.

"Your mama ..." Miss Adie stated, her eyes glancing up at the ceiling, searching for something.

Opal took a deep breath, holding it as if she had fallen into deep water and was sinking. Now, Eula would hear her hidden history.

Miss Adie's gaze returned to Opal's face. "Your mama," she repeated, "she would be so proud." Her bony hand limply shook Opal's.

"Thank you," Kylie Mae Applegate said, patting the hand and laying it gently on the quilt.

"Don't wait so long." Miss Adie said as Opal rose to

leave. "Can't believe how grown up you are; mustn't wait too long."

"I'll come back," Opal promised.

"She enjoy your visit," Eula said walking her to the door. "You see how it is. Sometime, she wander in that mind of hers trying to find the right road out. You did her some good. Thank you."

"Oh, no," Opal and Kylie Mae said, placing her hands on Eula's ample arms. "I'm the one who should be thanking her. Take care, Eula, and call me if you need me."

{ELEVEN}

HATTIE TURPIN SAT ALONE AT THE BREAKFAST table looking out the window onto the deck where the hummingbird feeder hung. An emerald-crested hummer like a tiny fairy sprite was busily hovering in the early summer air, dipping its long, narrow beak into the sugared water. How she loved spring and the hazy days of summer. She took a sip of her morning tea and looked toward the woods bordering the creek on her backyard. The trees looked nearly smoky, draped with the full bloom of bluish-purple wisteria. Just the other day, a goldfinch landed in the basket of marigolds that hung from an eave over the deck. It swooped in like a race car curving around a track as it pecked at the marigold's seeds.

She took another sip of tea. A book, Verabelle had said. Miss Adie, in a diminished state of mind, writing a book? Of all things! She hadn't seen Miss Adie in a long time, but perhaps it was time for a visit. Few, if any, except their daughter knew of Roy's affair with a clerk in their store. If the news got out, it would be like the goldfinch pecking away at the marigold's seed. She hadn't mentioned the news to Roy. Indeed, they never spoke of the incident, now long in the past.

The consequences of his heedless act of passion had nearly decimated their marriage. She threatened to leave, but there was Molly to consider. She adored her father. Often Hattie felt left out of the close bond between father and daughter. Roy firmly informed her early in their dating years that he wanted children.

"A field of children," he told her as she sat in the car with him, petting in the first phase of their romance. "I'll plant my seed," he teased, biting her neck, his hands pushing up her skirt as a delicious tingle crept up her spine. "We'll have a full crop."

But God granted them only one child before Hattie suffered multiple miscarriages and infections. Doc sent her to a specialist in Montgomery who told her she probably wouldn't be able to bear any more children.

"You're still my delicious," Roy reassured her, snuggling up to her in bed when she sank into a depressive state after the news. "It doesn't change what we are to each other."

Hattie yielded to his desire, but somehow their couplings were not the same. When she thought back on it, she realized that it hadn't been entirely Roy's fault. He was an ardent lover. Emotionally, she became as barren and fruitless as the once-fertile garden Doc and Miss Adie labored over. Everything they did together was a labor of love. Now that Doc was gone and Miss Adie bedridden, the garden became just a large expanse of earth spotted with clumps of weedy grass. Roy's attempts to make love to her had, if not completely stopped, diminished in frequency.

Awakened in the middle of the night by the touch of his hands on her body, she turned away, feigning sleep. Why then, should she have been surprised and angered when he sought solace in some other woman's arms? She walked unexpectedly into their store one afternoon. Roy had not been at the cash register or anywhere in the front of the store. Thinking that he was in the stockroom, she opened the door to find him and that prissy young thing they hired having at it against a store wall. They were standing: Roy's pants at his ankles and the girl's dress shoved up to her armpits. They looked like someone had glued them together. Roy's face, resting on the girl's breasts, had been turned away and the girl's eyes were shut, her head thrown back as if she were gulping air. Even now putting her hands over her ears to shut out the sounds of that day, Hattie could hear their panted breaths and moans of pleasure and then a loud cry: "No! No!"

Roy turned his head toward her and the girl, her eyes wide and startled, stared at her fearfully. As if a vacuum of air sucked them apart, they separated. The girl dropped her rumpled dress and raced past her out the door, leaving her panties on the stockroom's floor. Roy pulled up his pants, and with a flushed face and wide eyes approached her.

"Nothing," he tried to explain. "She . . . oh, Hattie . . . "

The girl's musky smell coated his body. His mouth was rouged with the girl's lipstick. His pants were unzipped.

Looking into his astonished pleading eyes, she advised, "Better zip up before a customer comes in the door."

With a crimson face and shaking hands, he pulled the zipper up.

"Don't," he called as she headed for the front door. "Please let me explain."

"What?" she said, turning to look back at him. "That you just screwed the help? I could see that."

"No, you don't understand. Lonely," he said. "Just a matter of . . . please, Hattie. Where are you going?"

"Home," she said. "Time to cook supper."

She opened the car door and got in, her hands shaking as she inserted the key in the ignition. Roy was still standing at the store's door watching, his eyes looking like a cocker spaniel that had just been scolded, as she pulled away from the curb. She didn't cry. The tears wouldn't come. They'd dried up long ago with the passion she once felt for her husband. Home, she said to him, "home," a word that used to represent comfort, stability. Now, it seemed as dried up as her womanhood, void of love or the need for it.

"Mom, what is it?" Molly, their fifteen-year-old daughter, asked when she came through the front door.

"Home early, aren't you?" she numbly stated. She looked up into her daughter's face as she plopped down on the sofa, placing her purse on the floor beside her as if she was a guest in this house.

Molly sat down beside her. She took one of her hands in hers. "Did someone die?" she asked.

"Die?" She laughed. "Why, yes, I suppose you could say that."

And then, she laughed again and again, convulsively, her body shaking. Only this laughter contained a cruel rumble like distant thunder rippling across the sky, warning of a coming storm.

"Mom!" Molly wrapped her arms around her. "Oh, Mom, I'm so sorry."

Then it dawned on her. Molly! Molly knew. How long had she known? She started helping in the store when she got out of school, but one day she announced that it was interfering with her homework and after-school activities. She thought that perhaps Molly was infatuated with some school boy, but now she recalled the looks she kept giving her father when he arrived home, as if he were a stranger walking in the door.

One day she mentioned Molly's strange new behavior to Roy. "I'm concerned," she said. "Have you noticed something different about Molly?"

His eyes slanted warily. "Teenage angst," he explained, picking up the evening paper and retreating to the den.

Their daughter must have walked in on her father and that girl just as she did.

"Oh, Molly," she said apologetically, taking her daughter into her arms as if her husband's indiscretion was her own.

They sat together in the silent understanding that someone they loved and looked up to had simply disappeared. "Has someone died?" Molly had inquired. What better way to describe the sorrow they shared as mother and daughter?

"It's over now," she comforted her daughter. "She's gone. Your father will be home soon and we'll go on."

"Will we?" Molly asked.

She understood that Molly's confidence in her father was shattered, but Molly's life was still beginning and with time, she would find a way to forgive. Her life, however, would remain altered, irretrievably changed. She wouldn't leave. There was her daughter to raise, even if life in this house with this man would never be the same. She felt as if she had once again lost a child, a life planned on, a love forsaken. She was in the kitchen preparing supper when Roy came home.

"I can explain," he said, touching her tentatively on the arm.

She backed away, opening the refrigerator to take out a congealed salad.

"Don't," she said in a warning tone, the salad shaking in her hands.

"What are you going to do?" he asked sheepishly.

"Put the rest of supper on the table," she replied, turning her back on him and walking into the dining room to put the quivering gelatin on the table.

That night, she started sleeping in the guest bedroom, but she found herself tossing and turning. If only there was someone she could talk to, someone who wouldn't divulge Roy's affair. Her mother taught her carefully the southern recipe: Never raise your voice, don't speak ill of anyone, keep family problems private. Life, like a fine coating of powder applied to the face, was to be dusted over, its flaws hidden. She began to lose weight; dark circles appeared beneath her eyes. Fearing she was suffering from a grave illness, she made an appointment with Doc.

"All your vitals are fine," he reassured her, his kind blue eyes searching her face. "Is anything else bothering you, Hattie?"

His voice contained the same kind, sincere timbre it always did on office visits as a child. When she started trembling, Miss Adie took her hand.

"Is Molly all right?" she asked.

When she nodded, Miss Adie inquired about Roy and suddenly Hattie found herself crying convulsively. While Miss Adie held her in her arms, Hattie told her and Doc everything. Doc prescribed a mild sedative and advised marriage counseling. The pills gave her the first peaceful night of sleep since discovering Roy's indiscretion, but she never mentioned marital counseling to him. She became accustomed to the nights spent alone, to the polite conversation between herself and the person she called husband. Sometimes in the midst of a deep sleep, she dreamed of another couple, one who once occupied this house, but in the light of day, they became passing shadows.

She began to crave chocolate. Somewhere, she read it was an aphrodisiac. She made fudge pies and chocolate marble cakes, scraping the sides of pans and pots with a spoon to lick up the remains. She bought chocolate bonbons and bars, secreting them away in the guest bedroom closet for late-night treats.

"Gaining a little weight, aren't you?" Roy inquired one morning in one of their limited attempts at communication.

"Perhaps," she answered nonchalantly, putting on the morning coffee before he left for work, where he had hired a male as an assistant.

Her girdles developed stretch marks on them where they fought to hide her bulges and she was forced long ago to give up on the clothes she used to wear. Elegant suits and dresses went into boxes to be taken to the church for rummage sales or charitable events. She ignored weight scales and Doc's advice on yearly checkups.

"Not healthy," Doc advised about her added weight. It's bad for your heart.

She wanted to tell him that the damage done to her heart was irreparable and that in a strange way she was happier in her new skin. She became someone else. The svelte self who used to wear her now-abandoned clothes walked out of her home the day she discovered her husband's affair.

Molly, however, busy with youthful plans for her future, had seemingly forgiven him and became her daddy's girl again. If Miss Adie in her altered state of mind should conjure up the past and reveal their carefully guarded secret, the town's cruel gossip would devastate her daughter. Perhaps it could even affect Roy's sales, money that would ensure that their daughter could go to a good college, the way she and Roy did.

The thought of college brought to mind once again the passionate joy she and Roy shared when they first met at the state university. Hattie recalled the excitement of walking across a tree-filled campus, her arms loaded with books, on her way to her next class. Suddenly, she stumbled across a broken brick in the pavement, landing on her knees, her books splayed across the grass bordering the walkway.

"Are you all right?" a male voice asked as she half-sat, half-lay, her skirt crumpled across the pavement and grass.

He was kneeling in front of her, a good-looking young man with high cheekbones, blue-green eyes, and a dimple in his chin. A freshman cap with a huge A on the front sat on a head of curly blond hair. His face was so close, she thought she could see sunlight reflected off the blue in those eyes. She blinked at the reflection.

"Should I call someone?" he asked, a frown between those brilliant eyes.

"No," she assured, "you're fine." A slight smile lifted the corners of her mouth.

"I'm fine," he said, humor in his voice. "The question is, are you all right?"

"Oh," she said, surprised as if she were dreaming and someone had just awakened her. "I mean ... could you help me up?"

His hands gently turned her as he lifted her to her feet with a warning: "Don't try to put too much pressure on your feet just yet."

Held in his arms, she looked up into his face. "Hello," she said inanely.

"Hello," he said in a jovial voice, grinning.

"I'm a freshman, too," she said, adding quickly before he disappeared, "from Simpsonville, Alabama."

"Simpsonville!" he exclaimed, his grin deepening. "Then I'm your neighbor, from Allenburg, one town over."

"Convenient," she responded inanely. "I mean, that's nice."

"Yes," he said, nodding, a huge smile on his face, "convenient and nice."

Smoothing down her skirt, Hattie discovered her knees were scratched and bleeding. He took her to the infirmary and waited for the nurse to see her, then with her knees bandaged, treated her to lunch. It was to be the first of many ardent dates and an amorous love affair.

Without warning, a tear tracked down her cheek. Strange, she thought laconically, that one wound should mark the beginning of a relationship that resulted in the greatest wound a man could inflict on his wife: a love affair with another woman. She couldn't allow Roy's affair to become public knowledge. She must protect Molly from the humiliation.

She needed to find a way to get past Eula and discover the contents of Miss Adie's book. She would take her prized vegetable soup to Miss Adie. Everyone in town tried to guess at the secret something that made it so special. Only her family knew the ingredients that went into a soup that had delighted generations. Several cartons were in the freezer. She would get one down and pay a call, a very important call.

{TWELVE}

EULA SAT TYPING PAGE AFTER PAGE OF THE
notes taken at Miss Adie's bedside. She stopped momentarily
to stand and stretch. News in a small town traveled faster than
a hummer's flight. Miss Adie's front doorbell was nearly plum
wore out with its constant *ding-dong*. Jest like she thought,
once the ladies heard about Miss Adie's book, they were flocking to her door like a bunch of gangling geese flapping their
wings, seeking out the seed of what was going into the rumored
book. In a town like Simpsonville rumor was as good as truth.

"Every life hold a secret all its own," she said aloud, repo-
sitioning her heinie on the chair and placing her nearly numb
fingers on the keyboard.

She was thankful now that she had taken a typing course
in school. She wasn't a speedy typist, but she got the job done
right well and she always made high marks in school for her
spelling and shorthand. If only she had listened to Lila Mae
and stuck it out, but no, she had to go and fall off a cliff for
that no good Jack.

"More like a jack of trades," she said to the keys as her
hands fumbled over the keyboard.

And how he knew his trades! More like a snake, slithering around her, climbing her body, sinking his poison in her skin. A school dropout, he slipped from one job to another as a yardman, working for the city picking up trash, slinging hash at a roadside café. She passed him one day on the walk home from school. He was leaning against a tree, smoking; his skin so dark, he seemed part of the tree's bark, and so tall he could reach up with one hand and snatch a bird's nest out of its branches. As soon as he saw her coming, he flicked the cigarette on the ground and put out its smoke with his boot.

"Whar you going, sweetheart?" he said, his voice as smoldering as the ashes at his feet.

Lila Mae constantly warned her about talking to strangers, so she picked up her pace to pass him by. He jumped out onto the roadway in front of her so fast she nearly bumped into his massive chest.

"You deaf or something?" he asked, his face so close, she could smell his cigarette breath. "You going to put out a fire, baby, or start one?"

And he grabbed her in his muscular arms and brought her up against him so hard she could feel the muscles in his legs and more.

"You see how it is," he said, knowingly, pressing her harder and lifting her chin until his lips were on hers.

And oh how that man could snuff the breath out of a girl and leave her moaning and wanting more. Even now, remembering, she could feel the heat of the moment, the quickening in her stomach that moved lower, making her feel a desperate need she never knew existed. She recalled she had thought of her mama and daddy; that this must have been what it was like with them; how they rushed into each other's arms, their bodies so close they looked like they could just walk through each other.

"I got to have you, girl," Jack said, his kisses on her neck and then her throat.

He pulled her that way toward the tree and placed her back to it underneath its low-lying branches.

"Umm, baby, what have we got here?" he said, lifting her skirt. "Something delicious," he said, sliding her down the tree.

Even now, she could feel the tree roots against her back and the root of him pressing on her. The sun had been particularly bright that day. It grew brighter and brighter as she rose through the branches of the tree and toward it.

"Lawd," Eula said to herself. "Memory has grabbed at me again."

She stood and walked into the kitchen for a glass of cold water.

"That man," she said to the kitchen walls.

Lila Mae was standing at the gate of their house looking down the road as she came home that day. Even from where she was up the road, Eula could sense the air around her felt like bad weather coming as if a storm was brewing out of Lila Mae's worry.

"Baby," Jack cried, taking little bites of her neck. "I got to have you. I'll be waiting right here," he said as she, startled by her emotions and the need for him, set out on the road again for home. "You hear?" he called after her, "tomorrow?"

Eula staggered down the road, smoothing down her clothes, her hands snatching at her hair, knowing that grass stains were probably on her dress, hoping that was all.

"Chile," Lila Mae rushed onto the road, grabbing her. "Where have you been?"

She made up a story about a truck that had swerved on the road, nearly hitting her, of how she jumped into a roadside bank to avoid injury. And Lila Mae had believed her.

"Lawd, you done looked out for my baby," she cried, taking her inside the house and pouring her a glass of lemonade. Bringing her the drink, she noticed her neck. "Eula," her voice sounded harsh. "What happened here?"

She hadn't even thought about her neck, about his bites. Just thinking about them made her want to run out the door and back for more of him.

"Briars," she lied. "A rose patch."

Lila Mae walked out of the room to get some antiseptic cream from the medicine cabinet. If only there had been some cure for the need that man had forced upon her, Eula's life would have been better. She would have graduated from high school, maybe had some chance for a good job somewhere. There was no one to blame but herself. If it hadn't been for her daddy coming to her rescue, she would probably be dead now. People were wrong when they spoke of the past being past. It was never really past; it was jest yesterday. Once a thing happened, bad or good, it became a part of you. If it was bad, real bad like Jack, you could somehow put it behind you and go on, but it was still a part of you. The good book spoke about forgiveness. It wasn't a saintly act, Eula believed. It was necessary, because it was really a selfish act. If you couldn't forgive something you could never forget, it was like a load of wash without any detergent. It still came out dirty and you weren't any better for it. It was a lesson she learned the hard way. When she told Lila Mae she'd landed in briars, it wasn't a lie, for that is exactly what happened when she decided to run away with Jack.

She shook her head as if she could shake away the memory,

but it did no good. Once a thing got hold of you, it never let go. You jest went on taking it day by day, knowing the good Lawd knew every secret thing about you and still loved you.

She packed a few things in a clothes bag. In the middle of the night, she sneaked out of the house and hid it near the hedge beside the road. On the way to school, she took a quick look behind to see if Lila Mae was watching, but she was inside cleaning up breakfast leavings. Grabbing the bag, she went on to school, putting it underneath her desk until it was time to go home. And there he was jest like before, having a smoke and waiting underneath the oak. His body quickened when he saw her coming down the road.

"Knew you'd come back for more," he smiled in a near-sneer, stepping out of the shade and toward her. "Liked it, didn't you? What you got here?" he asked, spying the bag in her hand.

"Came to stay," she said.

"Now, baby." His eyes widened. "It ain't that way with me. I don't ever stay. Life ain't got no hold on me or any woman."

"Oh." She felt stunned. Her face felt hot as if he had slapped her. "Well, then, we got nothing more to say or do here," she stated, her feet prepared to travel on.

He jumped out in front of her. "Hold on," he said, a big paw landing on her shoulder. His eyes studied hers, his forehead furrowed like a field newly plowed. "You mean what you say?"

"I do. Either you take me whole or you don't get any of me."

He threw his head back and laughed, a laugh that seemed to whip up a wind that rippled the tree leaves on the big oak. "Could take you anyway," he threatened.

Her spine tingled with ripples that sent a momentary shiver over her body. "If you do, won't be the same," she warned. "I won't be giving back what you give and you know it."

His eyes widened at her response and he bent his head as if in prayer and slapped one of his big paws on his forehead as if he was holding in a thought he didn't want spoken.

"You're a hant," he said at last. "Done gone and cast a spell. No woman I has known like you. You done got inside me some way. I'm not the marrying kind, if that what you think."

"I don't," she said, trying to hide her disappointment, but marry or no, she had to have this man. She couldn't imagine life without his hands roaming over her. His poison snatched away her very soul.

He reached for her hand holding the bag, taking it, then reached for her other hand, bringing her in close to his chest. The smell of him, the feel of his arms; he might be poison, but it was a poison she thought she couldn't live without. She walked away from all she had known with a man she didn't know at all, but for the claim he had over her body.

"Foolish," Eula said to the typewriter as if she was watching the young person she used to be walking down a road toward a terribly unstable future.

Later, she learned that Lila Mae called on every neighbor for miles around, had gone to the school and talked with her teachers, the principal, and even her daddy, but no one knew where she had gone. She simply went missing until the day Doc and Miss Adie came to her rescue, and by then, Jack had 'bout done her in to the point that even Eula had trouble recognizing the girl who took a wrong road, hand-in-hand with a man whose middle name was trouble.

{THIRTEEN}

THE SOUND OF THE DOORBELL BROUGHT EULA back to the present. She rose from her seat at the typewriter and bustled toward the front door.

"Can I help you?" she asked of the stolid woman on the doorstep wearing a green and pink striped pillbox hat and white gloves.

"Eula, it's Mrs. Turpin," the woman announced, tilting her head, a stiff smile on her face.

"Ms. Turpin, of course."

She tried to mask the surprise in her voice. The Ms. Turpin she remembered looked like she stepped out of a fashion magazine, so trim. But the woman who entered the living room had a pudgy face and body. Fleshy arms draped out of a paisley sleeveless dress with no waistline.

"I brought my vegetable soup for Miss Adie. How is she today?"

"She resting, but I know she mighty glad to see you. It's been a long time since you been here and your soup, my, what a treat! It always been tasty. Tried to cook it one day long ago, but something special left out," she said, taking the soup tureen from Ms. Turpin's hands. "Everybody in town favor this soup. Jest give me time to put it in the fridge."

Hattie followed Eula into the kitchen. "Did you brown the meat, chop up fresh tomatoes, put in okra, celery, carrots, potatoes, broth, green beans, and fresh corn off the husk?" she asked.

"Yes, mum, but this here soup taste better. Something missing in mine."

Hattie smiled. Everyone in town tried guessing what went into her family recipe, but none succeeded. No one knew the missing ingredient.

Eula opened the refrigerator. It was packed with food. Hattie spied boxes that must be cakes. She hadn't been the first and certainly would not be the last. The town was buzzing like a bunch of bees seeking out its hive with conjecture about Miss Adie's book. And no one wanted to be stung. No telling with her dementia and knowledge of the town's history what Miss Adie was putting in her book.

"Well," Eula said, closing the refrigerator door and opening the freezer. "There's room here."

"Townspeople have been good," Hattie said.

"Yessum," Eula agreed. "Let me check see if Miss Adie still resting."

Miss Adie was lying on her back snatching at the quilt that covered her, her hands still eager to be about something. Eula often wondered what was going on in that once-active mind. Were her hands sewing up some wound, working on a quilt, holding a newborn, or hoeing away in the once-fertile earth of her garden? Maybe they were searching for somebody's hand to hold, somebody like Doc.

"Got a visitor," Eula said. "Miss Hattie. She brought her special soup."

"Soup?" she asked. "Not hungry."

"She jest want to come say hello."

"Who's here?" she asked, the wrinkles on her forehead crinkling. "Who did you say?"

"Miss Hattie of the Mission Society. Her husband Mr. Roy Turpin runs the hardware store."

"I know her?"

"Yessum, you do, you and Doc watched her grow. Doc delivered their daughter, Molly."

Miss Adie's eyes did a twirly-whig in her mind like a projector in reverse searching backward for a picture slowly forming from the past. She blinked. "Hattie," she said, "lovely girl."

"It be all right," Eula walked around the corner to where Miss Hattie waited, "she ready to see you."

"Miss Adie." Hattie entered the room, a wide smile adding more plump to her pudgy cheeks.

"Who are *you?*" the shrunken figure in the bed asked.

Hattie frowned. It was worse than she thought. She didn't recognize the bony woman lying in the bed and Miss Adie didn't recognize her, but there was a slight resemblance to the once-robust person Hattie used to know.

"I'm Hattie Turpin," she said, taking the seat Eula directed her to beside the bed.

"No, you aren't!" Miss Adie refuted, "but I think you *are* someone I used to love," she added, an emaciated hand reaching out to her.

Hattie took the limp hand in hers, rubbing a finger across the bulging veins barely concealed behind a thin layer of flesh.

"Something about the eyes," Miss Adie said, peering into hers. "You have a sister?"

"No, there's just Roy, my husband, and Molly, our daughter.

You and Doc delivered her."

"Doc," she said, turning her head toward the window and the long-gone garden. "Children. Wish we had children." She looked behind Hattie at Eula standing guard. "Eula knows," she said.

"Knows?" Hattie asked.

"Everything," Miss Adie informed.

Eula drew in a breath and held it.

"She's a treasure," Hattie praised. "You're lucky to have her."

"Yes, we are," she said. "Doc and I, we would be lost without her, but we didn't know. I didn't know . . . "

"What's that?" Hattie inquired.

"'Love above all, the thing that lasts,'" Miss Adie quoted. "Don't forget," she said, withdrawing her withered hand from Hattie's. "So good of you to visit. Don't wait so long."

"I won't," she promised, rising to go.

"Life," Miss Adie said.

"Yes." Hattie raised an eyebrow in question.

"Tend it like a garden. That's what Doc always says. Isn't that right, Eula?"

"He do," she agreed.

"Come back soon," Miss Adie said as Hattie rose to leave. "You're a nice young lady, whoever you are."

"I'm sorry," Eula apologized, seeing Miss Hattie to the door, "One of her bad days. Some days be more better."

"Pickle juice," Hattie blurted out.

Eula raised an eyebrow in question. "Mam'n?"

"My vegetable soup," she said, "the missing ingredient is pickle juice."

"My, my, never would have guessed," Eula said.

"And Eula," Hattie added. "Don't worry about my visit

being a bad one. Miss Adie gave me something to consider. She gifted me."

"That be her, all right," Eula agreed.

She stood at the door watching Miss Hattie walk to her car. "Life do hand out all kind of surprises," she said to herself, returning to the typewriter and Miss Adie's book. "Pickle juice, of all things. Never would have thought that something vinegary could make something taste so good."

She sighed. For just a second there, she thought that Miss Adie might be 'bout to tell something that'd have the whole town fevered with talk. What was she thinking? Miss Adie didn't know—or did she? Her fingers searched the keys, but her mind was rewinding scenes from the past: the towns she lived in with Jack, the hovels that put a roof over their heads until they were thrown out because he couldn't pay the rent, the jobs she had taken as waitress, washwoman, and cook, to keep them in food and board, hiding money under the broken-down mattresses they slept on to keep him from spending it on drink. He had warned her and she should have listened. All the good of what she could remember of him was the thrill of his touch on her body, their bodies twining and intertwining on worn-out sheets. She tried not to think of that awful day that should have been her happiest. She had awakened feeling sick to her stomach and the sick kept coming day after day. She couldn't afford a regular doctor, so she went to a cheap clinic where she quickly discovered she was pregnant. It should have been a time of joy.

"Ain't no room in my life for some squalling parasite," Jack scolded as if she had gone and committed a crime. "Lose it."

A woman she worked with at the diner recommended a cheap clinic. "Safe, clean, and quick," she informed. "A day or two off yore feet; back to business."

It was quick, but not painless, physically or emotionally. She had trouble sleeping and getting out of bed to work at the diner. She kept wondering what the baby would have looked like. At night, she was often awakened by what she imagined was the cry of a baby, her baby. That child would be a young adult now, and all she had left of the love she once felt deeply for Jack.

What happens to love when it dies? Does it wither and dry up like Miss Adie and Doc's once fruitful garden because it's untended? Is it like a balloon ripped away by a sudden wind drifting on the air till it snags on a bush or tree limb? Her heart had been so full of love for that man, it nearly snuffed out the air she breathed. And then, she awakened one day to find it all used up along with the magic. He seemed a stranger, rough and cold, wandering through life with no map to guide him and not caring who or what he stomped on along the way.

"Come here, girl," he would say, snatching at her body, taking what he wanted and leaving her spent.

One night, she made the mistake of telling him she was too tired. He grabbed her by the hair, throwing her across the bed on her stomach, ripping aside her clothes, yelling in her ear, as he bent one of her arms behind her back, "When I wants something, I gits it."

When she screamed with the pain of it, he smacked one of his big paws up the side of her head. The room whirled like a merry-go-round. A large purple welt covered her cheek for weeks till it drained away down her side of her face just beneath the surface of her skin like colored tears of red and blue. When her co-workers, giving her suspicious and sometimes compassionate looks, asked her what wall she had stumbled into, she lied, telling them she tripped over her clothes basket and gone helter-skelter onto the floor, landing on her face.

He started drinking heavily. At such times, she tried to keep her distance, but even if she pretended to be in the bathroom doing her business, he would come after her, forcing himself on her over and over again. The only place to hide was work. She signed on for double duty, dreading the hour she would return home. Once she considered leaving and going back to Lila Mae's if she still lived in the old house, but her pride got in the way.

Eula shook her head, trying to forget the awful day it all ended, but the good Lawd put her on another pathway and here she sat trying to type up the beginnings of Miss Adie's book. Then there was the matter of a printer. Leaving Miss Adie with the girl Doc had hired from the quarters to spell Eula when she shopped for groceries or got medicine, Eula went to the library to the separate room set aside for her color to do some asking about a book on publishing.

"Publishing?" the woman at the desk asked, disdain in her voice.

"Yessum."

The woman was thin, with a long face and nose. She looked at Eula over the rim of itty-bitty glasses. Her eyes did spider tracks over Eula's face. "Don't know if there is such a book here," she informed. "Look on aisle six under P or W—P for publishing, W for writing. Can't check it out, you understand. Your ... well, your color ..."

"Yes'mum," Eula said.

"Do you know your alphabet?" she asked, her nose pinching tighter.

"I been to school," Eula replied, wanting to say more.

She headed down the aisle, murmuring under her breath. Some people didn't realize that by treating somebody as if they stupid, it jest make them look that way. She found an old book about to shed its bindings and sat in a corner writing down a few names, but most, like New York, were too far away. What she needed was someplace close in case there were telephone calls to make. Finally, one day looking through the newspaper, she found an ad for a book publisher in Montgomery. She wrote the company to see how much they charged, describing what she thought the book would come to be. For days, she fretted over it, checking and re-checking the mailbox. Then one day she received a contract telling how much money per page and asking if she wanted to hire an editor. She was a pretty good speller and grammar had never been much of a problem for her in school, so she sat down with the telephone directory writing down the names of the ladies Miss Adie wanted to see the book and tacking on the extras for the library and others just in case.

Long before Miss Adie became bad in her mind and worse in her body and Doc was still able, Miss Adie and Doc consulted with their lawyer. Eula and Doc were sitting on the porch in the early hours of a summer night rocking and listening to the *quank, quank* of tree frogs, the *cheeps* of birds bout to nest in for the night, and the *chitter-chatter* of crickets. Miss Adie, already wearing down like Doc, was slumbering away in her bed.

"Eula," he told her, "if I go first and Adie isn't able, I have made provisions for you to withdraw what you need from the bank. The same provision applies if Adie goes and I'm unable."

She didn't want to hear such talk and told him so, but he had gone on. "Don't be afraid. There will be no trouble. Do you understand? It's legal and binding. I have spoken with the bank president. All you have to do is sign your name. There's a piece of paper inside for your signature so all will be ready for when the time comes."

She put her hands over her ears to shut out such talk, but he reached over and took them in his own. "You will have to buy groceries, medicine, and whatever else is required. No one will bother you, I promise. My will details it all."

"Don't the crickets sound peaceful?" she said, trying to change the subject.

"Eula. You have been through enough to know that our time here on earth doesn't hold many guarantees, but what I have just told you does. It is all I, we, have to leave you."

They didn't say anything for a time—just sat rocking, the squeaking of their chairs joining the music of the night. Suddenly, the sky around them looked filmy and soft. The leaves had blurry edges. A flicker of light appeared above the front lawn, then another.

"Fireflies," Doc said, "summer's lanterns. An Indian chief nearing his death said 'What is life? It is the flash of a firefly in the night. It is the breath of a buffalo in the wintertime. It is the little shadow that runs across the grass and loses itself in the sunset.'"

Eula would never forget the sound of all the critters as they tuned up for the close of day, the firefly flicker like fairy lanterns in the dark or Doc's mellow voice quoting an Indian chief. She knew as long as she lived, she would never forget that night with Doc.

{FOURTEEN}

"HOW WAS YOUR VISIT WITH YOUR SISTER?" Jim asked Wynene, taking her suitcase from her hand and brushing her cheek with his lips as she entered the house.

"She's doing much better," she said as she started up the stairs to their bedroom, already regretting she wasn't still in Dan's arms.

"You seem different," he said following her with the suitcase.

"Different?" Her heart took an extra beat. Did Jim suspect something?

He set the suitcase on the bed for her to unpack. "You look rested and happy. The trip must have done you some good, too."

Wynene opened the closet to remove hangers. Keep busy, she said to herself. Try not to think about the frown on Dan's face as she left him.

"I know it's often difficult to be a pastor's wife," Jim added. "There are a lot of demands on your life. Guess I just want to say thank you and let you know you are appreciated. Quite a few members asked after you at services. They missed you, too."

Her face flushed. She suddenly felt guilty. "Jim ..."

He had already started down the stairs to his study. "Yes?" he asked, turning to look back up at her.

She hesitated. "Anything in particular happen while I was gone?"

"Just the usual, with one exception: I had to counsel a man, a very lonely one."

"Oh?"

"He was feeling a little depressed. His wife left town, but it was for a good cause. Her sister needed her." He grinned. "I really did miss you, Wynene. It's good, really good, to have you home."

She watched him continue down the stairs. Was missing the same as love? With Jim, she believed it was. He needed her in a spiritual way to fulfill his life. He had said he appreciated her and she knew it was true, but it wasn't enough. Love between a husband and wife was not complete without physical passion. Jim reserved his passion for his sermons, his congregation, his God. He was her God, also, and she believed that He wanted her to be happy. She sat down on the bed. Would God condemn her for finding completion with Dan? Adulteress, wasn't that what she had become? She had never been dishonest. Suddenly, she felt tired. She couldn't go on living two separate lives, but she didn't want to hurt Jim. She could imagine the talk. It would destroy his standing in this small community.

"Life is far too short," Dan had pleaded. "I have already lost years without you. I don't want you for only a weekend at a time. I want you forever."

Forever with Dan sounded like heaven; with Jim it would be a long friendship.

Home, she thought. I'm home. Was she really? She felt

more at home with Dan in temporary rooms than she did with Jim in her own house. She was only a few hours away from Dan and already she felt the loss of his presence. Without him, she felt as if she was walking around in someone else's house, in someone else's skin. Must stay busy, she said to herself, getting up off the bed. Suddenly, unbidden, an image of Doc and Miss Adie together in the garden came to her.

Over the years, the whole town became accustomed to seeing the couple, hats on their heads to shade them from the sun, hoe and spade in hand, turning the earth, planting the seed, season after season. The seed they planted had been so ordinary looking and non-productive until they inserted it into the waiting beds. Then, it became a living miracle with shoots of green. Now that Doc was gone and Miss Adie bedridden, did the dried-up beds that were once so fertile remember the touch of their hands, the loving care they gave to the once-rich soil? The garden was part of them and they were part of it. As they turned the earth, they awakened it. Now it seemed to be perpetually asleep, dormant, devoid of their touch. Did the sod that had once been a bountiful garden recall their voices, the scent of their bodies as they knelt side by side in a labor of love? She never saw them embrace in the garden or on her visits, but there was between them an atmosphere of completeness. Their lives were formed on fertile earth like their once-plentiful garden. Now she realized that she had always envied their companionship, the warmth of the looks they exchanged as they worked side by side in the garden or in the office.

Like the barren earth of their garden, she missed them. If Doc was still alive, she would have gone to him and unburdened her secret, one she was certain Miss Adie suspected since that day she happened upon her and Dan sitting hand-in-hand, gazing into each other's eyes. She hadn't paid a visit to Miss Adie in some time. Her Royal Legend cake—she would bake it and take it to her. Perhaps, just walking into her home, she would sense the completeness; the seed of a love like her own for Dan, and find the direction for her life.

As she neared the garden to the left of the house, she half-expected it to be blooming with Miss Adie's foxgloves, Shasta daisies, sweet William, daylilies, herbs, and Doc's vegetables. It lay forlorn, a wasted and weedy piece of land. Eula was out sweeping the walk. As she pulled her car into the driveway, Eula laid aside her broom and hustled toward the car.

"Why, Miss Wynene, mighty good to see you," she greeted.

"How is she today, Eula?" Wynene asked, going around to the other side of her car to remove the carefully boxed cake.

"Some days, they be better than others. Her mind do wander, never set in one place. She seem to remember the past better than the present. Don't be hurt if she don't remember you," she added, opening the door to the house.

"Brought her and you a little something," Wynene said, handing the box to Eula.

"My, how nice, let me see if she be awake. She doze quite a bit."

Wynene waited in the living room where a rocker sat in a corner with one of Miss Adie's carefully pieced and colorful quilts thrown over its seat. The room smelled slightly musty. A sofa against one wall seemed to still hold the impressions of Doc and Miss Adie's bodies as they sat reading or talking. She recalled the tall fresh Christmas trees that used to stand to the side of the fireplace and the crocheted snowflakes Miss Adie meticulously crafted dangling from the fragrant limbs. A picture of Doc in younger days sat on a corner table. The warmth of his smile flooded over her as if in a greeting. It felt like a blessing.

"She be awake," Eula informed, reentering the room. "I told her it was you. Jest don't be hurt if she forget by the time we turn the corner. My, it do my heart good to see you, Miss Wynene. It been a long time."

Miss Adie was propped up on pillows. The eyes were the same, but the body was terribly wasted. It barely made an impression under the quilt covering her. Wynene took the chair Eula placed for her by Miss Adie's bedside.

"You," Miss Adie reached a gnarled hand toward her.

"Ms. Wynene," Eula reminded.

"Pastor's wife," Miss Adie said.

Eula inhaled. A good day!

"Haven't been to church," Miss Adie said in an apologetic tone, "but Eula reads to me from my Bible. Still lovely," she added, patting Wynene's hand. "How is that young man of yours?"

Wynene caught her breath, then quickly recovered. "Jim is fine. He sends his love."

"Love," Miss Adie turned her head to look out the window toward the garden, "God's greatest gift, must be tended. You're in love," she said, turning back to Wynene.

"Yes, yes, I am," she said without hesitation.

"Not all are lucky," Miss Adie stated. She studied Wynene's face. "You are and Doc and I. That young man and you," she added. "I could tell you knew. Not everybody does. Don't let it go."

"I won't," she promised, patting the hand holding hers.

"It's a secret," Miss Adie added.

"Yes?"

"A miracle most don't have," she added, turning her face

toward the window overlooking the dried-up garden as if she could see something there no one else could. "Don't wait too long," she said, turning her face back toward Wynene's.

"Thank you," Wynene said, rising to go.

"It has to be tended. Don't wait too long," Miss Adie reminded her.

"She enjoy your visit so much," Eula said, walking her to the door. "You gave her one of her better days."

"No," Wynene said. "She gave it to me."

{FIFTEEN}

ELOISE SAT ON HER PATIO DRINKING A MORNING cup of coffee. *The last days of summer,* her garden seemed to say; *soon we go to seed.* The days were growing shorter. Yellow leaves from the tulip maples quilted the lawn. The lush pink blooms on her crepe myrtles reminiscent of the sticky cotton candy she bought as a child at county fairs had dried up into berries. Even the blooms on the zinnias were sparse. Hummers flitted furiously at her feeder, buzzing others treading on their territory as they filled up for what would soon be their long flights toward Central America and Mexico. Birdsong had quieted down. Their nesting season over, many birds were preparing to head south. Evening shadows lay differently across the grass as cicadas, grasshoppers, and crickets still strummed up for their nightly concerts.

August—a month of change. The flowers she may not have noticed in summer caught her eye in gardens and along the roadside: wildflowers, goldenrod, Queen Anne's lace. Another year without her son. He would be a young man now. Often on mornings like this, she felt him quite near her. He had loved nature as much as she did. Sometimes, she wondered how she got from there, the day he died, to here. Like a tree sealing off an injury, she had continued to grow beyond her wound and go on living. Doc and Miss Adie had been a blessing. Without their counsel, she might not have healed. She hadn't seen Miss Adie in nearly three months, since the day Verabelle mentioned she was writing a book.

She had taken her Southern Belle cake and been greeted at the door by the faithful Eula, whose life before Doc and Miss Adie remained a town mystery. Most looking at her face couldn't get past the elongated scar, but Eloise saw something in the warmth of her eyes and smile that made her seem familiar, like an old and trusted friend. She often felt like embracing her and would have if she thought Eula wouldn't consider it condescending.

Eula greeted her and ushered her into Miss Adie's bedroom.

"My dear," a diminished version of the robust woman she had known all her life said from beneath a bright quilt. A blush of color rose in the gray pallor of her cheeks. "It's been so long."

"Miss Adie . . . " She started to ask, 'How are you?' Instead she took the needlepoint chair Eula offered her beside the bed.

"How are the ladies?" Miss Adie asked.

"Fine. They send their love," she said, wondering if indeed most did or even thought about her until Verabelle's gossip about the book.

Since Doc's passing, Miss Adie had receded into the town's background like a piece of forgotten history. For awhile, she continued to come to church with Eula driving her and headed to the same pew where she and Doc had always sat near the front, where they could see and hear the pastor and choir.

"Should have come sooner," Eloise apologized.

"Well, here we are." Miss Adie's thin lips conjured up a smile that looked somewhat impish and nearly childlike. "How has it been with you, dear?"

For a moment, Eloise hadn't known how to answer her question. How indeed had she been? She survived. That is all she could think of saying. There was so little to tell of the months, the years since she last saw Miss Adie.

"I'm fine," she finally managed to say.

"Life," Miss Adie said, looking toward the window and the remnants of her garden. "It's out there. A gift," she added, "just waiting. God hasn't forgotten."

Hasn't he? Eloise wanted to ask, but Miss Adie reached out her hand for hers.

"Questions," she said as Eloise took the thin hand into her own.

"Excuse me," Eloise asked, perplexed, wondering if she should have come. She turned her head, looking for Eula, but she must have gone back into the kitchen.

"See it in your eyes," she stated, "never too late."

Eula bustled into the room with a tray of lemonade and two glasses.

"Isn't that so?" Miss Adie looked up at Eula.

Eula set the tray down on a bedside table. "Thought a glass of lemonade jest right for a hot day like this," she said, pouring a glass and handing it to Eloise, who took it gladly, thankful for the break in the wayward conversation.

"Love," Miss Adie said, looking up at Eloise. "To love someone is to have them forever. In the garden . . . "

"Let's try a little lemonade," Eula said, frowning and shaking her head in sympathy as she placed a straw in a glass.

"Don't want any," Miss Adie said firmly, waving the glass

away. "I saw him in the garden." She looked up at Eloise.

"One of those days," Eula mumbled in apology, shaking her head.

Eloise looked toward the window and the view it presented of the wasted earth. How many times had she, too, felt her son's presence as she stood in the kitchen baking for the Ladies Mission Society or for someone in need?

"It's all right," she whispered to Eula, who stood beside her chair. "I understand," she said to Miss Adie. "Jake would do his homework at the kitchen table while I cooked. It was a special time I looked forward to every day. He would share his day at school with me. Did you know that he wanted to be a chef?"

"My, my." Miss Adie smiled. "He would have been a good one."

Would have. Miss Adie remembered. Somewhere in her confused mind, she retained an image of Eloise's son. Somehow, it made him seem less distant. Eloise hadn't spoken of him to anyone in a long time. By compressing her grief, she sought to keep her son only to herself, but he had lived a life separate from hers. He made friends, shared laughter, and enjoyed God's earth. His life was not wasted. She continually denied him by not talking about him. Her anger at God had been an indirect anger at Jake. She hadn't forgiven him for leaving her. His life was a gift, would always be a gift. Doc had been right: Jake's death was not his fault. It was a mistake. She expected him to be perfect just because he was her son. No human being was perfect. She loved him so much. "To love someone is to have them forever," Miss Adie had said. Jake might not be with her, but the love she held for him and he for her was still there just below the surface, fertile earth, waiting to be nurtured like Miss Adie's garden.

That visit with Miss Adie brought absolution, and a plan began to form in Eloise's mind. A chimney swift flew overhead. Just yesterday, she spied a warbler in her birdbath. She had been busy filling up her hummingbird feeders to fatten the tiny jewels for their long trek. Over the next several weeks, the sky would be full of migrating birds and the oak trees would be dropping huge acorns on the ground. Soon the trees would display an artist's palette of colors, but there was still time to put her plan into effect.

Her thoughts were interrupted by the *ding-dong* of her front door bell. Getting up from her chair with renewed energy and purpose, she went to answer it.

"Yes?" she asked to the nice-looking young man who looked vaguely familiar on her doorstep.

"Excuse me, ma'am." He shifted on his feet. "I'm Bobby Hatteras. I went to school with Jake. We were . . . we were friends. I'm working in Atlanta. Was just passing through and thought . . . well, if you don't mind, I would pay a visit."

{SIXTEEN}

"HOW KIND OF YOU TO VISIT," ELOISE SAID offering the young man a seat in the living room. "You were in my son's class, weren't you?"

"Yes." Bobby sat down and looked around the room as if he expected Jake to appear at any moment. Clearing his throat, he apologized, "I hope I'm not intruding."

"Not at all, it's a pleasure meeting one of Jake's friends." She hesitated, took a breath, and asked, "Did you know him well?"

A perceptible color flushed his face. "Yes, I did."

Her clasped hands tightened in her lap at his reply. "And your parents? I didn't really know them. How are they?"

"They moved not long after I graduated from the university." He cleared his throat. "Actually, they divorced."

"I'm sorry," she responded.

"My mom lives in Atlanta, not far from me. My dad remarried. He lives in Birmingham."

She inhaled, then said, "Bobby, I need to ask you . . . *how* well did you know my son?"

He leaned over and put his elbows on his knees and his head on his chest as if he were praying.

Feeling an immediate sympathy, she said, "You don't need to . . . "

"No," he stated with resolve. He raised his head and looked directly into her eyes. "You deserve an answer. It's the reason my parents separated and finally divorced. They couldn't accept who I am. Jake told me so much about you and his dad. I remembered seeing you at school functions, but didn't have a chance to know you and my mom didn't run in your circle of friends. My folks worked a farm outside town and never became involved in town affairs. Do you mind that I came? It may have been selfish of me, but I felt it would make him seem alive to me in some way."

Eloise's heart flooded with sympathy. Here they sat, two people with divergent ages and backgrounds who loved a wonderful young man. "Of course I don't mind. Your visit is a gift to me."

"Then you knew?"

"Yes, I always suspected, although I don't think Jake's dad did and I didn't know about you. Jake never mentioned your name."

"I feel," his voice broke and his eyes looked teary, "that I was the cause of his death."

"Oh, no, you mustn't." She rose and went to him. Sitting on the armrest of his chair, she put her arm around him. Her understanding brought a deep sob as he rested his head on her shoulder. "It's not your fault," she comforted. "It's not Jake's, either. For a long while without realizing it, I resented my son for robbing me of his presence. A very wise woman recently revealed a truth to me. She told me that God hadn't forgotten; that life is a gift and to love someone is to have them forever. I am certain that Jake, if he could speak to you now, would say the same to you. What he did was a reactionary act. We mustn't blame him or ourselves. For all his wonderful attributes, Jake was like the rest of us, an imperfect human being."

"Then it wasn't an accident as the police ruled? I always suspected it wasn't an accident. He tried to distance himself from me."

"It's all right," she comforted. "You mustn't blame yourself."

"Then you don't mind my coming?" Bobby asked, looking up at her.

"Not at all; I'm pleased you did. You're obviously a wonderful young man. I can't fault you for loving my son, nor he for loving you."

"I wasn't actually passing through," he said.

"I didn't think so. That makes your visit even more special. Would you like to stay for dinner?"

"I wouldn't be imposing?"

"Not at all. Perhaps you would like to see Jake's room. I've kept it just like it was before . . . "

His face lit up like a boy's. "You actually wouldn't mind?" he asked, immediately standing up.

"Of course not."

He followed her down the hall. Jake would be his age, she thought, if he were alive. She had not visited her son's room in nearly a month. After the visit with Miss Adie, she, for some reason, didn't feel the need to look for her son there. She felt him everywhere she went. She could sense a slight hesitation from the young man before he stepped over the threshold, as if he were afraid of disturbing someone asleep. "Take your time," she said. "When you're through, meet me in the kitchen around the corner. Jake used to study at the table there watching me cook while he shared his day with me."

By the time Bobby walked into the kitchen to join her, a casserole was cooking in the oven and she was sitting on a stool snapping green beans.

"I don't know how to thank you," he said, taking the chair she offered him at the table. "I didn't expect someone like you. Guess I should have from the way Jake described you and his dad."

"Would you like a glass of wine?" she offered. "I would say a beer, but I'm afraid I don't have any on hand."

"A glass of wine sounds great."

"Red or white?" she asked, taking down two wine glasses.

"Whatever you like to drink."

"Then let's go for this red. It's one my husband always liked."

With the beans on the stove top and the rice in the lower oven, she sat down with him. "To you," she said, tapping his glass with hers, "with a grateful heart for your visit."

"To Jake's parents and to Jake," he responded. He took a sip, nodded his approval of the wine, and smiled for the first time since he appeared on her doorstep. By the time they finished their meal, they were laughing and talking together as if they had always known each other.

"You know," he said, gathering the dishes and helping her stack them in the dishwasher, "I feel as if Jake is here with us and that he's glad I came to visit."

"Would you like to spend the night?" she asked in a sudden gesture that surprised her.

"You wouldn't mind? I booked a room at the motel on the outskirts of town."

"Then call and cancel. It'll give us more time to talk about Jake and get to know each other. It's been a long time since

I've hosted someone in my home. And, if you don't mind my saying so, I feel as if I have always known you."

"Me, too," he responded, his eyes lighting up with a joy so reminiscent of Jake's that her heart did a sudden flip.

"It's a small house," she said, realizing that the only other bedroom besides her own was Jake's. "Would you mind sleeping in his room, or you can sleep on the living room sofa."

He shook his head in amazement. "You are something." He smiled. "If it really doesn't bother you, I'll stay in Jake's room."

"Then go get that suitcase out of your car and I'll do a quick dusting," she said, overwhelmed with gratitude that an empty room would once again have a young person in it. For too long, it seemed like a darkened tomb.

When Bobby met her in the kitchen for breakfast the next morning, she was flipping pancakes on the griddle and a pot of hot coffee sat on the stove. Since Jake and her husband passed Eloise had been used to toast and coffee and sitting at a solitary table or in the den with a TV for company. What a pleasure it was to be cooking for a man again.

"This lady," he said, woofing down a pancake with a man's hearty appetite, "the one you quoted yesterday. She sounds awfully wise. Who is she?"

"Miss Adie, the doc's wife."

"Miss Adie." He cocked his head. "I remember her; used to see her and the doc working away in their garden. He passed away, didn't he? What about her?"

"She's quite ill. Her mind comes and goes and her garden is just bare, stubby, stony earth."

"Horticulture," he said.

"Excuse me?" She took his cup and poured another coffee.

"That was my major. I work with the city on developing outlying counties. Gardens are my specialty."

Nearly dropping the pot of coffee, Eloise sat down at the table. "Then you would know how to take a neglected piece of ground and prepare it for planting?"

"Absolutely."

"Bobby," she laughed, placing a hand over one of his, "this may be your first visit, but for many reasons, I expect it will certainly not be your last."

{SEVENTEEN}

MISS ADIE KNELT ON THE GROUND. TAKING A deep breath, she inhaled the aroma of the soil, its moisture, warmth, and nutrients. *Time,* it said. *It's time to plant the seeds.* The mystique of the land never failed to amaze her. It lay dormant through the winter, its internal clock waiting for the proper change in the weather. She could almost feel its heartbeat beneath her hands. Is this how God felt, she often wondered, when He formed the earth? She patted the earth as if it were an old friend, testing it for softness. It would let her know what it needed to make it fertile. It would also let her know which bulbs or seeds to plant. The land talked to her. Its soil was not silent. Doc believed that a surgeon's hands could often define beneath the skin of the human body a temperature that offered clues to the human condition. It was the same with the land. It would take a common seed into its embrace and produce a miracle of color and aroma. Seeds that slept throughout the winter months would awake and germinate. They, too, knew the heartbeat of the earth. Green shoots would push up through the womb of the earth and flourish into an artist's palette. Vegetables nourished by the warming earth would germinate into fully grown bounty for their table. She had watched Doc perform his artistry on body and soul of those who came to him suffering, physically or spiritually. In the garden, they also worked side by side to bring to fruition the waiting land. Kneeling by her side, he would often place his gloved hand over hers and smile. We are one, his eyes said to her. This land, you, and I are part of God's miracle. The garden into which they poured their souls bore their handprints. In the evening, they stood at the border of the garden beneath a sky of stars to sense the silent communication of the living earth with bulb and seed.

She reached up to touch his face. Her hand snatched at air. The stars blinked, then vanished, taking him with them. "Where are you?" she called into the dark. "Why have you left me? Where have you gone?"

"Adie," his voice called from far away. "Look for me in the garden."

A light switched on. Eula, wide-eyed and in a nightgown, was standing over her bed. "Now, now," she said, filling a glass with water from a bedside pitcher and opening a bottle of pills. "It all right, you been dreaming again. Here, take this. You'll feel all better."

"Out there," she pointed to the window, but only darkness greeted her.

Lawd, where has her mind taken her this time, Eula thought, pulling a rocking chair close to the bedside to keep watch till the pill calmed Miss Adie down.

"Here we are," Eloise said, pulling into Miss Adie's driveway the next morning.

"And that would be the land," Bobby said, gesturing toward the barren earth bordered by a wooden fence leaning into itself beside the house.

"It used to be beautiful," she said, walking with him

toward the house, "when Doc was alive and Miss Adie still able to garden."

"I will need to test the soil," he said, nearly tripping over a loose brick in the walkway.

"Thought you might; that's why I brought a jar along," Eloise revealed, grinning, as she rang the doorbell.

He shook his head. "Once again, I have to say, an amazing woman," not informing her just yet that he would also need plastic bags.

"Miss Eloise." Eula appeared at the door. "What a pleasure to see you again, and so soon." She raised an eyebrow in question toward Bobby.

"Eula, this is Bobby Hatteras from Atlanta. He was . . . is a friend of Jake's. May we come in?"

"Why, of course, but if you be wanting to see Miss Adie, she plum wore herself out with some dream of hers last night and she be sleeping."

"Perfect." Eloise stated, bringing a questioning look from Eula as she and Bobby took the seats offered by Eula on the sofa. "Bobby," she said, giving an affectionate glance at the young man seated next to her, "is a county agent in plant cultivation. He's a horticulturist."

"No plants here to cultivate," Eula said, looking puzzled.

"None now," Eloise agreed, her eyes sparkling, "but there could be. That's why we're here."

Miss Eloise's eyes had a shine in them that Eula had never seen. She filled the room with an energy that for too long had been absent.

"Don't quite understand," Eula said, "what that got to do with Miss Adie. Would you like a cup of tea?"

"No, thank you." Eloise smiled at the perplexed expression on Eula's face. "But there is one thing you can do."

"What be that?"

"Could we have your permission to dig around a little in Miss Adie's garden? And in my hurry to get here, I forgot to get a spade. Do you think there's one in the old shed out back I could borrow? Also, do you have any plastic bags?"

"The garden?" Eula's eyebrows shot up. "What for? There's nothing there but bare earth."

"Bobby?" Eloise gestured to the young man seated beside her.

"You see, I, we would like to test the soil for cultivation; that is, for planting."

"Test the soil? You can't mean, Miss Eloise, that you think ..."

"That's right, Eula. We want to bring the garden back for Miss Adie and," she added, "for you."

"Lawd God almighty," Eula raised her arms in the air, a gesture that brought chuckles from Miss Eloise and her young friend. Then she frowned. "If it don't work, Miss Adie be plum disappointed."

"You say she's asleep?" Eloise questioned.

"I tiptoe in and check," offered Eula, getting up from her armchair. Eloise shared smiles with Bobby as Eula stepped softly out of the room. It had been a long time since she sat in this room. Doc was alive then. She looked around the room at Miss Adie's handicraft, her quilts and needlepoint pillows, and at Doc's picture smiling back at her. The room suddenly had a Christmas glow about it. The leaves on the dogwoods outside the window had all turned autumn colors. Even though the sun was shining, there was a hint of coming coolness in it.

"Camellias," she said to Bobby, "the state flower of Alabama. That will be one of the first flowers we will plant."

He smiled at her fervor and almost childlike excitement. "The first to rise and the perfect time to plant," he agreed, "but there's the land to prepare."

He hoped this trip wouldn't prove to be a disappointment. This gallant and giving woman had experienced enough of those in her life. She was a house gardener. It was a hobby. There were many factors to consider for this garden. The soil could have a high clay content, particularly since it lay dormant for as long as it had. The county extension office would give him an evaluation of the soil's composition and its pH level. Rocks, roots, and plant material would need to be removed. He hoped it wouldn't prove too arduous a task for her enthusiasm. And who would help her? The maid was obviously too busy with her nursing and housekeeping to be much of a help.

Eula hurried back into the room with a spade. "She asleep," she said, dangling a set of keys in her other hand and gesturing for them to follow her toward the front door. She hustled down the walk with Miss Eloise and her young friend behind her. "It been so long since that old shed be opened. I don't know which key is which," she said.

The dilapidated shed sat at the rear of the house, its shingles curling and many missing. A good heave-ho, Bobby thought, is all it would take, but he waited patiently for Eula to insert key after key with a shaking hand until she hit on the right one. When the door swung open, years of dust flung out, welcoming them. He was amazed at the order he found inside. Every rake, hoe, and spade was hung on the wall or set in niches along the wall. An old and crumbling bag of fertilizer still sat upright. A rusty rototiller sat at the back of the shed with a row of rakes. Gardening gloves were stacked neatly in a box on a shelf. A man's hat hung on a rack. He sensed a personality in the long-unused shed and immediately looked at the filmy floor, half-expecting footprints.

Eula coughed. "My, my," her voice quavered with emotion. "Like he jest walked out, finished with his gardening for the day."

Eloise patted her arm. "He kept his office the same way, neatly professional."

"He left us all the tools," Bobby said taking a spade off the wall and inspecting the rototiller. "A bit rusty, but with a little cleaning and oil, it should do fine."

"We can plant an herb garden close to the kitchen," Eula said, her voice excited and her face flushed.

"Vegetables will have to be placed away from the trees," Bobby informed her as they exited and relocked the dilapidated shed behind them. "It's important to choose a good site for drainage. Do you have any more plastic bags I could use?" he asked Eula.

While Eula scurried back into the house to get the bags and check on Miss Adie, Bobby walked over the land. He poked at the neglected dirt with the spade. Good, there didn't seem to be too high a percentage of clay. Eula hustled back to them with the requested plastic bags.

"She still asleep," she informed them, watching with interest as Bobby spaded the ground, dumping samples of soil from different areas of the land every 1,000 square feet into separate plastic bags.

"The county extension office will be able to evaluate the soil composition and the pH level," he informed Eloise and Eula, using a pen he withdrew from an inside pocket to mark the samples and keep them separate. "Then we can take it from there."

{EIGHTEEN}

VERABELLE LIFTED HER CHICKEN SCRAPPLE from the oven, trying to ignore her growing thirst for a drink. It wouldn't do to show up on Miss Adie's doorstep with whiskey on her breath. Miss Adie, at her age and with her diminishing sense of smell, wouldn't notice, but the omnipresent Eula would. She opened the fridge and took out the orange juice. Pouring a full glass, she downed it, hoping that the sugar would hold off her need. She knew the Mission Society ladies had been visiting, snooping out the mystery of Miss Adie's book. It was a chain reaction she set in motion months ago. They didn't mention seeing Miss Adie, but Verabelle knew she had piqued their curiosity. She licked her lips, her thirst for a stiff drink quickening. Nearly burning her fingers on the edge of the still-hot chicken dish, she wrapped it with foil and bustled up the stairs to change her clothes.

As she neared Miss Adie's house, she nearly slammed on the brakes at the sight of a large dark scarecrow standing in the long-vacant garden, but it was only Eula, who, at the sound of her car door closing, clumped across the cloddy earth.

"Miss Verabelle," she greeted, but her smile held no warmth.

Umm, umm, Eula thought, watching Miss Verabelle roll ponderously out of her car, good news followed by bad.

"Brought supper," Verabelle informed her, her gloved hands holding a large casserole.

"How nice," Eula thanked her. "Maybe it will perk up Miss Adie's appetite."

"How is she today?" Verabelle asked, charging into the house ahead of Eula.

"She be 'bout the same, with some days better than others."

"Visitors wearing her out?" Verabelle asked, snooping.

"You mean the ladies?" Eula dipped her head and looked up at Verabelle from underneath her eyebrows as the suggestion of a smile played about her lips.

It was a look that didn't go unnoticed by Verabelle. Eula found her visit, the second after months of absenteeism, suspicious. She must tread softly. No one thought Eula stupid. She had run this household long before Doc's passing and was like a guard dog when it came to her current charge. Eula opened the refrigerator, searching for a spot to place the casserole. Verabelle peeped around her. It was full of dishes and cakes baked, she was certain, by the Ladies Mission Society. She had been correct about their visits. The mention of Miss Adie's book set a bunch of bloodhounds on a trail toward her door.

"The ladies have been good," Verabelle stated.

"Yes, mum, they has. Let me check see if Miss Adie's sleeping."

I could lie and tell her that it's not a good day, Eula thought, turning the corner toward Miss Adie's bedroom, but she'd come back jest like a kudzu vine. Hack it back and it keep growing anyway, choking off whatever's in its path. Miss Adie was lying on her side but she was awake and looking out toward the wasteland that used to be her garden.

"Ms. Verabelle come visiting," she announced.

"Verabelle?"

Miss Adie turned the name over in her mind, searching Eula knew for a forgotten image.

"Guess you too tired," Eula suggested.

"Verabelle." A look of recognition came into Miss Adie's eyes. "Banker's wife."

"Yes, mum," Eula said, amazed at the memory connection. Perhaps Ms. Verabelle's visit would be a benefit anyway. "Do you feel up to seeing her?"

"Why, of course."

As soon as Verabelle heard "of course," she hustled triumphantly into the room from around the corner of the door where she was eavesdropping. "Miss Adie," she said, false affection slathered like honey on her tongue, "don't you look well today?"

"Don't rightly know." She frowned. "Do I?"

Verabelle took the chair offered by Eula next to the bed. "The ladies have been visiting, haven't they, my dear?"

"Ladies? Oh yes, they have, haven't they, Eula?" she looked up at Eula with the question.

"Yes, mum, they has."

"Let's see," Miss Adie puzzled, "seems like Eloise ... isn't that right, Eula, and that young man?"

"Young man?" Verabelle asked as Eula's eyebrows arched.

"Out in the garden; saw him." Miss Adie turned her head toward the window.

Verabelle looked up at Eula, a question in her eyes. Eula's lips were pursed and she looked like she had stepped on a tack.

"Why didn't you bring him in?" Miss Adie asked.

"Miss Verabelle brought us supper," Eula informed, hoping to change the subject.

"How kind." Miss Adie smiled affectionately at Verabelle. "Lucky to have such nice neighbors, but it seems for a long time, didn't see much of you. Not since Doc ..." She turned her face toward the window again.

"What young man?" Verabelle asked, not willing to let the subject disappear into the muddled corridors of Miss Adie's mind.

"Don't rightly know." Miss Adie frowned. "Never saw him before; kneeling on the ground. Eloise and you," she looked up at Eula, "were out there, too."

"I'll get some refreshment," Eula announced, scurrying out of the room.

Her heart racing, she sought sanctuary in the kitchen. Taking down two glasses, she opened the freezer and filled them with ice. The cool air fanned her flaming cheeks. All this time, Miss Adie hadn't mentioned a word about seeing them in the garden. And now, of all times, in front of Ms. Verabelle, who looked like a cat stalking a mouse. She poured sweetened tea into the glasses, set them on a tray, and taking a deep breath, returned to the bedroom.

"In the garden?" she heard Ms. Verabelle asking.

Setting the tray on a bedside table, she offered one to Ms. Verabelle.

"Ms. Verabelle's casserole look mighty good," she told Miss Adie.

"Not hungry," Miss Adie stated, taking a sip of tea through a straw Eula held to her mouth. Giving Verabelle a studied glance, she frowned. "Don't mean to hurt feelings, dear," she said, "but have to tell . . . "

"Yes," Verabelle sat forward on her chair, the tea glass rattling in her hand.

"You used to be so slim, dear. Haven't you put on a few pounds? Can't you do something, some little something?"

"Well!" Verabelle coughed. She stood up. "Must be going," she announced with pursed lips. She handed the tea glass to Eula, whose cheeks were puffed out. "Dick will be home soon, and there's dinner. Don't bother, Eula, I'll see my way out."

"Do come . . . " Miss Adie was saying, but the sentence vaporized in Verabelle's race for the door that slammed quickly behind her.

"Lawd," Eula guffawed, carrying the tray and glasses back to the kitchen, "you come through and saved the day. Ms. Eloise secret is safe. This be one time I'm happy to see Miss Adie's mind off track."

{NINETEEN}

RAIN SPLATTERED AGAINST THE TRAILER windows. Kylie Mae had forgotten to roll up the windows on the truck. Pa would be furious.

"Ain't no good," his voice slurred with beer. Drunk, he staggered from his chair toward her. "Think you better." He breathed on her neck. His beer-blown belly pushed her against the sink. "Thar's things you can't larn in no classroom." His hands were in her hair. "You done grown up," he said, pulling her hair to one side and placing his mouth against her neck.

Her body stiffened. "Pa, don't," she pleaded in a scared little girl's voice. "Let me make you some coffee."

A low chuckle like a growl issued from his throat. "All this book larnin' and you ain't larned one thing about a man." His arms encircled her waist.

"Pa, stop it! Let me go. You're drunk."

He began to pull at her jeans.

"Get away," she screamed.

"Hush, shoo," a voice called gently. "It's all right."

Opal's eyes popped open. A twisted sheet was caught in

her hand. Beyond the sheers and a rain-dappled deck bordering their bedroom, the silhouette of trees. She was at home in her bed.

"A nightmare," Hank said, his arms wrapped tightly around her as if he was afraid she would disappear.

"Yes," her voice quavered.

"You were yelling at someone. You were frightened."

She snuggled further into his embrace.

"You're shaking. Want to talk about it?"

"No." Her voice sounded too emphatic. "It was just a crazy dream. I'm all right now."

"The same dream?"

"Why do you say that?" she asked warily.

"Because of what you say."

"What?" she asked, her heart racing.

"You're telling someone to leave you alone, to go away. Are you worried about something, Opal? If you are, it might help to talk about it."

"No, Hank, just a nightmare. Everyone has nightmares."

"Not the same one. Look, Opal, this is the fourth time in at least that many weeks you have tossed in your sleep. If you've been threatened in some way, I need to know about it. Are you concerned about one of the children? I feel as if I'm sharing our bed with someone else, someone who is harassing you."

She faked a laugh. "No one else could share this bed," she said, her hands caressing his jaw, noting the overnight stubble growth. "It was just some stupid dream." She sat up and smoothed down her crumpled sheet. "And it has nothing to do with the children or with us. I'm sorry I awakened you. Go back to sleep."

With a frustrated sigh, he turned over on his side with his

back to her.

She closed her eyes in relief that she had at least partially mollified him, then opened them again to the rain-sheeted night and pine trees swaying in the wind. It had been raining that night, too—the night when Kylie Mae Applegate left behind her past to become Opal St. John. But the past was never truly in the past; like rock-laden baggage, it rode with her in that bumpy truck into the present. It would always be with her. Did Miss Adie remember too the little girl she had comforted after the loss of her mother? How much did she know about her pa and that awful night in the trailer when Kylie Mae left her father lying on a blood-slicked floor?

"*WHOO, WHOO?*"

Verabelle sat upright in her bed, her heart thumping. Dick, a lumpy-blanketed silhouette, was sleeping on his side, facing away from her.

"*Whoo*," the haunting call reverberated through the night sky. A hoot owl obviously perched on a tree near the house, that's all, she said to herself, lying back on the mattress, her head turned toward the windows where slanted shadows from wind-driven trees danced. The owl's call sounded like a taunting question. Who, indeed? Who had she become? She thought of Miss Adie's questioning of her weight gain. What happened to the hopeful slim young girl she had been when she first met Dick?

Verabelle had spotted him across the room at a fraternity mixer held at her college sorority house. He was standing with several of his fraternity brothers. One of them made a joke and Dick threw his head back in laughter. It was a laugh like sparkling champagne that made her tingle inside.

"Who is that?" Verabelle asked a sorority sister.

Then as if he could hear her across the noisy room, he turned and looked her way, his head slightly turned to the side as if he was studying her.

"I don't know," her sister said, "but he looks pretty interested in you."

"He's coming our way," Verabelle said, feeling suddenly timid.

She wanted to disappear into the crowd, but her feet seemed rooted to the floor. She turned to her sorority sister for help, but she had disappeared and then he was there, staring down at her, a mischievous grin creasing dark chocolate eyes. Dimples chiseled on each cheek deepened with his smile. She felt a strong urge to place her fingers there, draw his face toward hers, and kiss him.

"Haven't we met somewhere before?" he asked.

The question had seemed at first like a practiced line, but something about Dick seemed too genuine for trite conversation. They spent the rest of the evening at the mixer together talking, getting to know each other. In a few short hours, he made her feel as if she had known him for a lifetime. Their housemother's sudden appearance was the announcement that the gathering was over. Fearful that she might not see him again, Verabelle delayed their departure by walking with him to the front door, where he took one of her hands in his.

"I want to see you again," he announced. Then he smiled, dropped her hand, and backed slowly out the door and down the sorority steps to the walkway, never taking his eyes off hers. "And again, again, and yet again," he added, grinning mischievously.

When Dick reached the end of the walk, he half-stumbled over the curb onto the sidewalk. Recovering his balance, he held his arms out to his side, hands upward in an "oh well, clumsy me" gesture that made her giggle. They were engaged within a year, and when they married, Dick agreed to set up his practice in her hometown. What happened to that girl of twenty years past? With sorrow, she recalled the failed pregnancies and the annual visit to Doc when all hope of sustaining a pregnancy became impossible.

"There is a problem, Verabelle," Doc announced in a gentle voice with Miss Adie standing by his side.

"Problem? What kind of problem?"

"There are tumors," he explained. "Fibroids. Nothing to get concerned about, but a hysterectomy is necessary to prevent further infections."

"No!" she declared. "We want children."

"There is adoption," Doc recommended.

"I don't want someone else's child," she stated firmly. "I want our own. Can't you do something?"

He shook his head sadly and she started crying while Miss Adie wrapped her arms around Verabelle. At the time, she didn't stop to think about Doc and Miss Adie. Did they want children of their own and for some reason were unable to have them? Now, Doc was gone and the practice and the garden into which they poured their whole lives were gone also. And Miss Adie? Verabelle stared out the window at the undulating shadows of trees swaying in the wind. She had awakened in the hospital room after the hysterectomy to a filmy figure standing over her. A hand was on her arm. Something wet was running down Verabelle's cheeks. Tears, she realized. They were her tears.

"Are you in much pain?" a faraway yet familiar voice asked.

Unable to speak, Verabelle nodded. She tried to open her

eyes to see the person to whom the voice belonged, but they seemed glued shut. Her lips were dry and there was a funny taste in her mouth. She felt a quick twinge in her arm and she floated blessedly away. When she awoke, Miss Adie was sitting by her side, reading a book.

Turning her head toward her, Miss Adie asked, "How are you, my dear? Do you need anything?"

Shaking her head weakly, she fell asleep again. In the middle of the night, she tried to turn onto her side and awakened, screaming out in pain.

"It's all right, dear." Miss Adie's voice. "Take this."

She took the offered pill and swallowed a few sips of water while Miss Adie adjusted the pillows beside her to keep her from turning abruptly in her sleep.

"It will be better tomorrow," she promised, running a cool cloth over her forehead.

The next morning, Verabelle was disappointed to awaken and find Miss Adie gone.

"How long was she here?" she queried the young nurse attending her.

"All night," she responded. "She left about an hour ago."

"All night?"

"She's a regular when it comes to her patients. Most of them don't even know she's there, but I understand you had a pretty rough night. That Miss Adie, she's pretty special."

Had she ever thanked her for being there? No, instead Miss Adie faded into the background with the rest of her life when Verabelle left the hospital. Gone was all hope of bearing the children she and Dick had planned. Every time she passed a neighbor with her newest baby in a stroller or attended a baby shower, she returned home in tears. She tried to hide her disappointment from Dick, whose job at the bank was becoming more demanding. He never mentioned adoption to her again, and their marriage slowly became more of a partnership than a romance. If they had sex, it was seldom. Was it because she had shut him out, a subtle turning away from the need to express the love they once felt as ardently as they had the need to have a child? Communication also burned away with the desire to be together physically. Alcohol became the salve for her emotional wound. The first time Dick arrived home to find her slumped over her drink, apron-clad at the kitchen table, with the burned remnants of what was to be their evening meal strewn haphazardly on the counter and oven top, he turned on a cold shower and put her in it, clothes and all.

"You could have burned down the damn house," he screamed at her as she leaned against the shower wall to keep from falling down while water streamed through her sodden clothes and hair. "First thing tomorrow, you're seeing Doc."

Verabelle tried the pills Doc prescribed, but gave them up for the only pleasure she had in life, bottled elixir that dulled her senses and burned away all her desires. And she gained weight—so much of it that she no longer recognized the woman in the full-length mirrors she learned to avoid.

Dick snuffled and turned on his side. An arm fell across her thigh. A ripple of unexpected desire tingled up her spine. Careful not to awaken him, her hand lightly touched the hairs on his arm. In the first stages of their courtship and marriage, she used to affectionately stroke the hairs on his arm. His even breathing breezed across her face. Slowly positioning herself closer to his face, Verabelle studied the outline of his features. How long had it been since she had really looked at her husband, asleep or awake? The solidity of his bone structure was masked by the years with age, but he was still a nice-looking man. With longing, she recalled their first tentative touches when they were dating, the rush of desire to hold and be held so tightly their bodies blended as one, and the frenzy of their honeymoon night, their legs winding around each other. They had been so young. They were still not old. For the first time, she awakened without the need for a drink to dull her senses and drown the sorrow of her barren years. Alcohol had robbed her of the youthful body Dick once desired. It was time for her to try the pills again, time to fight the addiction that had robbed her life and was dissolving her marriage. If the promise of what they used to have was not possible, they could still build around the core and refine the structure. Dick turned over in his sleep again, this time away from her, but she followed, turning on her side so that her body was positioned just behind his as her breath fell lightly on his neck.

HIS LITHE BODY POISED ON THE DIVING BOARD, then spliced in an elegant arc through the blue sky and into the pool, sending a multitude of glittering ripples toward her. Treading water, she waited for a burst of spray somewhere near her as he broke through the surface, laughing. Stroking at air, she turned. She was lying on her side in a bed, her bed. Ted was snoring beside her and rain was falling on the roof. The young man of her youth disappeared. What happened to him? Did he fulfill his wishes to become a vet? Marry? Were there children? Norma Mae often dreamed of seeing Bart and wondered what the expression on his face would be when she told him that their summer day in the woods produced a child. Wherever he was, he continued after all these years to break through the surface of her life. However irrational, she had to know what happened to him. He was her first introduction to physical pleasure. A woman never forgot her first, she believed, and her first had produced a child. Her cousin Kat still lived in Atlanta with her husband and children. Perhaps she would know how she could contact him. She would call Kat in the morning. She closed her eyes. He still stood poised on the diving board, waiting.

As soon as Ted left for work the next morning, she called her cousin.

"Norma Mae, what a pleasant surprise. How are you, Ted, and the children? My, it has been a long time. Nothing's wrong, is there?"

"Wrong? No, just was thinking about you and wondered how you and the family were. Thought I would call for a chat to catch up on your news. And, yes, it has been a long time."

"Everybody is fine," Kat said, her voice light and happy. "The children are growing like weeds and Ben's insurance business is keeping him busy. Never hear from you except at Christmas. Wish you would plan a visit. Remember the fun we had as girls?" Kat laughed. "It seems like yesterday."

Norma Mae took a deep breath, then plunged. "You always made my visits fun," she agreed, "particularly that first summer I came for a visit."

"Goodness, you were in high school then, and now our girls are heading that way. You had a crush on Bart Richards that summer. Remember, the head lifeguard at the pool?"

A shiver went through Norma Mae at Kat's mention of his name. "Oh, yes," Norma Mae tried to make her voice sound nonchalant. "Whatever happened to him? I think I recall he was planning to become a vet."

"Oh, don't know about that, but it was pretty sad."

The shiver became a chill. He must have impregnated another girl and was forced to marry her. Kat was probably getting ready to tell her he was pumping gas at a filling station to support a family.

"He never made it to college?" she asked.

"No, he didn't. It happened not long after you left that summer."

"What happened?"

"He was always a wild card. Still . . . it was a terrible mistake."

"What?"

"He got drunk and wrapped his father's car around a tree going too fast around a curve. Killed instantly. Actually, now thinking about it, I believe it happened shortly after your visit that summer. Let's see, that was in June, and from what I recall he died that August shortly before he was to report to college. What a waste, lots of book smarts and not a lick of common sense." Kat sighed. "We were just kids then."

Just kids. The words swirled in Norma Mae's head. She sank into the armoire next to the telephone.

"All that potential wasted," Kat continued. "It nearly killed his parents. An only child, you know, or did you?"

"No, I didn't," Norma Mae said in a near-whisper.

"Oh, well, you really didn't know him, anyway. Now, tell me more about the girls."

Controlling her voice, Norma Mae continued to chat as she and her cousin swapped stories about their offspring, but all she could think of was the afternoon she walked slowly and fearfully up the walkway to Doc and Miss Adie's front door, carrying in her womb all that was left of a boy named Bart Richards. Her parents had mistaken her lack of appetite and lethargy to a flu bug and at first she did, too, until she realized she missed her period. A deep-rooted fear began growing in her mind even as her figure was being rearranged. She jumped a bra size and her skirts didn't zip as easily. When her period didn't occur for the second time and she would awaken nauseated, barely making it to the bathroom, she could no longer deny to herself that she was carrying Bart Richard's child. Foolishly, she considered getting his number from Kat and calling him. If he had still been alive, would it have made a difference? No, she decided now that she had talked to Kat and put her past into perspective. He was a spoiled, but intelligent boy with a scholarship to college and plans of furthering his education. He probably would have denied he was the father. Over the years, she had irrationally romanticized what amounted to a teenage tryst. She never meant anything to him other than another conquest.

She recalled the look of surprise on Ted's face on their honeymoon night when he discovered she wasn't a virgin, but it quickly dissipated and he never questioned her about it. She reasoned that it was because many women went to the altar with secrets, but what if he had been truly disappointed, and that disappointment fomented into a sexual neglect on his part, causing her to fantasize even more about what she erroneously considered a first love? In error, she had shortchanged her husband, a good man who loved their children and provided his family a comfortable existence. She shook her head. She wasn't a teenager anymore. How could she have been living in such a dream world?

{TWENTY}

SARAH ELLEN LAY IN BED SLEEPLESS, LISTENING to the storm. Through the bedroom sheers lightning slashed at the sky, but it wasn't the storm that kept her awake. She often tossed and turned ever since Verabelle's gossip about Miss Adie's book. It was Miss Adie's book that kept her awake and what it could disclose about her great-uncle, old gossip that thankfully had dissipated over the years since she was a child.

Her parents were not the ones to tell her of the horrific murder of the bank president. She happened upon it perchance. As a child, on rainy days she often entertained herself by going through her mother's desk, looking at old photographs and letters. Some of the black and white photographs portrayed staid-looking gentlemen with mustaches, dressed in suits, staring rigidly at the camera. Edges of the photographs mounted on cardboard were often frayed. The women in dresses that discreetly covered generous bosoms stared expressionless back at the camera. All looked bored and somehow unhappy. Later in life, she realized that cameras of their day were not advanced enough to capture a pose in any other way. One move and the camera would reflect a blurred image.

Some photographs had writing on the back in a neat, elegant script: Great-Uncle Hugh, Aunt Agnes, Rosalie. Some bore no identification. At the bottom of the stack of photographs, she came across one that immediately captured her attention and changed her life forever. It was of a nice-looking gentleman with a mustache. His eyes stared back at her rather defiantly, making her sense that smile or not, he wasn't one to get particularly close to people. Something about his looks piqued her interest. She took the photograph to her mother, whose eyes widened with seeming alarm.

"Where did you find that, Sarah Ellen? Have you been snooping around in my desk again?"

Only seven at the time, she timidly shook her head.

"Give that to me," her mother commanded. "Can't you find some other way to entertain yourself? Leave my things alone," she demanded, a scowl on her face.

"But mother . . . " she protested. "Who is he?"

"A great-uncle, and that is all you need to know. Now, go find some way to entertain yourself. I'm busy with supper." She added with a strict warning in her voice, "Don't mention this to your father. Do you understand? Now, get your crayons and draw or play with your dolls."

She meekly nodded, but her mother's last command only deepened her curiosity. Why was her mother so upset? It was just some old photograph, and since it was of a relative, why didn't she have a right to know who he was?

She waited until her mother took a shopping trip and she was left alone with the black maid to continue her snooping. Something forbidden was twice as intriguing. Stealthily, tiptoeing into her mother's bedroom, she pulled open the dresser drawer and took out all the photographs, spreading them across the floor, careful to keep them in the order she found them. If there was one picture of this relative, there must be more. Women in long dresses with latticed bodices stared back at her boldly. Many photos were group shots of families. She remembered thinking how lucky the children were in the photographs because they had multiple siblings. She, however, was an only child—a fact that made her even more curious to find something more interesting on a rainy day than playing with dolls or entertaining herself with crayons. This man with the bold eyes became a mystery, and one Sarah Ellen felt bound to unravel. What could be wrong about some man related to her family? After all, he was dead, a concept that seemed very distant and an impossibility to a seven-year-old just beginning her life.

Spread before her were pictures of relatives seated in high-back lattice chairs. The women for the most part wore their hair parted in the middle with large bows peeking behind frilly, lacy dresses with long sleeves. Some held infants in long dresses who stared back unaware at the camera lens. The pictures were often mounted on cardboard, imitating leather. Only one, a photo of a young woman holding a baby, displayed affection. The young woman, someone by the name of Ruth, had her age, fourteen, written on the back of the photograph, and she actually had a demure grin on her face. The baby was a girl. She knew that because she was identified as Rebecca, but there were no more pictures of the man with the demanding eyes. In fact, the picture had gone missing.

Then, to her amazement, Sarah Ellen came across a sheaf of aging paper. The handwriting had big loops and curlicues—fancy writing—some of it difficult to read. It seemed to concern her father's family. She went into the living room to get her father's magnifying glass, which was also old. She knew that, because her father told her so and that it was something she might get one day if she was "a good little girl." The paper was full of dates and names of people, boring until she came across the name Martin. A large "X" was before the name where someone had written a startling thing: prison. Sarah Ellen knew the word. Searching again through every drawer, she finally found the picture she had shown her mother, and it had writing on the back. Why she never noticed it before, she didn't know, except for the fact that the name was nearly unreadable. Her mother had hidden the picture in a bottom drawer beneath more recent photographs. Great-Uncle Martin was scrawled across the back of the photograph in nearly faded light pencil. Further searching resulted in a faded and yellowed newspaper article that described Martin's crime. He shot and killed the bank president in "broad daylight," the article said. What was broad daylight? Wasn't daylight just daylight, and why did he shoot and kill someone? What happened to him?

"Oh," Sarah Ellen recalled exclaiming, feeling somehow guilty, and then the realization hit her that in her small town everyone knew about her Great-Uncle Martin. She felt such shame and fear that tears rolled down her cheek.

No wonder her mother was so upset. Her family was marked. She felt as if she bore a large black wart—an "X" on her face that set her apart from everyone else in the town. She began to imagine on trips downtown with her mother that people looked at them strangely. If someone whispered near her, she was certain he or she was talking about THE family, her family, and what her Great-Uncle Martin did. When she stopped eating, her mother took her to see Doc.

"Perfectly healthy," he told her mother after a full checkup.

"How about some ice cream?" Miss Adie suggested, taking her by the hand into the kitchen. "It's homemade.

I churned it yesterday."

She gobbled up two bowls while Miss Adie sat beside her, lightly stroking her hair. "Did someone say something mean?" she asked, adding, "As a little girl, I often got my feelings hurt. Sometimes people just say things because they aren't happy."

"No," Sarah Ellen answered, looking up into a kind, gentle face, "no one told me, but I found it."

"Found what?" she asked.

Relieved that she could tell of her awful discovery, she told Miss Adie everything.

"You didn't do anything wrong," Miss Adie reassured her. "You're a good girl from a good family. We can't control what other people do. Now, if you start eating again and make good grades in school, I'll treat you to more ice cream on your next checkup."

And she had treated her more than once, but now Miss Adie was bedridden and writing about the town. In her addled state, was the family tragedy long-forgotten by the town about to be dredged up again? It could destroy the lives of her two children: Becky, only ten, and Mark, thirteen. She knew what that kind of shame could do to a young person. She didn't want them to feel as marked as she had once felt. She wouldn't have the family scandal served on a platter for the town gossips to digest.

{TWENTY-ONE}

STRAIGHTENING THE NURSE'S CAP ON WHAT
had been her carefully coiffed curls and running her fingers
through her disheveled hair, Adie stepped into the hospital
corridor. It was such a windy day in early spring. As she
waited for the elevator she wondered how her patients were
doing. The doctors would be doing their rounds soon. Dr.
Rogers would be waiting for her at the nurses' station. Would
Mr. Galvos be released? His wife had not left his side. They
were such a devoted older couple; she would miss Mr. Galvos' sense of humor. And the little girl with the tonsillectomy;
it was time for her to go home, too. Over the past few months
since moving to Atlanta and joining the staff at Emory, Adie
had grown fond of many of her patients. Oh, of course, there
were those who were trying. She recalled the words of Mrs.
McMillan, one of her nursing school instructors: "You will
be heavily tasked with the old codgers and the young ones
who try, and often do, pinch, or worse. Of course, some of
them won't recall this behavior because of heavy medication
or disorientation, but most grabs or attempts at sexual ad-
vances will be intentional."

Many of the girls had cast glances at each other as they tried to stifle giggles.

"Laugh now," Mrs. McMillan had stated, "but you will encounter these kinds of personalities. Keep in mind, however, that you must keep a professional decorum. If possible, keep the door open when you enter a room. You may be young ladies, but remember the status of your uniform. You will be asked for phone numbers or where you live. Never give this information. And that brings up another matter: doctors, single or married. Many look at young nurses as easy. Just because you are familiar with the human body doesn't mean that others have a right to be familiar with yours."

That last phrase had become a popular saying in the nurses' dorm. Standing with legs askew, the other student nurses would wag a finger in the air mocking "McMillan," as they called her.

"Just because you are familiar with the human body doesn't mean . . . " here a pause for effect, "that others have a right to be familiar with YOURS!"

"And don't become too attached to your patients, especially the severely ill or old. A ward is for the living and the dying. You will encounter both. Leave the heavy counseling to the visiting pastor or the chaplain on staff. Nursing is not an easy job. Encountering suffering will be a daily regimen. Keep a professional decorum and try not to take on the misery of those you serve."

That last admonition had been especially difficult for Adie. The first time she lost a patient had been particularly painful. As a trainee, she had been stationed in a small community as a visiting nurse. She received a call to go to the outskirts of town to help a woman delivering a child in a trailer park. The call came from the community's doctor, who was in surgery.

"Routine," he said over the telephone. "She's healthy and already has a second child. These people! They expect to deliver at home. Although I tell them there could be complications, they will not come into the hospital, but you should have no trouble."

But there was trouble, and severe hemorrhaging. Adie lost the patient and had to comfort the husband and tell the other child, a little girl, that her mother was gone, as was her stillborn baby brother. She found the child sitting underneath a tree looking at the ground studying something there or simply deep in thought, waiting. She had to have heard her mother's cries during the protracted labor. The father, whose breath smelled strongly of beer when she first entered the small but pristinely neat trailer, became almost comatose with grief and drink at his wife's passing. She was forced to go out to find the child by herself. The girl turned and watched Adie walk down the trailer steps toward her. Even before she reached her side, she stood up, a rigid little person, poised for the awful truth. "Keep a professional decorum," McMillan's words reverberated in the stillness of the air. Even before she left the trailer steps, she prayed for courage to tell that little girl she had lost her mother. The child's courage gave her strength, but when she reached her side and spoke words of comfort; it was her eyes that imprinted on her memory. They were luminous eyes full of pain, shock, and something else indescribable, a loss that bordered on near-hatred toward the one delivering the terrible news. She reached past the misdirected hate and took the girl into her arms. The child rested her head on her uniform, but her arms remained as frozen and rigid as the rest of her little body. It was a moment she never forgot. McMillan had been wrong. It was impossible not to become emotionally engaged, uniform or not.

The elevator door opened.

"Morning, miss," the attendant said, smiling. "Little breezy out there?" A gold front tooth gleamed from the bronze face as he slid the door shut. "Third floor, right?"

"Yes, and yes." Adie smiled as the elevator door clanged shut.

It had taken weeks to get a smile out of Holcomb. He sat, no, overflowed, the stool he sat on as he pushed the elevator doors shut. He became so used to most of the staff barking out orders and considering him just another fixture in the small confines of the elevator that his features seemed permanently frozen on his face. When she asked him his name the first day, he half-mumbled a response not truly believing she was interested in his life outside the confines of the elevator. Now she knew he was working another job at night slinging hash at a local diner trying to support a family that consisted of two small children and a wife who took in washing. He carried a worn black and white photo of his family in his billfold.

"How's the family?" Adie asked.

"Lawd." Holcomb chuckled, then smiled, proudly. "They going to sure 'nough be the death of me."

The elevator stopped. Several young doctors stepped on. From the clipboards they held in their hands, they must be students doing their residence, particularly because Dr. Wallace walked on behind them. Adie could almost smell the starch in their new uniforms.

"Good morning, Adie!" Dr. Wallace greeted. "Gusty day out there. Be careful that wind doesn't carry away one of our best nurses. It wouldn't take much to pick up our tiny pixie. Gentlemen, if you're lucky, you might get Miss Miles' floor."

"I want that floor," one said, causing several to laugh.

"Depends totally on your specialty and if you make the grade," Wallace quipped, winking at Adie from behind his bifocals.

"More incentive," one of the interns standing next to her said.

She turned to look up at him. His eyes were a deep brown and they had a mischievous twinkle in them that made her want to smile. She had an immediate sensation that they had met before.

"Lester Seabrook," he said, offering her his hand.

A spontaneous moan went up from the rest of the interns as she took it in hers. Dr. Wallace laughed. "Seems Seabrook has beat you all to home plate."

The elevator door opened.

"Excuse me," Adie said to the interns in front of her. "My floor. Good to see you Dr. Wallace, and nice to meet you, Dr. . . . ?"

"Seabrook," he said. "Lester Seabrook."

When she stepped off the elevator, she resisted the urge to turn and look back. Why, she wondered, would such a chance encounter affect her? She had never seen him before, but there was something familiar about this Lester Seabrook—something that made her feel as if they had known each other for quite a while. It was a comfortable something like a visit long-delayed but very much anticipated. And she knew that most of those interns probably wouldn't have made such a fuss over her if Dr. Wallace hadn't been present. It was all for his benefit. She knew she wasn't particularly pretty, only attractive at best. She recalled the words of an elementary school friend's mother, who on first meeting Adie, stated that she had interesting looks and that it was "Far better to be interesting-looking than pretty." The words stung. She must have blushed, because her friend had exclaimed, "Mother!" to which the mother had added, "Look at Katherine Hepburn. She's not pretty, but she's interesting-looking. Wait until you grow up, you'll understand."

Adie hadn't really thought at the time about how she looked, but when she came home from the visit to her friend's home, she rushed to her bedroom mirror to study her features. Her face was long and narrow, as was her nose. Her eyes were unremarkable except for their size and the way they tilted upward. Now she had to wear glasses most of the time. None of the young men she dated had ever accused her of being pretty. "You're different," one had said. "Most of the girls I date don't listen the way you do." "Good conversationalist," was another one's opinion. She often found herself sitting with a good book while her nursing student friends went out on multiple dates. And she never had any boy tell her he was in love with her. Not that she thought about marriage a lot. None of the boys she dated held much appeal for her. But she would like to get married someday, to the right man, and have children. Now her days were preoccupied with her patients. By the time, she returned home to the small apartment she rented with two other nurses, she was so tired she ate the takeout from the hospital's cafeteria and fell into bed, exhausted.

"Lester. Lester Seabrook," she said to herself, walking down the hall to the nurses' station to meet Dr. Rogers.

For the first time in her life, Adie wished she was pretty, really pretty, but soon her day was so busy with dismissals and new patients that she put the name and the chance encounter out of her mind. Before she realized the day was gone, she was clocking out and walking back to the elevator. When she turned the hall corridor headed for the elevator, a doctor was leaning against the wall. Him, she said to herself. It's him!

"Adie," Lester greeted, approaching her. "It is Adie, isn't it? Or should I be more formal and call you Miss Miles?" he added, cocking his head while a slight grin played across his lips.

Taking a deep breath and trying to keep her voice steady, she said, "Adie is fine."

"I hope you don't mind," he said, walking with her toward the elevator. "I could have checked at the desk to see when you got off, but I was afraid the other nurses wouldn't give me the information, so I just decided to wait here in the hall until you showed up. And here you are."

"Yes," she said, struggling to keep her voice calm. "Here I am. Have you been waiting long?"

"All my life," he said, looking down into her eyes.

{TWENTY-TWO}

ADIE SAT ACROSS THE TABLE FROM THIS LESTER Seabrook in the small hospital cafeteria watching him stir sugar into his coffee. He had surgeon's hands, the fingers long and slim. Catching her studied glance, he smiled up at her and placed his spoon aside. One eyebrow lifted in question.

"Adie," he said, placing a hand, an open invitation, on the table.

She put her hand in his and sat mesmerized as those long slim fingers curled around hers. It was such a simple act, but one that made her face flush.

"Tell me about yourself," he said.

"What do you want to know?" she asked, looking into eyes she had never seen until this morning, but ones she felt she had looked into many times.

"Everything."

She soon discovered they were both from small towns. He grew up in a small town in Alabama, where his father was a doctor as had been his grandfather. He was an only child. His mother was deceased—a bad heart. Adie's parents were farmers in North Carolina. Her younger brother died from a burst appendix.

"My mother thought it was stomach flu and there was no doctor nearby. Rodney was gone by the time my father rode into town and came back with one. My mother and I . . . " she looked down at her coffee cup, "held him in our arms. He was only seven."

"And you have wanted to be a nurse ever since?" he asked, his hand tightening gently on hers.

She nodded. "Ever since. And, of course, there were all the animals to tend. I was nursing even as a child. I used to help my dog deliver her pups."

"Was it a large farm?" he asked.

"Oh, no, it's just enough land for some gardening and vegetables—corn, beans, that kind of thing. I'm your typical farm girl. Poke sallet all the way. I bet you don't know what poke sallet is."

"There's nothing typical about you," he said with warm conviction. "And poke sallet is a dish of cooked young greens from the pokeweed plant."

She laughed in affirmation.

"My parents, in their spare time, had a garden," he explained, "and Adie, I am a small town southern boy."

"Lester," she said, startled somehow at how familiar his name sounded spoken, "you seem ..."

"Yes?" His eyebrows lifted in question.

"Well, sophisticated," she said.

"Do you like to read, Adie?"

"Oh, yes, yes, I do."

"And here you are, a young woman, a career woman, in a difficult, often challenging career. An intelligent young woman who likes animals, cares about people, reads books. That's sophisticated. At least, it is from where I come from. Will you have dinner with me?"

"When?"

"Tonight and many nights thereafter."

Her two roommates were inquisitive as she fussed over what she should wear the night of that first date. In her excited confusion, she laid out three dresses, the only ones she owned, on the bed.

"Much be pretty special," Nan said, "never have seen you in such a titter before."

"Wear the black," Janet suggested, plopping down at the foot of Adie's bed. "Then no matter where this Mr. Mysterious takes you, you'll fit in. And is he?"

"What? Is he what?" Adie placed the dress in front of her and eyed the figure in the dresser's mirror. At first she felt as if she was looking at someone else's reflection instead of her own. The woman looking back had a sheen on her complexion that could almost be called radiant. Her eyes had a luminosity that made them seem a clearer blue.

"Yep, I was right," Nan laughed. "Something special. When do we get to meet him?"

"He's just a date," Adie said, discarding her nurse's uniform on the bed and slipping the black dress over her head, "a dinner date." And then she added with a tone of resignation, "I may never see him again."

"Then you won't mind if we meet Mr. Excitement?" Janet questioned, winking at Nan. "Since we won't have another chance?"

Janet had loaned her a handbag and Nan had helped her with her makeup, applying blush on her cheekbones and a hint of it across her forehead and chin, "to highlight your bone structure." They sat giggling on the sofa waiting in anticipation for his arrival at the door. When the doorbell rang,

Janet and Nan jumped to their feet, while Adie sat rigidly on the sofa.

"Come on," Nan urged, but Adie felt suddenly paralyzed.

"What's wrong, honey?" Janet asked, sitting down beside her.

"Life," Adie said. "My life ..."

"Then if you feel that way," Janet said firmly, putting her arm around her, "take a deep breath and plunge. For God's sake, Adie, answer the door and go get it."

The doorbell, she must answer the doorbell. Lester was waiting. She tried to get up, but she couldn't. She turned toward Janet but she had disappeared and the room slowly receded into the distance. The doorbell rang again.

"I'm coming," a voice, a woman's, called. It wasn't Janet's or Nan's, but she knew that voice. "Goodness," she heard the voice say. "That fridge 'bout to bust. What now?"

Voices, one was a male's. Lester? She tried to get up, but somehow she couldn't. There was a coverlet over her. It was familiar and the furniture in the room, it too, was familiar: a dresser, a nightstand. There was a picture of a man on the nightstand. Lester? It was a much older man, but the features resembled Lester's.

She *had* opened the door, and there he stood, wearing a suit, a smile on his face. It was a smile that made something bubble up inside her, like a suppressed laugh waiting for release.

"Adie," Lester said, stepping inside the room. Just her name, but it had a sparkly, happy sound. And then he added, "You look great!"

She introduced him to Janet and Nan, who were hovering near the door. And then he took her arm and walked her to his car. It had been a beautiful night.

"A full moon," he said, opening her car door. "I ordered it just for you."

All her apprehension disappeared in the warmth of his presence and she laughed at its release. They both laughed as if they were sharing a secret joke. He took her to a small Italian restaurant where he ordered wine to toast, "Our first date, the first of many, I hope," and they spent the evening together as if they always spent evenings together at a cozy corner table sharing the stories of their former lives before they met.

She picked at the colorful squares of the quilt that covered her. Where had he gone? She turned her head to look out a window to her left. The garden? They had a garden. They spoke about gardens on that first night. She took him home to meet her parents, and he had gone into their garden to admire the flowers and the vegetables. Her father showed him around the small farm while she and her mother sat in the kitchen talking.

"Nice young man," her mother said, stirring sugar into her teacup. She took a sip and then, cocking her head to one side, looked up at Adie. "Your father seems to like him."

"And you, Mom?"

"Well." She set her teacup down. "I think . . . " She paused, giving Adie's face a studied glance. "I think he just might do."

They married in the garden of her parents' home. It was a small wedding with Nan and Janet as her attendants, Lester's father as best man, and a few of her parents' friends in attendance. When Lester completed his residency, they settled in his small town, living in his childhood home, where they assisted in his father's practice until his death a few years after Lester took over the practice. Once a month, they traveled to the outlying countryside to give free medical care to the needy. Sometimes the practice demanded that Adie stay behind in Simpsonville to give patient care while Lester served in the rural areas outside town. When he was gone, she missed him terribly. Simpsonville had welcomed her as the wife of Dr. Lester Seabrook and the daughter-in-law of their beloved and prestigious Dr. Samuel Seabrook, but it was obvious she didn't really fit in. Though a small town, Simpsonville's families were basically well-to-do, and in the minds of the ladies who made up the town's social life, she was nothing more than a farm girl who managed, somehow, to snare their prized male. She was, in their minds, a necessity as she was Doc's wife and nurse, but not an asset. They weren't exactly unkind; some of them were very kind, but she was never included in their social circle except when it included her husband. Most she came to know only because they were patients. She helped mend their wounds and birth their babies, many of whom were young men and women now. The practice and the garden she and Lester grew beside the house kept her more than busy. She never regretted leaving the big city to marry him.

And then there had been the nights. She ran her hands over the quilt. Sometimes, they would go into the garden to stand beneath the stars. Gazing up, she would lean her back against him while he wrapped his arms around her, his breath warm against her neck. She would turn to pull his face toward hers. Alone, with only the earth and the sky, they would lie down on the grass, the aroma of it and the rich dark earth an erotic perfume.

"Adam," he said, laughing with joy on one such night, "never had such an Eve."

Sadly, the pleasure they gave each other never produced a child. He came home from one of his weekends away to find her kneeling in the garden crying as she pruned plants.

"Look at all this life," she said looking up at him wistfully. "We did this and we can't . . . "

He knelt beside her, taking her into his arms.

"Adie." He placed his mouth against her neck. "I don't love you less."

"Oh, Lester, why? Every time we deliver a baby, I wish . . . "

"Look at me," he said, taking her face in his hands. "We have each other. You haven't failed me any more than I have you. It just wasn't to be."

Often after a delivery, she would coddle the small pink creature swaddled in its blanket in her arms and pretend it was hers. With time, she adjusted to the fact that as Lester said, "it just wasn't to be." What they did have was each other. She knew that many of the married women who walked into their office had never known, would probably never know, the kind of fulfillment in their love that she and Lester had. Many nights she would awaken to his touch, his hand reaching for hers, his fingers lacing through hers. Running her hand up his arm, she would feel a sensuous pleasure as she stroked skin, hair, and muscle. And when he took her into his arms, she knew no regret.

{TWENTY-THREE}

"MISS ELOISE, MR. HATTERAS," EULA SAID answering the door, "how good to see you. Miss Adie, she still be asleep, but I can . . ."

"No, don't wake her," Eloise said. "You're the one we came to see. Bobby has some good news from the soil samples."

"The earth has been barren for some time," Bobby said, sitting down on the sofa beside Eloise as Eula settled into a nearby rocker. "It will take work. Most plants grow best at a neutral pH from 5.5 to 7.5. The pH is the chemical balance of the soil. The pH in the best areas of the garden barely makes a 5, but that in itself is amazing since it has lain dormant for so long."

"It's survived along with Miss Adie," Eula said, a wide smile on her face. "Do that mean it can be planted again?"

"With a lot of work," Bobby said. "It will have to be prepped, and pretty soon."

"But Miss Adie, she take such care," Eula said, wrinkling her brow. "Don't know how I can do much."

"I have a plan," Eloise said. "If you don't mind all the fuss and if you don't think it will bother Miss Adie too much, I think I can manage getting some extra hands to help, and

Bobby has offered to take some of his vacation time to get us started."

"Lawd," Eula exclaimed, looking toward the living room window. Beyond the fence lay the clumpy earth that once yielded the fruit of Doc's and Miss Adie's labor. It had been a labor of love. Suddenly, a vision of the two of them kneeling side by side over the earth was so vivid she blinked.

"Vegetables," she said, "and flowers in the garden again?"

"Certainly," Bobby said smiling, "as soon as we get the ground ready. Here in south Alabama, peas, beans, turnips, and rutabagas can be planted from seed in August for a winter harvest. With its mild climate, high rainfall, and eight-month growing season, Alabama is one of the best in the nation for gardens."

"And celery and Brussels sprouts?" Eula added.

"That also and plenty more; they'll mature in three months. Even if we have to plant in September, you will have a harvest for the holidays."

"Pansies," Eloise said, looking toward the window and the barren garden outside. She could visualize their contrasting faces and those with ruffles. She could already see the blues, purples, and reds pushing up through the earth, gracing the garden. "We can plant them in fall, and snapdragons. They can go in the middle of a cottage garden border. In the winter, we should see blooms." How pretty they will look, she thought, with their apple blossom pinks, roses, yellows, and multiple other colors. "And crocus can be planted in mid-October. Azaleas, wouldn't they look pretty in the front yard? We can get the container grown and plant the Alabama azalea with its creamy white flowers in October."

"We'll have to improve the acidity of the soil for the azaleas," Bobby informed them, "and yes, they would look great in the front of the house. It needs some focus."

"Iris. They were one of Doc's favorites," Eula said, visualizing their spring bloom. Doc loved the lemon yellows and the lavender blues. "Lawd!" she exclaimed, taking a deep breath. "Miss Adie, she might not be ..."

"She could," said Eloise. "Look at how long she has lasted, and Eula, think of the spider lilies planted in September and blooming in the fall. Lenten roses," she added enthusiastically, "planted in the fall near the tree line in full shade. The Christmas rose—it will bloom in late winter—and the hybrid tea rose. 'The Fairy' will bloom nearly all season long, from mid-June to November."

Eula's face felt flushed. "The Lawd sent you," she said to Bobby. "He must intend for Miss Adie to live long enough to see her and Doc's garden flourish again."

"It won't be easy," Bobby warned. "We should make a sketch of the garden and draw in where each seed or plant is to be placed. Then there's the matter of the soil. We will have to rake out all the rocks, leaves, and grass, spade out the weeds, and then prep the soil. I believe I saw a tiller in Doc's shed. Lime will improve the soil and three inches of composted manure will aid its biological and chemical properties."

"She got to see it bloom. Every bit of it," Eula stated. "She all the time waiting, staring out the bedroom window."

"Then, Eula," Eloise said, her voice softly reassuring, "part of that wait, with God's help, is about to end."

Eula frowned. "How do we keep it a secret from Miss Adie?"

"Oh." Eloise pursed her lips. "Is there no way you could move her to another bedroom or pull the drapes closed?"

"She wouldn't take to the drapes closed. She got to see out the window, though God knows what she see except clumpy grass, weeds, and old stalks of some long-forgotten plant trying to grow itself back. There is another bedroom, closer to the kitchen. Doc had to sleep there when she became more ill. And," she added. "I can move her with her wheelchair."

"Will she still be able to hear our comings and goings out in the garden?" Bobby asked.

"Her hearing not that good. Company must come close for her to hear what they say," Eula said. "I'll have to come up with some excuse why I'm moving her."

"What if you had some painting done or window washing and wanted her nap time uninterrupted? That is until we have tilled the soil and started our planting," Eloise offered. "After that, she will, of course, know that the land looks different, particularly in a few months when the first flowers start to show."

Eula cocked her head and grinned. She felt suddenly childlike, as if she was seeing her father bounding up the stairs again to take her and her mama in his embrace. Life did have its surprises, bad and good, and this day was bringing her one of its best.

The last of the day's sun splashed the tops of the trees with gold as if the waning heat of the day were collected there. In the distance a nightingale sang its poignant song. Eula stood in the kitchen warming up a pot of coffee and the last of one of the ladies' casseroles. On such an evening, Doc would sit in the kitchen with her drinking a cup of coffee. Often, she half-expected to turn and see him there as she busied herself about the kitchen preparing the evening meal. In the days before Miss Adie became bedridden, he would comment hopefully on her health, although it was waning.

"She'll be up early," he would say, stirring sugar into his coffee. "You'll see," he added, trying to encourage Eula and convince himself, "spading away in the cool of morning."

"She close her eyes soon as I pulled down the spread; she that tired," Eula replied.

"Rest, that's all she needs," he added, attempting to dispense hope as easily as he had medicine to cure someone's ailment.

As Eula set his dinner before him, Doc looked up into her eyes, searching for a glimmer of hope. Knowing how much he needed it, she agreed that "yes, rest be the answer," but no amount of rest could cure the heart or restore the boundless energy that had been so much a part of the woman they both loved. And as her energy waned, so did his. The garden, a legacy of Doc and Miss Adie's love, also slowly withered away. Eula turned and looked at the empty table behind her.

"My fault," Doc's words echoed across the years.

He lost weight during Miss Adie's illness. His clothes hung on his thin frame as if they were draped over nothing more than a hanger.

"Look at all the good you done for Miss Adie, for the town, for me," she encouraged. "We're all soiled laundry waiting for His cleansing. God is all 'bout love and forgiving. Miss Adie know you treasure her."

She sat down in his empty chair and placed her plate in front of her, half-expecting the seat to be warm from his presence.

"Your love's not wasted," she said to the otherwise empty room. "Not like mine," she added in regret for the years she spent with that no-good Jack.

If only she had listened to Lila Mae.

After a particularly brutal beating, Eula packed the small bag she took when she ran away with Jack and sneaked out in the middle of the night from their rented hovel, expecting any second to be snatched by the hair and thrown across the room, but Jack, in another of his drunken stupors, remained asleep. A rickety bus ride took her back into the countryside and dropped her off at its last stop. Half-dragging the case, she shuffled down the dusty roads she and Jack had traveled when she ran away with him. Then she was a young girl. She had never been as pretty as her mother, but she did have her slimness. Now, her figure was as lumpy as an old pillow. She wondered if Lila Mae would recognize the woman on her doorstep. The tree where she and Jack first made love was still there. Even after all the disappointments of living with that man, she felt a surge of heat remembering the push of his body sliding her down the bark of the tree.

The hot sun had taken a toll on her as her calloused feet kicked up the dry red earth of the road, but Lila Mae's was not far now. Eula licked her lips. The canteen of water strapped around her waist was dry. When the fence came into view, her feet picked up speed. The house looked as saggy as her shape and several of the fence's posts were broken and tilted. She expected curtains, the pretty patterned ones Lila Mae hung at the windows, but instead the windows were empty and some of its panes were missing. The stones leading to the front porch were full of dead leaves and twigs, as was the front yard. The front porch rockers where Lila Mae used to sit shelling peas were missing. Pushing open a rickety gate badly in need of paint and dropping the suitcase, she called out hopefully, "Lila Mae. It's me, Eula." The house's bare windows stared back at her blankly. She tried to turn the knob on the door, but it wouldn't give. Someone had locked it.

Distraught and bone tired, she crumpled onto a stair step. The house was abandoned and the yard full of nature's debris, but a vision of how it used to be swept before her eyes. There on that beech tree was a hemp rope swing and from it a wisp of a girl was kicking her feet at the ground in a hopeful sweep of flight to touch a branch, and on the porch behind her was the sound of a rocker and the hum of an old spiritual as Lila Mae's nimble fingers snapped beans or worked on a piece of needlepoint. A car's engine brought the girl's flight to a halt as she jumped off the swing and ran to greet a young man wearing a suit and a hat getting out of a car.

"My girl," his voice rang through the years as he swooped her up in his embrace, twirling her around the yard laughing as she, giggling with pleasure, breathed in the smell of his cologne.

"Good. So good," Lila Mae always said, smiling, putting down what she was working on and coming down the steps to greet him.

They both tried to give Eula a good life, but as she became older, her heart hardened. She rejected the man who fathered her and ran away from Lila Mae with a man who would give Satan a race for his money. She didn't even know where her father lived or if he was still alive, and Lila Mae, what had happened to her?

"I waited too long," she said to the unkempt yard.

The rattle of wheels on the roadbed brought her head up. An old, bearded farmer and his dray horse pulling a wagon full of hay stopped on the roadway. The farmer peered at her from beneath a tattered straw hat.

"You looking for something, girl?" he called.

"Lila Mae Whatley," she said, getting up quickly and walking toward the gate. "She owned this house."

He shook his head. "Name don't mean nothing to me. Heard tell the woman who lived here passed some nine, ten, or more year ago. I never knowed her."

Eula turned and looked back at the vacant windows. All

the warmth she had known and hoped to find again was gone. The house was a crumbling shell, just like her life. She leaned against a porch railing badly in need of paint. Her head hurt and her vision clouded.

"You all right, girl?" the old farmer asked, swinging down from his wagon and tying the horse to a tree.

"Water," she said through parched lips. "I could use some water."

Turning back to his wagon, he lifted out a jug and a tin cup. "No need to drink so fast," he said. "I got plenty more. How did you get here?" he asked, looking down at her dusty shoes and swollen feet.

"Walked mostly," she answered, taking another long swig of the water, "then took a bus part of the way."

"You got some place you want to go?" the man asked.

There was nothing to do but go back. She would find some way to get away from Jack, make some excuse about missing work, and hope they would retain her. It was all she knew to do. So she had the old man take her as far as he could to catch the bus.

Eula shook her head. If she had known what trouble was waiting, she would have taken another road, but then she wouldn't have come to know Doc and Miss Adie.

"God do work in mysterious ways," she said to the empty kitchen as she set her dishes in the sink and turned to go check on Miss Adie. Passing the chair where Doc used to sit, she said, knowing that somehow he could hear her. "Doc, the earth is 'bout to remember."

{TWENTY- FOUR}

ELOISE FELT AS EXCITED AS A TEENAGER ON her first date as she parked at Wynene's curb for the meeting of the Ladies Mission Society. She knew all the ladies wouldn't want to be a part of her and Bobby's plan to restore Miss Adie's garden. Many would have their excuses, but she already knew who she *could* count on: Wynene for one, Opal, Norma Mae, and possibly Hattie. She regretted Bobby was forced to return to Atlanta and couldn't be present to explain all the details of their plan, but he did have a job. She still couldn't believe that this wonderful young man had come into her life. He opened a door long closed. Joy, that is what she felt, and a renewed interest in living. Before his arrival, she existed in a gray area. Now her life took on color again. Bobby inspired her with the expectation that by merely turning the earth and fertilizing it, some of Doc's plants might even take on life again and bloom.

"Isn't that, after all," she said to herself as she parked at Wynene's curb, "what Bobby's appearance at my doorstep and our plan to bring back Miss Adie's garden has done for me?"

Her life had been like barren earth since her son's death. She lived in shadows—the stones and weeds of sorrow weighing her down. The seed of her existence was buried and unyielding, until Bobby appeared at her front door and the plan to bring back Miss Adie's garden gained momentum.

"Eloise," Wynene greeted, swinging wide the door and taking her covered plate of freshly baked cupcakes, "my, you look especially happy today."

"After you open the meeting," Eloise said, "I would like to make an announcement."

"An announcement?" Wynene raised an eyebrow as she placed the plate of cupcakes on the dining room table. "Now, you do have me intrigued. What . . . ?"

The doorbell interrupted her question and soon the living room was full of the Mission Society ladies and the buzz of their conversations over the clink-chink of their cups on saucers. Wynene brought the meeting to order as the ladies took their places on sofas and chairs.

"Eloise," she gestured toward her friend, "has some news for all of us, so before we begin our meeting, I yield the floor to her."

Several of the ladies gave each other mystified expressions. Eloise was usually the quiet one. Many of the ladies put down their plates and cups and saucers on nearby coffee tables or trays set up around the room near their seating.

"A few weeks ago," Eloise began, her eyes bright and her voice conveying enthusiasm, "a young man appeared at my door. He grew up in Simpsonville and graduated in my son's high school class. He's a horticultural specialist. We have a plan to restore Doc's and Miss Adie's garden."

"Restore her garden?" Verabelle questioned. "But how? Why, it's nothing but stony ground and twigs."

"That's a huge project," Hattie stated. "How would you go about it?"

"What's his name?" Sarah Ellen asked. "Did we know his parents?"

"His name is Bobby Hatteras and his folks lived and worked on their farm outside town. His mom lives in Atlanta now."

"Hatteras," Wynene said, cocking her head. "I believe they came to Jim's church. I don't know the young man."

"He's a fine person," Eloise said. "All of you would like him."

"What was he doing in this neck of the woods?" Verabelle asked.

Eloise took a deep breath. "He made a special visit to come see me," she informed them, her voice quavering.

"Because of Jake," Wynene quickly intervened. "He wanted to check on you. He has to be a very special young man to come all this way."

Eloise cast a thankful glance at her friend. "Yes, and perhaps make a nostalgic trip to his old hometown. His visit came at such a providential time, because I had just been thinking of some way to restore the garden for Miss Adie. I didn't know he was a horticulturist until I told him of my interest in bringing it back. He's a wonderful young man. He took a sample of the soil back to Atlanta and just this past week, we went to see Eula with our plan."

"And Miss Adie," Opal asked, "does she know about it?"

"No, we want it to be a surprise, a gift for all of Doc's devotion and hers."

"How long will it take?" Sarah Ellen asked. "She's pretty frail."

"Seeds won't bloom till later, but shrubs should produce

fairly quickly here in south Alabama, but all of you know that from your own gardening." Her voice quavered with emotion. "Within a few months, Miss Adie should see blooms on the shrubs and green shoots pushing up through fertile earth. That is, if we start amending the ground now."

"We?" Verabelle raised an eyebrow, a snap in her voice.

"That is any of you who are able or willing to fit it into your schedules. We don't have to go on the same days once the ground is prepped."

Verabelle was thirsty and not for the sweet punch Wynene provided for refreshment. She began to quiver inside. What she needed was a good stiff drink. This was going to be harder than she thought. Right after the meeting, she would call her doctor and get a refill on the medicine to help her stay dry. Perhaps a project such as the one Eloise was outlining would help, keeping her busier and outside away from the temptation to have a toddy. Yes, perhaps working the earth could help. The image of Miss Adie sitting with her the night of her surgery resurfaced.

"Count me in," she said, the first to volunteer.

Eloise's eyes met the widened, surprised eyes of Wynene's. They noticed the same reaction from some of the other ladies. Life *was* full of surprises.

"It's a wonderful idea," Opal stated. "High time we paid Miss Adie back for all her service to this town as Doc's nurse."

"I'll be glad to help," Norma Mae said.

"Count me in, too," Hattie joined other voices in the room, calling out a resounding chorus.

Eloise was astonished and fought hard to control her emotions. She expected that a handful of the ladies might volunteer, but not the entire room. The ladies in a spontaneous display were on their feet, clapping, words of congratulations and questions on their lips: "One of the best ideas yet," "Can't wait to meet this young man," "What tools should I bring?" "When do we start?"

Eloise could feel her mouth quiver. "We can start as soon as Bobby comes back with the proper fertilizers to prep the soil. He's taking some early vacation time to help. He has also offered to bring some tools. I'll check with him on what else is needed. We'll have to pass the hat for money to fund the shrubs, seeds, and whatever else is needed. I can't ..." her voice faltered as she swallowed hard, "thank you enough."

"Her room," Opal said, her brow wrinkling, "is right near the garden. How do we hide the fact we are there if we are to keep this a surprise?"

"Eula and Bobby brought that up. There's the room where Doc started sleeping when Miss Adie's health worsened. Eula has already offered to chintz it up and move Miss Adie in her wheelchair. She's working on an excuse—painting or some other renovation."

"Then," Wynene offered, "perhaps we should take up a collection to help with that expense also."

All the ladies agreed, and the meeting was adjourned while Eloise went around the room hugging each woman. She couldn't recall feeling closer to all of them. She and Wynene stood at the door seeing them out to their cars and listening to their chatter, a birdsong trill in their voices.

"Well," Wynene put her arm around Eloise, "you are full of surprises. I can honestly say this is one meeting of the Mission Society where I haven't been bored."

Eloise laughed happily. "Or more surprised at the idea's reception?"

"That too, absolutely! And, Eloise, my heart gladdens that you have met and made a friend of your son's. Your life has taken on a new vibrancy."

"You understand, don't you?" She looked wistfully into Wynene's eyes.

"I do. Jake was a sensitive, loving boy. This young man sounds as if he is also, to come all this way to help restore an old lady's garden, and to bring a greater closure for you. We all have our imperfections."

"You're a perfect friend and pastor's wife," Estelle congratulated, hugging her dearest friend.

"I'm not perfect. Don't ever think of me that way."

"Is anything wrong?" Eloise looked into her friend's eyes, noting a certain reluctance to accept her compliment.

"Someday . . ." She hesitated. "Nothing to bother your mind with," she added. "Just don't think me perfect. I could disappoint you."

"That's something you could never do." Eloise hugged her friend again and climbed into her car. "I'm so happy this meeting took place in your home. Thanks for your support. Sorry I sort of took over the meeting without warning."

"No apologies needed. It was the best for its lovely surprises."

Waving goodbye, Wynene couldn't help thinking as Eloise drove away how much of the offered support she witnessed in her living room had an ulterior purpose—to dredge out the secrets of the book Miss Adie was reputedly working on.

{TWENTY-FIVE}

Eula SAT TYPING AWAY AT HER MANUAL typewriter. Beside her sat the stack of notes dictated from the often-meandering memories of Miss Adie. It was amazing that with her dementia, Miss Adie could recall so many details from the past and the early history of the town, much of it before she married Doc and moved to Simpsonville. It was the present that confused her. Eula was surprised by many of the stories of the ladies' lives, but of course, they were also a part of the town's history and Miss Adie and Doc's lives. As Eula typed away, a plan fomented in her mind. This book could become even more interesting with some information Eula could toss in: magic ingredients to add some spice to the book.

A man in coveralls appeared at the entrance to the library where she sat typing away. She was so involved and enticed with her new idea about what to include in the book, she temporarily forgot that she was not alone.

"Didn't mean to scare you," he said, when wide-eyed, she jumped out of her seat.

She unclenched her fists. "Sorry. What can I do for you?"

"We're through with the painting. It should dry in a day or two. Want to check out the color?"

She walked with him back to Miss Adie's room. All the windows were open to help air out the room. The color, an eggshell blue, looked like an early summer morning's sky. Blue was one of Miss Adie's favorite colors. In the past, she'd often commented to her and Doc about how clear the sky looked on sunlit mornings, "as if the sky is like a lake and just on the other side we can see a vision of heaven." It hadn't been easy to convince her she needed to be moved to another room, the one next to the kitchen where Doc had slept when she became bedridden.

"Jest for a little while," Eula told her, "till the painting's done. The fumes aren't good for you."

"Why?" she argued. "Why, Eula? He won't be able to find me."

"Oh, he knows all the time where you be," she reassured.

"But, in the garden." Miss Adie looked wide-eyed toward the windows overlooking the barren, stony earth outside her bedroom window.

"It's his old room," she appeased. "And I've put the quilt you made for him on the foot of the bed."

"The quilt?" Miss Adie turned the word over in her mind before the glimmer of a sparkle came into her eyes. "Took a long time; gave it to him one Christmas."

"Yes, you did, and how he went on . . . he so delighted."

The memory of that Christmas brought a smile to Miss Adie's face that lit up her face as if an inner flame flickered in the hearth of her mind. There was a Yule log burning in the fireplace on that Christmas as it did every Christmas morning, warm weather or cold, because Doc considered it a tradition. Her face had a childlike glee as Doc unwrapped a large, bulky package, one of her carefully and painstakingly stitched quilts. She had worked on it in the late hours of the night while he was sleeping, secreting it away in the antique cedar chest at the foot of their bed.

Doc, too, had trouble adjusting away from her. Often during the night, Eula would hear the shuffle of feet pass her room and knew he was going to check on Miss Adie. A few times, when she went in to wake Miss Adie in the morning, she found him there, his arms around her, their bodies close and way too skinny. Together, they seemed like one person lying underneath the blanket. Sometimes at night, even now, years after Doc was gone, Eula would awaken to the shuffle of feet in the hallway. Her heart would skip an extra beat and she would go into the hallway half-expecting to see him sneaking down the hall like an errant child on a forbidden mission on his way to Miss Adie's room.

It took a good bit of work to move Miss Adie to Doc's old bedroom. Miss Wynene and Miss Estelle spent one afternoon helping. They removed her favorite pictures from the wall and the dresser picture of Doc, unloaded her closet, and removed all the knickknacks on her dresser and table tops, packing them carefully in tissue paper to be stored in boxes until the painting was done. When Eula lifted Miss Adie's frail body in her arms and placed her in the wheelchair, they were present to reassure her about how pleased she would be to see fresh paint on her bedroom walls. They tried to hide it, but Eula could see on their faces how startled they were to see how emaciated Miss Adie looked beneath her gown, her flesh draped on her arms like wet crumpled clothing hanging from a clothesline.

"Oh, how lovely," they exclaimed comfortingly as they entered Doc's old bedroom, where Eula had moved Miss

Adie's favorite rocker from her room and covered the bed with a lace coverlet, one of her quilts folded neatly at the foot of the bed.

Hung on the walls were all the pictures from her room, and Doc's picture sat on the dresser across from the bed where Miss Adie could always see it. Miss Adie seemed too exhausted from the short move to comment, but that night she called out for Eula.

"The garden," she exclaimed, her voice shaking. "Eula, where is the garden?"

"Jest out there," Eula reassured.

"Where?" Her eyes were wide with confusion. "I can't see it."

"You're in Doc's room," Eula explained again. "It's jest for a little while. As soon as your room is freshly done up with new paint, you'll be back there."

"Doc's room." An expression of warmth suffused her face. She patted the quilt over her, pulling it up to her nose. "Smells like him still." Putting it over one cheek, she fell peacefully asleep and never complained again.

"Eula," a man's voice called softly from the living room.

Mr. Bobby. Eula got up excitedly from her chair and met him in the living room. He was standing jest outside the screen door on the stair stoop, his jeans and shirt smudged with earth. His knees were damp from the soil. A brown smudge on his left cheek gave him even more of a boyish look. From the open door, Eula could hear the excited voices of the ladies like little children at play in the freshly turned earth of the old garden. For over a month, they had come by turns going down on hands and knees pulling out weeds, stalks of old plants, and removing stones. With handheld tillers, they put in compost manure, working it in with a hoe to prepare the once-forgotten earth for planting. Even Miss Verabelle had gotten her knees dirty. Her once-well-manicured nails were encrusted with soil and broken off from hours of mending the land. Calluses had formed on her hands and her somewhat pasty face had become tan. She even lost fat, as most of the ladies had—their faces and limbs trimmer.

Eula took a deep breath. The smell of the freshly turned earth was intoxicating. It reminded her suddenly of her mother planting the seed and shrubs for vegetables and flowers in their small patch of land. On special days, daddy days, he would get into work clothes, rolling his sleeves up, and getting on his knees beside her mama, helped with the planting. Often, as they worked row by row, they would stop and Eula would find them in a close embrace, their hands touching each other's faces, leaving the same smudge marks Bobby bore on his cheek. Then they would laugh, a bubbly sound that Eula could feel tingle in her tummy. Eula could see her mama's lovely face before her, the high cheekbones, the large brown eyes, and the dimpled chin her father often took in his hand to bring her lips close to his.

She blinked as Bobby's face blurred before her eyes.

"Anything wrong?" he asked, frowning.

"What? No, nothing." She wiped at her eyes. "Sorry. It's jest that I still can't believe all this. What can I do, Mr. Bobby? You need something, a glass of water, food?"

"Can you come out for a second? I, we," he said, his voice full of enthusiasm, "want you to see the beginnings of the garden."

"Let me go check on Miss Adie first."

Slipping down the hallway, she peeped into Doc's old room. Miss Adie was asleep, the quilt underneath her chin. Exchanging her shoes for an old pair, Eula met Bobby at the front door. "She be fast asleep," she said, slipping out the screen door.

Even though she had watched the ladies and Bobby digging out roots and stones, raking in fertilizer, and mulching to control weeds, she was unprepared for the results of their work. The ladies were on their knees dropping seeds carefully into shallow furrows dug into the earth. Many of the rows were already marked with Popsicle sticks to indicate the flower or vegetable that would push up from the newly cleared and fertilized soil.

"Eula," Miss Eloise called, kneeling over a freshly planted bed. Her face looked bronzed from the sun and nearly childlike with pleasure.

Another woman, her face buried beneath a huge straw hat, stood up from the earth. "Oh, Eula," she called, carefully stepping between rows toward her. It was Miss Hattie. Not only did the hat disguise her, but she also seemed slimmer. Eula could see her cheekbones again. Her face was glistening with sweat. "Walk between the rows and see the vegetables we have planted: rutabagas, collards, broccoli, peas, beans, and more. In three months, you will have a harvest for the holidays."

"In October, turnips, mustard, spinach, and kale can be planted," Bobby added. "Spinach will mature early and be ready to pick in a month."

"Come look," a voice, Miss Wynene's, called from the shade of pine trees on the side of the house. What appeared to be evergreen shrubs had been set down into open holes onto a mound of soil and pine bark.

"Camellias?" Eula asked in an astounded voice.

"The soil here is somewhat acidic, semimoist, and well-drained. Perfect," Bobby said with a wide grin.

A sense of joyful anticipation seemed to permeate the freshly tilled and planted soil. Eula looked over the beginnings of the garden, expecting Doc at any moment to appear over the horizon wearing his weathered hat and gardening gloves. This earth had known the healing touch of his hands; these women had known it also. He was still a part of them all and not that far away.

{TWENTY-SIX}

WYNENE SAT IN THE DEN READING A BOOK while Jim sat at his desk nearby working on a sermon. She was delightfully exhausted, though energized, from her day in Miss Adie's garden. Muscles she didn't realize were there ached pleasantly. Jim sighed, putting his pen down. He swiveled his chair around toward her.

"Let's have a child," he declared abruptly, a nearly pleading sound in his voice.

"What?"

"A baby. It's not too late. You're still in your thirties."

"Why? Why now? You've never seemed interested before."

"Well, I am now. A part of you, a part of me."

"But Jim . . ." Her face blanched.

He got out of his chair and came toward her. A sudden sensation swept over her that if he tried to touch her, she would get up and run. She couldn't recall the last time they had sex. All she could think about was Dan waiting for her return. Did Jim suspect and this was his way of forcing her hand? No, that wouldn't be his way. Jim wasn't a vindictive or devious human being. He knelt at her feet, a shocking gesture that nearly brought tears to her eyes.

"I know I haven't been much of a husband to you lately," he said, laying his head in her lap and putting his arms around her knees. "My congregation and all its duties have gotten in the way. We aren't getting any younger, and a child, our child, could make such a difference. Don't you want a baby, Wynene? I thought you liked children. You're always volunteering for the church nursery."

"I do . . . it's just that I need some time to think," she said, resisting a sudden urge to put a hand on his head and run it through his blond curls, the way she did when they were dating. "I've been busy helping out with Miss Adie's garden, and," she added, her voice quavering, "my sister expects me to come up again. Her health isn't any better."

"What's wrong with right now?"

"Oh, Jim, I'm just too tired."

Taking a deep breath, he stood up. "All right," he said, a remorseful tone in his voice, his arms at his side, the palms of his hands turned out toward her as if in question. "All I'm asking is think about it."

He stayed there, a handsome man, her husband, staring down at her with those clear blue eyes that made her feel drawn by them as they did when they first met. He seemed to be studying her. It was a look that penetrated her soul. More than plaintive, he seemed puzzled, as if the woman seated in front of him was someone he felt he recognized, but now wasn't quite certain. Then he turned and left the room, leaving her with a sense of overwhelming grief as if she had just lost the best friend she ever had.

WYNENE LAY IN DAN'S ARMS WHILE HE continued to gently stroke her cheek. The sheets were crumpled from their lovemaking. She took a deep breath, let it out and sat up.

"He wants a child."

"What?"

"Jim. He announced a couple of days ago that he wants a child."

"And . . ."

She turned and looked down at him. "Oh, Dan, that's out of the question."

"I've never asked you," he said, pulling her down beside him again. "You can have children, can't you? If you can't, I'm fine with that, too, as long as I have you. If you can, I want them with you. I never felt that way with Laurel. A child with you would be an extension of our love, and when grandchildren came ..."

"Of course I want children. I love children. I would adore your children."

"Our children," he said, running a hand down her bare leg and turning her over so he lay on top of her looking down into her eyes. "Tell him, Wynene, it's time you told him. You can't go on living with a lie and I can't go on living without you beside me every day."

VERABELLE FELT TIRED, BUT IT WAS A NICE KIND of tired. She drank a glass of water and took another pill to fight off any desire she had for a drink. Lately, though, she had noticed that hours would go by without an irresistible urge for a drink. She and the ladies had been working on the garden since August. They were now nearing the end of

September. Nearly two months since a drink.

"Hello," a voice called.

"In the kitchen," she answered.

Dick placed his briefcase on the kitchen table. "Something smells good."

"Thought I would cook the chicken and broccoli supreme," she announced, opening the oven door and leaning over to test the casserole with a fork. "It's almost done," she said, smiling up at him, the heat from the oven and the sun she had gotten that day flushing her face.

"You look different." The hint of a smile played across his lips. "And you're acting different, a nice kind of different."

It had been so long since he smiled at her that she felt suddenly giddy, like the schoolgirl she was when they first met. He came closer and took her face in his hands. "You've been out in the sun. It looks good. And haven't you lost weight? Your clothes seem looser and your face thinner." His hands slipped down onto her hips. "Yep, definitely slimmer." Pulling her closer, he placed his mouth on her lips. Fearful he might step away, she wrapped her arms snugly around him. "How long till dinner?" he whispered into her ear.

"Ready. It's ready," she murmured into his neck.

"Put it on warm," he said. "It can wait."

HATTIE MAE LEANED BACK AGAINST THE TUB'S edge. The warm water flowing from the tap felt luxurious to her aching muscles. Frothy rainbowed bubbles rose to her chin. She wiggled her toes, raising one leg into the air to stretch out her soreness. She felt pleasantly fatigued. Miss Adie's garden was quickly taking shape. She felt as light and free as the bubbles flowing around her. Bobby had warned them that Miss Adie's garden would be an ongoing project as Eula was far too busy nursing to weed, spray, and fertilize the developing plants and vegetables. She didn't mind. Working the garden gave her a peace she had not sensed in a long time, and she was discovering muscles in her body she didn't know existed. Every time she sprinkled seed into a furrow or helped the other ladies lower a balled plant into the waiting earth, she felt worthy—a sensation she hadn't experienced in a long time, since the discovery of Roy's affair. Like an amnesiac, she had wandered through her days fulfilling her duties without any true knowledge of who she was. The garden had given back to her a sense of self. Often, she would return home almost too tired to eat and when she did, it was a light meal. The chocolates she favored were a thing of the past and her clothes were becoming too large. She had to fish through her closet to retrieve old clothing.

"You look good," Roy commented. "You seem content and trimmer."

"I am," she replied.

Noticing the inquiring glance that accompanied his compliment, she stifled an inward giggle. Did he suspect her of an indiscretion? The despair and anger that followed the discovery of his affair had disappeared.

"When did my anger disappear and why?" she said aloud to the swirling bubbles.

A gradual release, it fully took fruition with the preparing and planting of Miss Adie's garden. In the clumps and clods, the weight of her grief, there was no space to grow. Was it possible to retrieve, as she did her old clothes from the closet, the love she once felt for her husband? Perhaps not as it used to be, but she was learning at least to forgive, an act that was itself a tremendous release.

TWENTY-SEVEN

OPAL KNELT ON THE EARTH. PACKETS OF SEED were in a large basket near her. It was time to plant turnips, mustard, and spinach and start beds of strawberries. The chatter of the other ladies working nearby had a joyful note to it. They were all busy mulching and spraying to protect the garden from scale and mites. The summer had passed quickly. With its passing and the planting of Miss Adie's garden, a greater comradeship developed among the Mission Society ladies. The laughter they shared as they worked the garden sounded like the trill of birds. They had worked on many projects before, but none had given them as much delight as being outside digging in the dirt to restore Miss Adie's garden. The ladies had never looked better, even with straggly hair shoved beneath broad hats and sweat on their brows. Raking, mulching, and removing debris also pruned away weight.

October already! Turnips, mustard, spinach, and kale would be ready for picking in November when roses were planted, and in December, rutabagas, collards, broccoli, peas, and beans could be harvested. Tree leaves were beginning to lose their green pigment. Goodness, Opal thought, December and Christmas only two months away. She would have to get the children's wish lists; make a trip to Montgomery. She sat back on her heels and wiped her brow. Christmas! The very thought of it projected across the garden's landscape an image of her ma dragging a spindly pine tree she chopped into the trailer.

"Look, baby," she would call, excitement in her voice, "setting at the edge of the woods waiting for me and just right."

Rummaging around in her bedroom closet, her mother pulled out a small box and a tiny stand. Kylie Mae felt all tingly inside as she helped her set the tree into the stand in the kitchen corner. Soon, the trailer smelled deliciously of pine and corn popping in a pot on the stove. Helping her ma string the corn and drape it around the pine was always a special treat.

"Now, don't go spoiling your supper," her ma would warn with humor in her voice. "Save some of that popped corn for the tree."

Then came the ornament hangers for the pecan shells handpainted by her mother in vibrant reds, greens, and purples, and for the final touch, a small package of recycled tinsel. There were no lights.

"Such fuss," Pa always scolded. "Don't go thinking I'm allowing no damn electricity."

"Are you all right?" Wynene, working nearby, asked.

"What? Oh, yes, thanks. I just got some dirt in my eye."

Wynene smiled. "Can you believe all this?" She swept her gloved hands across the garden full of greenery and beginning bloom.

Opal cocked her head. Wynene's face glowed. More than sun and sweat, it was a luminous joy that Opal had never seen on her face. It reminded her of her ma's radiant face and smile as they hung the last handmade ornaments on the spindly pine in a tiny backwoods trailer. On Christmas Eve, she lay the long stocking her mother had knitted on the worn trailer sofa in the kitchen/living room.

"Bunch of silliness," her father snorted, mashing a beer can in one hand and tossing it into the garbage.

Ignoring his comment, they lit two red candles on the kitchen table to celebrate "the birth of a child," her ma told her, "sent by God Himself to teach us about love."

"Love," her father sneered, grinding out a cigarette butt with his boot on the trailer floor and swigging the dregs of his beer. "I'll show you 'bout love." Heaving his massive bulk out of the chair, nearly knocking over the candles, he snatched her mother about the waist.

"No," she protested, her face paling as he twisted her around, bending her backward, "Hal, not here! Kylie Mae, go on now. Bedtime!"

"That's right," he snarled, his face burrowed in her mother's neck, "bedtime."

"Mama," she cried.

"It's all right, baby," she said, still struggling, as she was shoved toward the sofa where the stocking lay waiting for Santa. "Go on now like a good girl, Santa's coming."

"Santa," her father slurred. "He's coming, all right."

Kylie Mae crawled into bed, disappearing beneath a blanket. She pulled a pillow over her head so she wouldn't hear the strange sounds from the other room: her father's voice like an animal's low growl; her mother's plaintive, painful pleas. Safely hidden, she could see stars twinkling in a Christmas Eve sky beyond the worn window sheers. The next morning, her mother came into her room, a bulging stocking in her hand. Purple bruises were on her neck.

"Look, angel," she said in a tinny voice, "Santa."

"Ma," she asked, tightening her hand on the cover held rigidly over her head. "Is he still here?"

"Oh, no, sugah, he never stays. A world full of children to gift, but he'll be back next year."

"No," she said, "not Santa, Pa."

Her mama's eyes widened. "Oh." She plopped down on the bed. "No, baby, he's gone," she said flatly, stroking Kylie Mae's hair. "Let's you and me eat breakfast. Made your favorite, blueberry pancakes. It's Christmas. Don't you want to see what ole Santa put in your stocking?" She smiled, but it was not a happy smile.

"Opal?"

Opal blinked. Wynene was kneeling in front of her. She was in a garden, a spade in her hand. She was Opal St. John, married to a wonderful man. She had two lovely children and a more than good life. Kylie Mae disappeared long ago on a stormy night, leaving on a blood-slick floor the man who suffocated her mother's life and had nearly taken hers.

"Are you all right?" Wynene asked. "Your face … you turned pale. You've been working too hard. Perhaps you should take a rest, drink some water."

"Nothing, it's nothing." She sat back on her heels. "You're right. I should take a break."

"I'll get you some water," Wynene said, leading her to a garden bench beneath a beech tree.

Opal leaned her head back, looking up into the copper-colored leaves that even in winter would still be there. She sat up and looked across the garden. A hazy cloud lay across her vision, shutting out the sunlight and beginning buds. Layer upon layer of Miss Adie's unfertile earth had been transformed into fruitful ground, but no matter where Opal went or what she accomplished, she would always be that frightened girl racing through a stormy night in a beat-up truck, carrying the past with her.

VERABELLE SMILED AS SHE WEEDED THE FLOWER beds. She ccouldn't recall being this content since she first married Dick. The garden gave her life new purpose and direction. She hadn't had a drink in months, and with every passing day, her figure became trimmer. She took a deep breath. How good the mineral-rich earth smelled. It was like an elixir. Every morning, she awakened with renewed vigor, and the nights . . . She giggled like a schoolgirl. Dick had been more than ardent. She felt as if they were having a second honeymoon.

"Treat yourself to some new clothes," he said last night, grinning as he slid his arm around her waist. "I want to show off my new bride."

"You seem jolly today," Sarah Ellen, working nearby, commented. "Actually, Verabelle, if you don't mind my saying so, I can't recall seeing you happier."

She blushed as if Sarah Ellen could read her mind. "It's all this fresh air."

"You're right. It's been good for all of us." Sarah Ellen added, dropping seed into a furrow and thinking that working to restore Miss Adie's garden gave her life new meaning. How could she have blamed herself for a murder her great-uncle was responsible for in the distant past before she was ever born? Life with her parents, husband, and children was more than good, and wonderful friends were another blessing. Taking this barren earth and hopefully restoring it to its former abundance of flower, vegetables, and fruit for Miss Adie was a creative and heartfelt plan. She awakened each day with new vigor, excited to give back to Miss Adie a portion of the compassion Miss Adie had given her as a child, when her life felt horribly blemished by a relative she had never met.

"My small garden plot doesn't hold a candle to Miss Adie's; can't wait for her to see it. She will, won't she?" Sarah Ellen added plaintively.

"She has to. She must." A slight frown creased Verabelle's brow. "After all she and Doc have done for this town, for us."

Sarah Ellen's eyes widened. Verabelle never spoke kindly of Miss Adie—or anyone, for that matter. Transforming her garden was working wonders for them all. A warm October breeze blew through her hair. She smiled at the soft warble of a mourning dove calling from a nearby branch. In it she could hear a plaintive cry of hope.

{TWENTY-EIGHT}

EULA STOOD IN THE GARDEN. THE AIR AND earth emitted the clean, fresh scent of life growing all around her. The ladies had performed a miracle. This past week, they had been busy planting hardy annuals: larkspur, poppies, candytuft, and pansies. Lilies of the valley had been placed in shady places. A cold frame held cabbage and lettuce. The garden was already yielding a harvest of vegetables and forget-me-not roses were in full bloom as were camellias, the state flower. She particularly loved the vivid bright pinks and reds. She peeked into the face of a fluffy Lady Kay. A light breeze waved the petals as if it were saying good morning. The garden was flooded with the purples and yellows of crocus that would thrive through the winter months. A nip in the air signaled coming December.

Miss Adie's book was growing, too. A year ago, she couldn't have imagined the return of Miss Adie and Doc's garden or a book about the town and the ladies. When the book first began, she didn't worry about how the ladies would receive it, but since then she had gotten to know many of them. They seemed changed, as changed as the garden: a barren landscape without color suddenly bursting with it and Miss Adie, with all her ailments and dementia, was still alive and settled in Doc's old bedroom. Life did have its surprises.

Eula knew all about surprises. Some of them came in good packages, a lot in bad. Jack had been a bad one. She should have seen that one coming as clear as a tornado surging through the sky picking up everything in its path, tossing trailers, houses off concrete blocks, sucking out the very air. After her disappointing trip back to find Lila Mae to seek her forgiveness for running out on her, she went back to see about her old job at the diner.

"What you doing here, girl?" Ruth Ann, a waitress who used to work with her, asked Eula. "You jest asking to be killed." Jack had come looking for her, barging through the back door into the kitchen, sending pots and pans clattering to the floor. "Where is my woman?" he demanded. "You know, you bettah tell or else."

"The police came," the staff told her. "You bettah be a gone thing 'fore he beats your ass."

She hurried back to gather up what few things she had left behind while he was still out somewhere. Hands trembling, she emptied all she owned from a drawer into a bag, but it was too late. She heard feet clattering up the wrought iron staircase. She tried to run past him, but he snatched her hair with a large paw, twisting one of her arms painfully behind her.

"Whar you goin,' darlin'?" he grunted as she screamed in pain.

"Jack, no," she pleaded.

He dragged her down the stairwell. She gripped one of the bars on the staircase, but he pried her fingers loose, yelling,

"Bitch!" She saw a woman's face peeping fearfully around an apartment window curtain.

"Police, call the police," she screamed.

The curtain fell. Bumping her knees and arms across the parking lot, Jack tossed her into their broken-down excuse of a car. Forcing her down on the seat, he screeched out of the parking lot going 90 to nothing. When she tried to sit up, he slammed one of his giant paws onto her head, forcing her face into the shredded vinyl of the seat cover.

"No one leaves," he sneered. "I been left all my life, woman."

"Pl . . . eas . . . ee," she begged. "Don't . . . "

"Don't what, darlin'? Kill you? When I git through with you, you gonna beg to be dead."

She didn't see the car he hit, but she remembered the fierce cry of a horn and a massive crushing sound. Suddenly, she was catapulted through glass and metal, landing heavily on a hard surface. The acrid taste of blood was in her mouth. She coughed.

"My God, she's alive," a woman's voice said. "It's going to be all right, honey." She tried to focus on the woman's face, but the sky had turned dark and large chunks of it were falling heavily on her chest.

"Do you need anything for pain?" a faraway voice called.

She opened her eyes to see eyes peering down at her from above a white face mask.

She tried to open her mouth to speak, but nothing came out. Weakly, she nodded. Dizzy—she felt so dizzy. She tried to focus on the nurse's face, but it faded away. She was on a swing going higher and higher into the sky toward a bright blue sky.

"More. More, Daddy," she said, her tummy tingling.

"Look, Mommy," she called, tuning her head toward the porch where her mother sat, laughing. "I'm flying."

"Come down little bird," her mother called, "it's time to hit the nest."

Her father grabbed the swing, stopping it, and lifted her in his arms, but she still felt as if she were spinning through the sky toward the hazy sunlit green of trees. She awoke painfully to an antiseptic odor. She was lying in a hospital bed. A needle was in her arm attached to a long tube and a bag of liquid hung above it. Her face throbbed. She wiggled her toes. They worked. Then she tried her legs. They hurt, but they, too, moved. Her lips felt parched and cracked. She tried to open her mouth. The left side of her face felt as if hot ashes were placed on it. Footsteps. She tried to turn her head, but it hurt too much.

"Well now, we are awake."

She looked up into a woman's face. A white cap sat on her head and beside her stood a man in white.

"I'm Dr. Logan," the man said, checking her pulse before he parted her gown to place a stethoscope on her chest.

He wrote something on a chart and handed it to the nurse. He placed a hand lightly on her left cheek. Eula grimaced in pain.

"Lucky," the doctor reassured, "you could have been killed. The left side of your face took the brunt of your accident. We worked on it for a long time. Other than that, you suffered massive bruising. You will have some difficulty talking, but when your cheek heals, you'll be fine. Nurse Polk will take good care of you, and I'll come back again tomorrow morning to check on your progress. Try to rest now."

The nurse switched the bag feeding fluids into her arm and wrote something down on her chart.

"What?" she asked of Eula's painful mumbling. "Here, don't try to talk just yet," she advised, handing her a piece of chalk and a small blackboard.

"Bad?" she printed in a childlike slant.

"Just as Dr. Logan explained, it could have been a lot worse."

She scribbled on the black slate. "Man with me?"

"Sorry, I can't answer that question, but I'll send someone who can. Now, how's your pain level?"

"Bad," the chalk scrawled erratically. "The man. Must know."

"Let's treat your pain first. I can do that intravenously through your bag. You're also getting nutrients through the IV. Later, when you're better, you'll be able to eat on your own."

Eula wrote on the pad again. "The man?"

Her nurse's footsteps receded into the background as she fell into what must have been a drugged sleep, for when she awoke, a man with a chaplain's collar was standing over her. Beside him stood Eula's nurse. Before he pulled a chair close to her bed, Eula's suspicions were confirmed: Jack had been killed instantly, as had the man in the pickup truck he hit.

"Is there anyone we should notify?" the chaplain asked.

"No one," her hand shook as she wrote the words on the slate.

Eula faulted herself for the only emotion she felt—an immediate and ecstatic rush of freedom. Jack had been a no one whose only ambition was to remain a no one who belonged to no one or anything. He had succeeded in his only non-ambition.

It took weeks for her face to heal. There were no mirrors in her room and she was flat on her back, so there wasn't any way to check the damage the windshield and fall had caused, and bandages still covered her face. The first time she asked the nurse about her face, the nurse hesitated.

"I'll have to ask the doctor first," she stated, placing a cuff on her arm to check her blood pressure.

"We're making progress," the doctor said when he made his rounds later that afternoon. "Let's check on your facial healing."

The nurse handed him a pair of scissors and what looked like tweezers of some sort.

"This will sting," the doctor warned, gently removing her bandages.

Eula steeled herself for the worst, but when the doctor started removing the stitches, tears came to her eyes.

"Sorry," the doctor said in a gentle voice. "You're lucky it wasn't a lot worse."

The nurse tried to keep a composed face as the doctor pulled out stitch after stitch, but Eula noticed a compressing of her lips as she flinched.

"There, all done," the doctor reported, "nicely healed, although you'll have to apply a salve on it for some time."

"Can I have a mirror?" Eula asked, steeling herself.

The woman staring back at her wide-eyed was unrecognizable. An elongated and enflamed flap of skin folded over like a ropy coil lay on the left side of her face. Her mother's lovely features appeared before her. She was never as pretty as her mother, but she inherited her high cheekbones and her eyes. 'A handsome gal,' Jack used to call her before drink totally consumed him. She was no longer even that. The only things recognizable in the mirror were her mother's eyes. She began to shiver.

"It's all right," the doctor comforted, placing a blood

pressure cuff on her arm. "Nurse."

She was handed two pills and a glass of water by the nurse, who said in a compassionate tone, "Swallow, please."

That evening the chaplain paid her another call, trying to console her with the thought that who we are is not what people see, "what comes from within is the true character of a person." Kind words, but Eula couldn't bring herself to look in a mirror again for a long time, and she still had difficulty recognizing the face looking back at her.

When she was finally released from the charity ward, she confronted other problems. She had no job, no place to live, and little money except what she had managed to hide from Jack. Her only option was to call on her co-workers, whose faces registered astonishment and repulsion.

"Don't go thinking the boss man goin' to take you back," she was warned by one dunking dishes in suds. "If he walk in here, you bettah be a gone thing."

"I got a friend," another offered, sympathy in her voice.

She suddenly felt like a street person, maimed and pitiful, but she was in no position to turn down help. She was told about a woman living down in south Alabama who rented out row houses.

"She could help find you a job, maybe, taking in washing, ironing. I'll write and see. I put you up till we hear."

Within a week, Eula was on a bus heading for some town called Simpsonville. This was one time she didn't mind sitting in the back of the bus where she could hide her face, already partially draped with a scarf. Dragging her suitcase, she found the quarters and the woman who rented her a small wooden frame house with a workable stove and a tiny icebox. The bed was more like a cot with a lumpy mattress, but she was used to all that from the hovels shared with Jack. She bought the weekly newspaper and started looking for some kind of work where someone wouldn't mind her misshapen face. Her scar began itching—normal, she knew, when healing—but then she woke up one night in pain. Placing a cool cloth over the wound didn't help. If anything, the pain grew to the point where she couldn't leave her small hovel to look for the much-needed job. The scar looked festered. It began to ooze. The groceries she bought the first week she moved in were nearly gone, but even walking the floor, which she did every night to stave off the hurt, seemed to make the pain worse. She was sitting on the sofa's broken springs swaying back and forth in pain when her landlady knocked on the door.

"My God, girl," she exclaimed, "no wonder I hadn't seen you about. You got a 'fecton. You needs a doctor."

"Can't afford one," Eula said, "and besides, don't know one. Give it some time; it got to get better."

"Don't know who beat you or what trouble you seen, but you want that thing eating up the rest of your face? There's a doctor and his nurse, his wife, who come by weekly, tomorrow actually, checking on the quarters' peoples."

Eula moaned as she shook her head, "Can't pay."

"He don't never charge. I'm sending him; you bettah answer your door."

Eula spent the whole night fevered, walking the floor, stumbling over her feet, her fists balled up in pain. "Lawd," she cried, "why didn't you let me die quick like in that car?"

She was slumped on the sofa moaning when the knock came on her door the next morning. She sank deeper into the broken-down sofa, having already decided the best way out of her troubles was to let nature take her out.

"Eula, you open this door," her landlady called. "We is coming in one way or'nother."

She sank even deeper as far as the sprung sofa would allow, but the knocking became louder. Then the door swung open. She should have figured the landlady would have a key. She sighed and closed her eyes. When she opened them, she was looking up into a man's.

"My Lord!" he said, blinking.

Eula could barely see his face for the tears flowing down her face. That day, she went home with Doc and Miss Adie. They couldn't repair the damage done to her face or her life, but they gave her a job and a real home. First, she had been the patient, then Doc, and now Miss Adie. God did have a strange way of answering prayer.

{TWENTY-NINE}

HATTIE MAE CRAWLED INTO BED. WORKING in the garden energized her. She should have been exhausted. Instead, she stayed up late reading a book. The moon through the guest room sheers spread an ethereal blue light across the backyard, reminding her of childhood fantasies: fairies prancing across dew-laced grass. She stretched her legs and arms; they were more flexible and far slimmer than they had been in a long time. Plumping her pillow beneath her head, she fell into a deep sleep.

She awakened to a breath of air on her cheek and a hand on her shoulder. Heart pounding, she sat up. "What?" she demanded, her arms flailing in the air.

Roy was standing over the bed. "I didn't mean to frighten you," he apologized, sitting on the edge of the bed.

"Are you all right?" she asked, wondering why he had awakened her.

"Yes . . . no. I miss you; I miss us."

"Roy, I'm tired," she said, exasperated. "There is nothing to discuss." She lay down and turned her back to him.

"It's not that simple," he said, slipping into bed beside her and putting his arms gently around her.

His touch aroused a pang of passion, a remembrance of who they used to be before the discovery of his affair with that bimbo clerk. He lightly kissed her forehead. "Roy," she whispered, surprised at the rush of warmth she felt. He hugged her closer.

"I miss you so much. I want my wife back. Is it possible? Can you finally forgive me for being such a fool?"

She ran her hands through his hair, kissed him. She had forgotten how right it felt to be in his arms. "You won't ask me to forget? I can't forget."

"Just forgive. That's all I'm asking. I know it's a lot."

She wrapped her arms around him, kissed his neck. "If I don't, I will just be punishing myself."

EULA WAS IN THE ATTIC GATHERING UP BOXES of Christmas ornaments. That morning, Bobby had arrived in his car, followed by a truck with two men in it. Tied securely on the truck bed was a massive balsam tree. He also brought a large stand for the tree.

"Better put some sheets down for stray needles," Bobby advised, watching the two men struggle to lift the tree.

Wynene and Eloise, taking a break from the garden, stood with Eula watching in awe as the men struggled to lift the tree, bring it over the threshold, and set it into the stand in a corner of the living room near a window that overlooked Doc's crumbling fountain. They wobbled the tree from side to side to check its stability.

"It's so fat and tall," Eula exclaimed. "Almost touch the ceiling, jest enough room for a star."

"Hope it's not too big for you," Bobby said.

"I'll help decorate," Wynene offered.

"Count me in," added Eloise. "Don't get a chance anymore to decorate a lot since . . . " She paused, breathed deeply
before adding, "Jake's passing."

"Is Miss Adie still content in Doc's old room?" Wynene
asked.

"Not one word of complaint. She be happy holding onto
the quilt she made for Doc. When do you think I should move
her?" Eula asked, fluffing a fragrant branch on the tree.

"Let's get the tree decorated first," Bobby offered. "Then
when we wheel her out, she'll have two surprises. The weather should hold to take her outside to view the garden. I can't
recall many cool Decembers this far south."

Satisfied the tree was well situated in its stand, Bobby
paid the men who delivered the tree and helped set it into
the stand. Wynene and Eloise returned to their work in the
garden with a promise to be back when Eula gathered up the
ornaments. The garden was yielding a harvest of vegetables,
and the other ladies were there now adding roses, mulching
the other plants, and planting hardy annuals. After a quick
check on Miss Adie, who was sleeping, Eula started up the
stairs eager to gather up ornaments long stored in the attic.

"Now, where is the star?" Eula murmured to herself,
shifting boxes full of ornaments stored years ago when Doc
and Miss Adie's health began to deteriorate. She felt as excited as a small child. For years the only Christmas tree in
the house was a small potted one she bought to decorate for
a living room side table. What a delight to have a real tree
to decorate. Even when she was cooking, she would be able
to smell the woodsy aroma from the living room. She could
imagine her mama standing in front of the massive tree, her
head tilted way back to see the top, could almost hear her say,

"Baby, that tree still be growing."

"Mama," she said, opening a box to discover an angel ornament, "where you are, every day is Christmas day."

Holding onto the bannister with one hand and carrying her boxed Christmas treasures with the other, she took the stairs one by one, careful not to trip. Wouldn't do Miss Adie no good if she was to end with a sprain or worse.

"Eula." Wynene was standing at the bottom of the attic stairway. "You shouldn't be doing that by yourself. Let me help."

"Lawdy," she exclaimed, setting the boxes on the living room sofa. "I has forgotten how many ornaments Miss Adie and Doc stored away."

She opened a box of crocheted snowflakes. They would be Miss Adie's. Another revealed a collection of glass ornaments from Santa Clauses to snowmen and everything in between. She finally found the glass garlands.

"I'll go get Eloise and Bobby," Wynene said. "He can place the star on top and start the lights and strands of garland. Did you find ornament hangers in any of those boxes? Bobby forgot to get some."

"Yes, mum, I did. This be only half of what I opened so far, but that fat tree need every bit."

Bobby and Eloise came through the door after changing their shoes from their garden work and placing them in a large basket Eula kept near the door just for that purpose. He climbed the tall ladder while they held it steady, admonishing, "Careful, don't you fall." Leaning into the tree, he grabbed the top branch to set on the star. Carefully handing him up the lights and the garland, Eula, Wynene, and Eloise watched him wind them meticulously around the tree. Then they all began hanging ornaments, stopping occasionally to hold up those they considered particularly unusual or beautiful. When one box was empty, they started in on another, with many trips to the attic to retrieve more. The snowflakes were the last things to go on, starting with the smallest at the top, the medium size near the middle, and the largest hung on the lowest branches. When they were finished, Bobby switched on the tree lights. The ladies fell back on the sofa, their mouths open in awe.

"We did that?" Eloise asked.

"Majestically beautiful," Wynene added with awe in her voice.

Bobby's eyes shone with delight like a small boy who had just hit his first home run.

"It's . . . it's . . . " Eula said, her voice shaking, "like something in a storybook. How can I thank you?"

"Don't," Bobby said, his eyes crinkling with delight. "All of you helped."

"Let's call in the other ladies," Wynene said, rushing out the door.

The ladies' enthusiasm over the magnificent tree matched their own. They sat on the sofa, in chairs, or on the floor drinking hot chocolate and eating the cookies Eula brought in from the kitchen. They all agreed that Miss Adie would be amazed. The delight in their eyes reminded Eula of little children's.

"This going to be one fine Christmas," Eula said to herself when they left for the day.

She awoke in the middle of the night feeling like a small child as she tiptoed into the living room, careful not to awaken Miss Adie, who had given her a start when she was feeding her that night.

"Voices," she said. "Eula. A lot of voices: the ladies. Was it a dream?"

Eula inhaled and thought quickly. "No," she finally said. "They all the time coming checking on you, but you was sleeping."

She held her breath, waiting for Miss Adie to ask her about her room, when she could go back, but she didn't.

Turning on the Christmas tree lights, she sat back on the sofa and squinted her eyes to blur all the pretty colors and the sheen of the ornaments. "Lawd," she prayed, "Jest let her live to see the tree and her and Doc's garden brought back to life."

THIRTY

"DON'T BE TOO LATE," HANK SAID, LEANING through the car window to give Opal a kiss. "Be careful," he added, placing a hand on her cheek.

Putting one of her own over his, she reminded him, "There's a pot roast in the refrigerator. Just heat it and the vegetables with it."

"I don't really like you driving home at dark," he stated, frowning. "Try to get home sooner and keep your car door locked."

"I'll be fine." She smiled at his concern. "Look for Santa's sleigh full of Christmas on my return."

He flipped his pants pocket inside out, giving her a remorseful grimace. Laughing at his mock gesture, she backed out of the driveway. Hank always worried when she made an occasional trip to Montgomery, one that concerned her too in case she should see a face from her past, but the girl she used to be and the people she knew then had gone on to other lives. Still, she regretted the angst she knew the trip would bring. On past shopping forays, Wynene would often accompany her, but she had been busy of late visiting her ailing sister when she made trips to the city. As the car ate up the miles, Opal regretted as she always did that Simpsonville's shops offered few choices in clothes and other items on the children's Christmas wish lists. As soon as she entered the outskirts of Montgomery, a very young and frightened girl joined her in the car. Opal expected her. When Wynene was her fellow passenger, the girl had less room in her thoughts. It was easier to keep her away. If it had been storming as it had been that night Kylie Mae left her father bleeding on the trailer floor, she would have turned around immediately and returned home, but it was a bright, sunny day in early December.

"It's all in the past," she said out loud to her invisible passenger. "No one knows us. One of us is dead, buried in that cemetery, and the other girl—she escaped into a new identity."

It wasn't true; it would never be fully true. Opal had grown around the persona she had adopted, but she would always be that frightened girl, grabbing her purse and stepping over her father's body. She didn't know how long he had been dead, but his lips had turned blue. His blank eyes stared up at her as she yanked open the trailer door and dashed into the rain-soaked night. Shocked and nauseated, she jumped into the battered truck. Her hands were shaking so violently, she had trouble inserting the key into the starter. Spinning the wheels in the mud-soaked earth, she gunned the engine and slid onto the road.

"Care–ful," Kylie Mae stuttered, noticing her speedometer. "A cop . . . She swung her head from right to left, cut her eyes to the rearview mirror. No one. "Slow, must go slow."

How did it happen? She was stunned. Her head hurt. One moment she was unpacking groceries after placing the knife on the counter. Her father grabbed her. Twisting away, she hit her head on the counter and passed out. Did she grab the knife to protect herself or was she turning to give it to him? He was drunk; he was going to rape her, would have raped her. She tried to swallow, but she felt as if she was choking. An acrid taste of bile rose in her mouth. Pulling the truck over quickly, she opened the door and retched. Grabbing the towel thrown over the torn passenger seat, she held it in the rain and wiped her face, then tossed it in a ditch. She felt the back of her head. A goose egg was forming. Spinning away, she headed back on the road. Where was she going? She was never allowed to drive the truck anywhere except to the small grocery nearby. She didn't even have a license.

"Careful," she repeated to herself, "must be careful."

How long would it take for someone to discover her father's body? He wouldn't appear for work. Someone would start looking for him and then for her.

"Don't think," she said to herself. "Take deep breaths; keep driving. Find a town, any town . . . no, somewhere safer, far away."

It was raining harder. The night was so dark. How much gas? She checked the gauge. At some point, she would have to stop. Suddenly, she was very thirsty. When she found a filling station, she would get some water, and crackers for later when her stomach settled. She rifled quickly through her purse. Money … she didn't put the money left over from her purchases on the counter. Her father coming at her; there was no time. "He's gone, Ma," she said into the darkness broken only by her lights and one or two cars passing in the other lane. Sudden tears—not for her father, but for her mother and for school, her counselor's promise of a scholarship, a ticket to a life she would never have. She would have liked to tell Miss Rollins goodbye, to thank her, to explain, but explain what, that she had killed her father? And the future ... it was as blank as the road down which she traveled.

"No," Kylie Mae said at the thought, "I'm alive. That could be me back there on that floor, dead, or wanting to be after what he would have done."

She was heading somewhere now, but where, she didn't have a clue, and suddenly, she was exhausted. She slapped her cheeks.

"Stay awake," she ordered. "Don't know where we are or where we're going, but we're going to get there."

She drove on through the stormy night, wincing as lightning streaks like burning spears slashed through the sky. How long had her father lain on the floor, she wondered. Did he bleed to death suffering for a long time or was his death a quick one? Don't, she commanded herself, mustn't dwell on it. If he had succeeded in doing to her what he'd wanted, she would want to die. Thank God for the truck, she said to herself, gripping the wheel tighter with each flash of lightning. If she didn't have it, there would be no escaping unless she simply ran, and then what? The truck! At some point, she would have to abandon it. The police would be looking for it once her father's body was discovered.

At daybreak, a brilliant rose-hued glow filled the sky. She was entering the outskirts of a small town. Lights began to glow from the sparse houses she passed. Hunger gnawed at her stomach. She had eaten the few crackers she had bought, but nothing since. She stopped at the first open service station.

The solitary occupant, a man behind the counter, looked up as if startled from sleep. "Good morning," he said listlessly, "restroom in the back."

Locking the door, she used the toilet, then ran water onto a paper towel to wash her face and hands. Startled, she watched the water turn pink. Blood on her hands drained down the sink. The haggard girl with circles under her eyes barely resembled someone she left behind. Carefully unlocking the door, alert to whoever might be on the other side, she took a deep breath and stepped out.

"Mighty early to be out," the man behind the checkout counter said, depositing her money into his cash register for a box of crackers, a wedge of packaged cheese, and over-the-counter headache tablets for the persistent throb from the welt on her head. "Care for a cup of fresh coffee, jest brewed?"

"Thank you," she answered, nodding.

"Guess you headed for the big city?" he said, pouring the coffee. "Most traffic I git through these parts is headed thataway."

She nodded again and breathed a "thank you" for the fragrant coffee as she fished in her pocket for change.

"On the house, on me," he said, waving aside the money. "Yep, little town like our'n don't git but those passing through on their way to Mountgumery." He looked her up and down. "Lookers like you—don't see many . . ."

She backed toward the door, pushed it open with her heinie, and heard him call, "You be careful like."

Back on the road, she went a safe distance, then pulled off near what looked to be an abandoned roadside church to drink her coffee. Parking the car behind the church, she bit off a huge chunk of cheese and ate some crackers. Suddenly, she felt an urge to walk. The rain had slacked off to a slight drizzle. She opened the door and wandered behind the church. On a mottled, moss-grown gravestone near a crumbling brick wall, she discovered a name: Opal St. John. It sounded like a jewel.

"Opal St. John," she said, getting back into the truck, feeling the name was an omen, perhaps the beginning of a new life from one past and buried like her own.

She was very thirsty. Water, she thought, forgot about water. On her next stop, she would use a restroom, find a drinking fountain, and ask about the exit for "Mountgumery." Luckily, she didn't have to ask. She came upon a small bus station some distance down the road. Whipping the car around, she drove a few blocks back, parked it off the side of the road, left the keys in the ignition, and with her box of crackers and cheese, slammed the rattling door on one part of her past.

"Morning, miss," the ticket agent greeted her. "Guess you going to the city?"

"Yes."

"Round trip?"

"One way," she answered.

"Be by 'bout thirty minutes," he said, handing her the ticket. "Restrooms inside. Luggage?"

She shook her head. "Could use some water," she said.

"There's a fountain inside and coffee. White one near the door. Have a good trip. You welcome to wait inside or out. Weather nice now. Purty nasty bit earlier."

She nodded and pushed the door open to find the fountain, guzzling the water as fast as it spouted, spilling down her chin. Wiping the water off her face, she turned to find a place to sit. A black woman cradling a baby sat in the colored section of the station. Kylie Mae smiled at the comforting scene. The woman nodded.

"Pretty child," Kylie Mae complimented.

The woman smiled shyly, but her face glowed at the compliment. "Thank you, miss."

"Do you mind if I join you?" Kylie Mae asked, suddenly craving the comfort of the family scene, but also realizing that anyone looking for her wouldn't suspect a white woman traveling with a black woman and baby.

The other blacks sitting nearby looked at her queerly, but made room for her when the woman said, "Course not."

They made little or no conversation, laughing occasionally at the antics of small children, black and white, restless with waiting, racing across the station floor with parents in pursuit.

"Montgomery!" a loud voice finally announced, and Kylie Mae found herself taking the stairs up into a bus that smelled of worn vinyl and exhaust fumes.

"You have a good one, now," the black mother said, heading to the back of the bus.

"You, too," Kylie Mae said, smiling, feeling suddenly buoyant as she took an outside seat near an exit.

"Plenty up front, miss," the driver announced.

"This one's fine, thanks," she said, hoping that no one would take the window seat where she placed her food.

The bus doors closed and the engine revved up. Kylie Mae put her head back on the seat and smiled. "Mountgumery," the store owner had called it. However Montgomery was pronounced, her next destination was called "Escape." She yawned and stretched her feet out, tension slowly receding from her neck muscles and her shoulders. Ignoring the babble of noise around her from fellow passengers, she gave into the sleep long-neglected.

"Montgomery, last stop," a voice in the distance announced.

Feet shuffled past her.

"Miss?"

She sat up. The bus driver was looking down at her.

"Where?" she asked, sitting up, slaking sleep and the relief it brought.

"This be your stop," the driver said.

"Oh."

"You all right, miss?"

"Yes, yes, fine," she answered, "thank you."

Gathering the remainder of her food, she tottered into the aisle and down the steps into the station, thinking "now what?" The cheese in her package emitted a rank odor. A greasy stain showed through the brown package.

"You have any luggage?" the driver asked.

She shook her head as she looked around. People were greeting each other with warm embraces and laughter. Suddenly, she felt very alone.

"Anybody meeting you?" the driver asked, still standing beside her in a protective stance. She must not look vulnerable, although she certainly was with no one there to enthusiastically greet her and no place to go.

"I came a day early," she found herself saying. "I'm a ... surprise."

"And a very nice one," the driver said. "Guess you gone to need a cab?"

"Yes." She looked around the station through the mass of people.

"Then Eugene be your man."

"Eugene?"

"He my friend and the best, safe driver there be. He won't try to run you up. I introduce you."

Taking her arm, he walked her through the people thronging around them, coming and going, and took her past the station toward the end where a line of cabs were parked.

"Eugene," he called, tapping on the car door, the passenger side.

"My man!" a voice hooted, as the cab door opened. The two men clapped each other on the back. A gold tooth in the mouth of the man named Eugene sparkled in the sunlight. "What's up, man?"

"This here young lady need a ride."

"Glad to oblige," Eugene said, taking off a beat-up cap and bending from the waist toward Kylie Mae. "Yore luggage?"

"She got none," the bus driver said, opening the backseat of the cab for Kylie Mae to take a seat, which she promptly did.

"Thank you," she said, fishing for some money to tip him.

"No, miss," the bus driver said, "thanks jest the same. You has a good visit."

"Where to, miss?" Eugene asked.

Where exactly? Kylie Mae ran the question over in her mind. She hadn't known where she was going and now that she was here, she didn't know what to do. Finally, she said to the gold-toothed man still looking at her from the driver's seat, patiently waiting with a smile on his face, "I need a place to stay . . . somewhere cheap while I look for a job."

"Oh," Eugene said. "You never been here?"

"No."

"Safe and cheap?"

"Exactly."

"While you looks for a job."

"Yes."

"Then I takes you there, don't you worry none. Lots 'bout yore age come to the city looking. This place put you up. Might have to share a room with other young ladies jest like you, but it's safe and clean. All right?"

Kylie Mae inwardly quivered. She had no other option and very little money. There was really no other choice. "All right," she responded, as Eugene put the taxi in gear and pulled around the other cabs.

She crunched into the seat as Eugene took her away from the station, one more step away from her past and a blood-drenched trailer.

{THIRTY-ONE}

THE DRIVER PULLED UP IN FRONT OF THE YWCA. "You take care now," the driver said, his gold tooth gleaming as Kylie Mae got out of the cab to take the stairs of the building. "God bless."

"Good morning, young lady," a rotund, older white woman with hair dyed too black said from behind the front desk. "You be wanting a room?"

"Yes, please."

"And for how long?"

Kylie Mae searched her mind. How long would it take to find a job when she was inexperienced and didn't know if she had enough money?

"Can you do weekly?" she asked. "I'm looking for a job."

The woman smiled kindly. A familiar response, and the girl looked exhausted. "Where's your luggage, honey?"

"Didn't bring any."

She frowned. *This* was a bit unusual.

"Where can I get breakfast?" Kylie Mae asked noticing the woman's expression and wanting to change the subject of why she appeared on the doorstep without any other clothes.

"There's a café just down the street to the left," she said. "Just register here and I'll show you to the room first. You'll be sharing."

Kylie Mae winced: share a room and come up with a name, two more obstacles. A name? She was reluctant to use the one on the gravestone. Somehow, she felt it would come in handy at some future time, but what for now? Then an image of her mother appeared, sitting at the table writing on a tablet a list of names for the baby.

"If it's a girl . . ." Her mother looked out the trailer window at the bird feeder. A robin sat there seemingly peering back at her, waiting to hear. Her mother laughed. "Then, of course: Robin."

"Ain't goin' to be a girl this time," her pa said, snapping the lid of a beer can. "This un's a boy. Goin' to be called Joey."

"Robin?" the woman behind the counter asked.

Kylie Mae nodded.

"Robin what?" She waited patiently, giving the girl time, a familiar scenario.

Ma had been a Shanks. "Robin Shanks," she could almost hear her mother whispering the name in her ear, feel her smile as she took the pen from the woman and wrote the name on the registry. She followed the woman up two flights of stairs to a spare room with two lumpy mattress beds.

"This one taken," she said, pointing to the bed on the left, "the other is your'n. Your roomie won't be home till later," she said handing Kylie Mae a key. She turned toward the door. "Miss Shanks."

Kylie Mae took a seat on the bed and looked around the pristine room for some sign of warmth, a bit of color. An orange trash can sat in a corner.

"Miss Shanks," the attendant called again in a somewhat louder voice.

"Oh, sorry," Kylie Mae looked up.

"Lights out at ten; no gentlemen callers allowed except downstairs; bath down the hall; bed linens and towels changed once a week; diner serves from 7 a.m. till 10 p.m. When you leave, turn in the key. The desk is manned 24 hours. Just remember to sign in and out."

"Thank you," she said.

The attendant turned to look back at the forlorn figure with disheveled hair and dark circles beneath her eyes. Another lost soul trying to find herself. She had seen them come and go. The expression on her face didn't fail to register with Kylie Mae.

"It's going to work out," the attendant said, sympathy in her voice. "Look toward tomorrow. My name is Miss Dot. Your roommate is Susan Wade. Try to get some rest," she added, softly closing the door behind her.

Kylie Mae stood at the window looking down on a rooftop and all those beyond. The hunger that had been gnawing at her stomach turned into a state of near-nausea. She had to slake her feelings of isolation and fear. There was no trace of Kylie Mae Applegate except a body on a trailer floor. Everything from this point on was a new beginning. There was no way for the police to find her. Somehow, she would find a job and though she had no means of transportation, there must be a bus station somewhere nearby. She would ask her roommate when she returned. Now, even though she didn't feel like eating, she would go to the diner. She couldn't afford to become ill. A new future demanded a healthy body even though she could never mentally put her past totally behind her.

"Have a good dinner?" Miss Dot asked, handing over her room key on her return. "Not that you will need it. Miss Wade is already there."

Kylie Mae slowly took the stairs wary of the roommate and whatever questions she would ask. Wearing a pair of faded striped pajamas, Susan Wade was on her bed, her face obscured behind a paperback book whose cover portrayed a couple in an amorous embrace.

"Oh, hi," she said, setting the book aside on the lopsided mattress. "You're Robin Shanks," she added with a trace of sarcasm in her voice as she swung long legs over the edge of the lumpy mattress. Shoulder-length blonde hair framed a plump face. The hint of acne on her complexion didn't detract from the large brown eyes studying Kylie Mae with a trace of amusement. There were flecks of gold in the eyes fringed by the longest eyelashes Kylie Mae had ever seen. Her eyes reminded Kylie Mae of the deer that used to roam near the trailer looking for the crumbs her mother put out, but there were no traces of wariness in these eyes, nor in her demeanor that seemed open, accepting.

"Just to get things straight," this Susan Wade said with a grin, "I won't be asking where you came from or why and I expect the same. Okay?"

"Okay," Kylie Mae said, a wave of relief in her voice.

"Just one question, all right?" she added. "Do you need a job?'

She nodded.

"If you're not particular," Susan Wade said, the grin deepening, "there's a dance studio . . ."

Kylie Mae cut her sentence short. "I don't know how to dance."

"No problem. All it is is a shuffle step and plenty of takers to learn."

"I'm not that type," she responded firmly, frowning.

The girl laughed. "You misunderstood my meaning. There's nothing shoddy about the studio. It's well-supervised. All they want are attractive young women to draw in paying customers. After you get a certain quota, the pay goes up. Granted it's not much to start out, but it's something. Helps pay for these deluxe quarters," she added sarcastically, her arms flung out to the sides.

A sound filled the room. It bubbled up from some tamped-down spot in Kylie Mae's soul. It took a shocked moment before she recognized the sound as laughter, her laughter. And, quickly behind it came tears.

"It's going to be all right," Susan said, wrapping an arm around her shoulders. "This ain't heaven, but, honey, it sure beats hell."

Kylie Mae fell into an exhausted sleep that night, but not before she began to wonder what to do about clothes. She had borrowed some soap powder from Susan to wash her underwear so that would be one thing clean, but she needed clothes.

"Not to worry," Susan informed her, "if the boss likes you and there's no question he won't hire someone who's a sure draw for his business, he'll advance you enough to buy a few clothes. Too bad mine won't fit."

They ate breakfast at the diner the next morning and caught a nearby bus for the dance studio. Kylie Mae began to feel better knowing that transportation was nearby. If the need arrived, she could always get out of town. The dance studio sat on a corner in the center of the city. The man who interviewed her asked if she knew how to type, and very few personal questions.

"Not bad," he said, sitting back in his swivel chair, "looks with a manual skill."

Then he went on to describe how much she would make until she got a certain number of clients. It was very little, but enough to purchase a few clothes and keep her from starving. She felt awkward learning the few dance steps from a male instructor who held her in his arms while he guided her around the room. She had never been held in a man's arms before and she could feel her body stiffen when his arms went around her.

"Relax," the instructor told her. "Concentrate on your feet and the moves."

There was consolation in the ever-present female supervisor who called out certain dance routines, but she still became edgy the first full day on the job.

"Think of something pleasant," Susan recommended, "and bypass personal questions. Ask the men about their jobs, hobbies, anything to keep them moving. Half the time they enjoy talking about their own lives anyway. If anyone gives you trouble, let Ms. Jackson know. She'll cut the hassle."

Her first full week left her with swollen, aching feet, but she had a job, a little money, and she began to feel more comfortable twirling around a dance floor with strangers. She learned to fake laughter at corny jokes and to ignore those that bordered on lewd. Whenever she felt an urge to quit, she recalled the gnawing hunger of her desperate flight. When she had enough money to get by on, she began to set aside a little each week, hiding it between her mattress and the box spring. She noticed a small business school on her bus route. Already an acceptable typist, she needed to up the ante on her skills to move on to a better job position and more pay. It would mean extending her schedule with later evening hours and no weekends, but it could lead to more money and perhaps, with luck, a better place to live. The plan did present problems: She would miss Susan and the camaraderie they shared, and she lacked evidence of a legal name. One evening on the bus as she and Susan were returning to the boardinghouse, she decided to divulge her desire to change jobs.

"Good plan," Susan congratulated. "You're way too bright for a dance floor."

"It's not that I'm ungrateful."

"Got to look out for yourself, honey."

"There is one problem," Kylie Mae added.

"Robin Shanks isn't your name," Susan said, grinning.

Kylie Mae's eyes widened as her body stiffened.

"Oh, quit," Susan half-whispered. "Susan Wade isn't my moniker, either."

"It isn't?"

"Look, honey. I don't know your history and you don't know mine. Let's keep it that way; makes it a lot more comfortable all the way round. What you need for that class is identification. I know someone who can make it a whole lot easier, but it will cost you."

"You mean a forger?"

"Yep, darn good one: birth certificate, full nine yards."

Kylie Mae gave her a jaundiced eye.

"Nope," Susan stated, raising her right hand. "I don't get a cut, if that's what you're thinking, and I won't ever know what your new handle is. I've roomed with you long enough to realize you're just another girl running away from hard times. We're all refugees. You're not the thieving or murdering kind."

Though relieved, Kylie Mae winced. Not the murdering kind. She turned her face toward the window. Reflected back

at her from the bus window was her father's ashen face staring with blinded eyes. Kylie Mae slumped farther into the
seat. A hand took one of hers.

"It's going to be all right, doll," Susan's voice soothed,
"we're all running away from something or someone."

Opal parked at the curb and readied her change for the
meter. "We've come a long way," she said to her invisible passenger, opening the door and locking it temporarily on Kylie
Mae Applegate vs. Robin Shanks.

Walking into Saxtons, the biggest store in Montgomery,
Opal wondered what had happened to the girl who called
herself Susan Wade. Did she find happiness? Without her
help, Kylie Mae wouldn't have found her first paying job or
the man who skillfully faked her new ID on a birth certificate.
The day she met him, she stood at the bottom of the stairs
on the outside of a downtown building. Kylie Mae tentatively took the stairs not knowing what to expect at the top of
the stairway.

"Come in," a man's voice called.

The door swung open to a middle-aged man with a bald-
ing spot on the back of his head. Humped-shouldered, he was
wearing glasses and peering down at something he was working on at his desk. The sleeves on his shirt were rolled up,
revealing hairy arms.

"Yes?" he queried.

"I'm Robin, Robin Shanks," she said, not moving from
the open door. "We have an appointment," she timidly
reminded.

"Close the door, please," he ordered, his eyes still focused
on whatever he was closely inspecting. "Then take a chair."

She did as he ordered and waited patiently as he continued scrutinizing whatever he was working on. Finally, he

swiveled his chair around to face her. "So," he said, his eyes surveying her face as carefully as he had the paperwork. "Who sent you?"

"We spoke on the telephone ... I set up the appointment," she responded, hesitantly, not quite understanding his question.

"Young lady," he said, frowning, "I asked who sent you?"

"Susan. Susan Wade."

"Come closer," he said, finally standing and moving a chair closer to his.

"Name?" he inquired as she took the seat he placed next to his.

"Robin Shanks," she repeated.

The thick glasses he wore over grayish eyes had a hint of humor in them as they crinkled at the corners. "Of course you are," he said. "Now, who do you want to be?"

Dead leaves rattling like the bones of skeletons over an overgrown moss-covered grave with crumbling stone in a wayside churchyard; the name still plainly visible: Opal St. John.

"Opal St. John," she stated without hesitation.

"Opal St. John," he repeated, scribbling it on a piece of paper. "Sounds rather regal; suits you." Then, turning to peer into her eyes again, he said in an assertive tone, "It'll cost you. Are you prepared to pay, and in cash? Of course, until you get my paperwork, you probably can't pay any other way."

"We discussed this over the telephone," she reminded, "and I know what Susan paid. I have just enough cash, no less, no more."

The eyes behind the spectacles narrowed, but not menacingly. "Rather assertive, aren't you. I could turn you down, you know."

Kylie Mae returned his gaze. "There are others," she stated, her fingers lacing tighter in her lap. She held her breath, praying he wouldn't detect a bluff as he continued to scrutinize her face.

"Feisty," he said, his lower lip curling in a near-smile. "All right, young woman, Opal St. John it is, but first the cash."

"No," she said. "Not until you finish the paperwork."

Something hollow and raspy crawled up his throat. A laugh, she realized, her face reddening.

Nearly jumping out of the chair, she stood over him. "This isn't a game, mister, and I'm not playing," she shouted, her voice shaking with rage. "My paperwork and then you get yours."

"Young woman, I don't know who you are or what you have done, but you have spirit. You win, and I retract my original statement about the choice of your name. Opal St. John isn't strong enough for someone with such spirit."

Within a month, Kylie Mae had a birth certificate that led to her registration at a business school. Armed with better typing skills and a secretarial degree, she finally found a decent job as a secretary at a small advertising agency. There she met a young woman living at home who wanted someone to share an apartment. It had been difficult to tell Susan goodbye. They embraced at the door of the boardinghouse before the taxi came to take Kylie Mae to her new living quarters.

"I couldn't have made it this far," she told her, "without your strength and help."

Susan, her eyes misting with tears, shook her head. "You have the kind of guts that would have found a way."

As the cab pulled away, Kylie Mae waved from the backseat, watching the figure of her first real friend recede into the distance. Keeping their respective pasts a secret from each other, they had shared a room and a common courage. Susan never inquired about her new name or where she was going. Ultimate trust bonded them together forever, but they were faithful to an unspoken commitment that forbade ever seeing each other again.

Fighting a lump in her throat, Kylie Mae whispered to the diminishing figure: "I'll never forget."

{THIRTY-TWO}

ARMS LADEN WITH SAXTON'S SEASONAL shopping bags decorated in bright reds and greens, Opal finally completed her Christmas shopping. Her feet were aching and she was weary of fighting jostling, complaining crowds; time to head home before the traffic got too heavy. She shoved her back against the department store doors to head toward her car. Someone or something thumped against her shoulder, sending her packages sailing onto the pavement.

"Oh, I'm so sorry," a woman apologized, leaning over to retrieve Opal's packages and her own scattered across the sidewalk. "I didn't see you coming."

"I should have been looking," Opal said, squatting, her head bent, as she separated her purchases from the ones the woman had spilled.

"My fault," the woman said as they both stood up. Are you all . . . ?" Stunned eyes stared into hers. Eyes, familiar eyes, lit with recognition as she was grabbed in an enthusiastic embrace. "Robin, it's you, really you!"

Opal sat across from her old friend in a nearby sandwich shop. She wondered how to begin. However delighted she was to finally see the woman who called herself Susan Wade, she felt hesitant. Teary-eyed and carrying their parcels, they had sought the sanctuary of a nearby restaurant to share a cup of coffee, but beyond that, Opal hadn't thought ahead. Susan poured cream in her coffee, her eyes suffused with a nearly childlike joy at seeing her old friend of so long ago. Her face was still as open as the girl who dropped her book to greet a very frightened stray calling herself Robin Shanks, who had timidly walked into the room they shared all those years ago. They had been two young women running away from fractured pasts attempting to take the pieces of their respective puzzles and put them back together again.

Opal decided to break their happy silence. "I couldn't have done it without you. Actually, before I did my shopping, I was thinking of you, wondering, and no, that doesn't mean you have to divulge anything. Let's just enjoy each other's company." She laughed. "I feel so odd, as if all these years that stand between us . . . it seems only yesterday."

"It's like a Christmas present," Susan stated, reaching across the table to grab her hand.

"I've never had a closer friend except well, my husband and children."

"I finally found someone, too," Susan said.

"And children?" Opal inquired, regretting the question instantly when Susan's smile turned into a grimace. An aura of sorrow seemed to surround her as she stared into her coffee cup. Opal squeezed her hand. "It's all right," she said, realizing how lame it must sound.

Susan met her eyes. "I wasn't always the girl you met all those years ago. Hung out with the wrong crowd, got into lots of trouble: sneaking out at night, crawling out my bedroom window with boys while my parents were sleeping, experimenting with drugs. Then I got pregnant. I was terrified, but I kept it a secret from my parents. My mother heard me talking about it in my sleep during a nightmare. An abortion was arranged. Here I was fifteen, almost a child myself, and I found myself actually wanting to keep my baby. Somehow, the doctor screwed up. There were complications that eventually led to my losing the uterus, too. When I recovered, I ran away from home. It took me years before I contacted my parents. You actually were my inspiration when I did. There was something about you and your determination, taking those classes, trying to make a better life whatever your history was. After you left, I called my family. I didn't know what to expect, but figured what did I have to lose? All that time, they had been looking for me. They came for me, took me home. Eventually, I finished school and went on to college. That's when I met Josh. He knows the whole story. You would like him; he would like you, and don't worry, he has never heard me speak of Robin Shanks except that a girl I used to know gave me the courage to turn my life around."

Opal looked at her friend with renewed pride in her spunk. "You're a strong gal."

"So are you, my friend. I don't know why our lives intertwined or what you were running away from, but you seem content. More than that, very happy, and you really haven't aged, just a different hairstyle and a new stability."

"I wish," Opal said, sighing, "I could be as honest with you as you have just been with me."

"If you think I won't admire you as much, nothing can destroy that."

Opal studied the face of her friend. She knew she meant it, but there were the children and Hank. She wouldn't do or say anything to compromise their welfare.

"It's something I haven't even told my husband."

"Then don't tell me. You don't need to. I'm not offended; you'll always be my friend. We've shared too much. I would like to see pictures, if you have any. I have one of Josh." She rifled in her purse and pulled out a photo holder, handing it across the table.

A nice-looking man smiled up at her.

"I like his eyes," Opal said, "and without meeting him, I like him for making you so happy."

"We live on the outskirts of the city. He's the vice president of an insurance agency."

"And you?"

"Oh, I forgot to tell you, I'm a school administrator."

Opal's first thought was wouldn't Hank as a school principal be pleased to hear that her old friend held such a responsible position in a school system, but of course, she couldn't tell him that or anything about seeing her dear friend from the past. Instead, she sighed and said, "I'm just an ordinary housewife now."

"There's nothing ordinary about you," Susan said, eyes crinkling with merriment.

Opal looked at her watch. "I hate to . . ."

"I know, and I don't want you to go. It reminds me of what seems like yesterday. Will I see you again?"

The eyes studying her across the table looked sad as if she anticipated her response. They mirrored the angst Opal felt in her soul. How could she find an old friend and lose her again? Avoiding the question, she opened her pocketbook to retrieve her billfold with pictures of Hank and the children. Not wanting Susan to see her driver's license, she slid the pictures out of their plastic sheath and handed them across the table.

"The girl looks like you, the same eyes and high cheek-bones," Susan said, studying the photos closely. "The boy is a combination of both you and your good-looking hubby. You're blessed."

"They wouldn't be possible without your help. My whole life changed the day I met you."

Susan smiled, her face suffused with warmth at the compliment. "You would have made it with or without me, but I'm grateful we shared part of our lives together."

They stood simultaneously and embraced. Opal fought to maintain her composure. How could she find the dearest friend she ever made and turn her back on her? When they parted, she studied Susan's face, taking a mental snapshot. It was one that would never fade or yellow with time like an old photograph. With her arms laden once again with Christmas packages, she walked out of the restaurant with Susan, whose eyes glistened with tears.

"Don't forget," Susan said in a beseeching tone.

Opal shook her head. Her throat throbbed with withheld emotion. "That's something I could never do."

Taking a last mental photo of her dearest friend, she turned to head to the car, praying that Susan wouldn't follow. She had gone half a block when a voice called, "Wait!" Susan was nearly sprinting toward her.

"You want to keep your privacy and I can understand," she said, restrained tears flowing down her cheeks, "but I can't just let you leave like that. You don't have to tell me what you were running away from or why, even though nothing could mar my high esteem of you and I can understand your reluctance to let me know where you live, but I can't let you just walk away. Not after all we went through together as two displaced young girls." She pulled a card from her purse and dropped it into one of Opal's shopping bags. "Don't lose it. It contains my office and home numbers, also my business and home addresses. Please promise you will reconsider. We shared too much to just simply walk away from each other. I'll always be your friend."

"Oh, Susan, I wish, I really do."

"Then keep the card. Now, get on your way to that good-looking family of yours," she added, turning to retrace her steps. Then she stopped and turned to take one last look back at the girl she knew as Robin Shanks, who stood silently watching. "And have a Merry Christmas. Mine has already begun."

As soon as she reached the car, Opal retrieved the card from the bag.

"Alice," she said to the empty car. "Alice Johnson."

She opened her purse and slid the card behind Hank's photograph, where she was certain it couldn't be lost. "Alice," she said again as she turned onto the highway leading home.

A name was such a simple thing until the mind associated it with the warmth and courage of a girl who once called herself Susan Wade.

{THIRTY-THREE}

CAMELLIAS, "THE ROSE OF WINTER," WERE blooming. Their dark green shiny foliage contrasted beautifully with the blooms' varying shades of pink, red, and white. Winter jasmine was also beginning to sprout. Their bright yellow flowers would reach their peak in January. A light breeze blew through Wynene's hair as she and several of the ladies knelt in the garden adding plants to the rose garden while the rest were nearby, busy planting viola seeds and other hardy annual seeds. She smiled with pleasure as daylilies nodded with the slight wind shift. The weather had turned cooler overnight. Christmas in south Alabama could often be too warm for a toasty fire in the hearth. That would not be the case this season, but then, so much was different this year. She sat back on her heels and smiled, taking a deep breath of the sweetly perfumed fresh air and the rich earth on which she knelt. The moment had arrived to reveal the ladies' surprise package. She and Eula had agreed it was time to move Miss Adie back into her bedroom and draw aside the drapes on the windows that overlooked the new landscape.

"And the tree," Eula added with childlike enthusiasm. "Or do you think, Miss Wynene, that the excitement of two

surprises in one day will be too much? Course she could spy
the garden from the windows when we roll her wheelchair
into the living room. Once she catches a glimpse, she'll have
a fit to see it."

"How alert has she been the past few days?" Wynene
inquired.

"'Bout the same. Her memory flitters like a bee after
nectar. Sometime I hear her speaking to Doc jest like he in
the room."

"Then her memory is kind."

Eula smiled. "Yes mum, it seems so. It keeps her company."

"Theirs was an unusual marriage," Wynene added wistfully, missing Dan, the sound of his voice, his touch. "Not
many are so blessed."

"No mum, not many," Eula agreed, a tone of regret in her
voice that was not lost on Wynene.

Eula's life before she came to live with Doc and Miss Adie
was a mystery, but it occurred to Wynene as she studied Eula's scarred face that all of the ladies' lives probably harbored
secrets of one kind or another. How much did one truly know
another? The garden, however, brought them closer together
and made many more trim and fit. No project undertaken
in the Mission Society had produced such pleasure. Most
had come because of the rumored book Miss Adie was writing, but as they worked side by side restoring the earth and
garden, the book and its subject matter seemingly receded
into the distance. Wynene began to believe that the ladies'
endeavor to bring Miss Adie and Doc's garden back was an
altruistic one.

"Do you feel she is able to be wheeled into the garden?"
she inquired of Eula, patiently awaiting a reply.

"She all the time talking about it. Sometime I think she is

already more there than in that bed."

"Isn't there a back door from the kitchen?"

"Yes, mum." Eula's face shone with an almost childish excitement.

"Good. I will get the ladies ready. Miss Adie can see the garden first; the tree we will save for later just in case it's too much excitement for her heart in one day."

Now that the big day had arrived, Wynene found she was a little nervous. What if the garden's evolution from barren earth to a colorful landscape of flowers and plants proved to be too much excitement for Miss Adie's faltering health? Miss Adie had worked day by day at her husband's side witnessing birth, death, and every manner of illness, but she was a much younger woman then. Might she be disappointed in the ladies' efforts to restore her and Doc's garden? Many of the plants and flowers she and Doc tended struggled to push through the dormant earth after years of neglect, but there were several varieties the ladies had planted that were probably never there when she and Doc knelt on their garden's fertile earth. She told Eula that memory was kind. Perhaps the ladies' efforts to restore the garden wouldn't fulfill the vision Miss Adie still held of her and Doc's efforts? She felt as nervous as a little girl waiting to play her first piano recital.

"Miss Wynene," Eula's voice interrupted her faint-hearted thoughts. Her face was flushed with excitement. "Miss Adie's in a warm robe. I'm ready to put her into the wheelchair. Are the ladies ready?"

"Have you explained where she's going?"

"I haven't mentioned the garden, jest a short ride outside to get some fresh air."

"I'll get the ladies ready and turn on the fountain Bobby restored. I wish he were here to witness her first glimpse of it and the garden, but there will be other days."

"Yes, mum," Eula affirmed reassuringly, "don't you worry none. Mr. Bobby will understand we had to pick a sunny pleasant day before the chill sets in."

"You're taking her out the back door?"

"Yes, mum."

Wynene smiled at the enthusiasm in Eula's voice. She too felt nearly giddy now that it was time to unveil their secret. Its excitement erased her earlier concerns.

The ladies, their gardening tools set aside, were all gathered to the side of the garden near the walkway that led from Miss Adie's kitchen door up the side yard to the front and the fenced-in garden. Excited whispers fluttered through the air as softly as pirouetting fall leaves.

"I feel like a child on Christmas morning," Opal said as she clasped one of Wynene's hands in hers.

"Are you comfortable?" they heard Eula ask as the wheelchair slowly rattled up the side yard walkway.

Miss Adie mumbled a reply. To Wynene, the only decipherable word was "Doc." One of the ladies muffled a nervous cough. The wheelchair and its ashen-faced occupant covered with a thick blanket finally came into view.

"What?" Miss Adie questioned, her face scanning the figures of the ladies. "Oh," she said, blinking in the bright light of the morning sun as she turned her wan face toward the garden's blooms and rows of vegetables, "you came to see the garden." She smiled. "Lester will be pleased."

Opal's hand tightened on Wynene's.

"The ladies . . ." Eula said, frowning.

"Couldn't be more pleased," Wynene completed her sentence. "Doc always planted the most beautiful garden in Simpsonville."

"Yes," Miss Adie agreed with a thin-lipped smile. "Would you all like a cup of tea?"

"I'm sorry 'bout all that," Eula said apologetically as she took down the tea kettle from a cabinet shelf while the ladies took turns washing up at the kitchen sink.

She had discreetly returned Miss Adie down the walkway beside the house to avoid her seeing the Christmas tree. The ladies decided to enter the house the same way, leaving their gardening shoes at the back step and cleaning up at the kitchen sink before Miss Adie was wheeled into the living room to see the tree for what they hoped this time would truly be a surprise. Miss Adie was resting in Doc's room, waiting for Eula to announce that tea was ready for her guests.

"Apologies aren't necessary," Eloise said comfortingly. "The rest of the ladies and I agree we were only completing a project that Miss Adie and Doc started. The garden remembers the touch of their hands. They were the first to kneel on its earth. Many of the flowers and vegetables they planted so long ago are struggling to return. Bobby's design and ours may not be as original as we thought."

"Oh," Eula said, a tremor in her voice, as she sifted tea leaves into the pot. "Maybe then, Miss Eloise, it was jest waiting?"

"For all of us," Norma Mae said, sitting at the kitchen table with the rest of the ladies, who smiled and nodded their heads in agreement.

"It just took some planning," Wynene said, "and perhaps not our own."

"Then," Eula added, placing warmed-up biscuits onto a tray with a pot of jam, "maybe we're like the garden, something waiting to be completed."

"I couldn't have expressed it any better, Eula," Opal said, eyes misty.

"We'll take care of the tray and bring in the cups and saucers," Verabelle offered, "if you think Miss Adie is ready."

"And don't you worry, now," added Hattie, "if she thinks the tree is one of Doc's projects, we won't be disappointed. It may just be."

The woodsy fragrance of the tree and a hearth fire greeted them as they entered the living room. Eula switched on the tree's lights, which sparkled with colorful warmth against the green boughs. While the ladies seated themselves comfortably on sofas and chairs around the tree, Hattie poured tea.

Norma Mae's hand shook as she lifted the cup to her lips. She looked down at the buttered biscuit on her plate, but was too excited to take a bite.

"I don't know about the rest of you," Hattie stated, "but I feel as jittery as a child on Christmas Day."

"Guests, how nice," they heard Miss Adie say as Eula wheeled her down the hallway leading to the living room. "Lester and I, just the two of us and the garden until that day . . . remember that day, the day you came."

"Yes, mum," Eula mumbled, praying, dear Lord, don't let her say more. Just as they crossed the threshold, a shaft of sunlight through a window sheer fell across the tree's star, sending a radiant beam across the room and its occupants.

Hattie nearly dropped her teacup. Norma Mae's plate fell from her lap, spilling its half-eaten biscuit on the carpet while several of the ladies sat transfixed in astonishment.

Lawd," Eula exclaimed.

"Oh," Miss Adie stated, leaning dangerously forward in her wheelchair as if she were straining to get out of the chair to greet a visitor.

Eula gently grabbed her by the shoulder, steadying her as the rest of the ladies, their plates and cups set aside, stood up prepared to help.

"You?" Miss Adie questioned looking up at Eula, "You and Lester?"

"The ladies," Eula corrected. "I jest brought down the ornaments. They did the rest. Mr. Bobby, he and some men delivered the tree."

"Mr. Bobby?"

"He's a young friend of Ms. Eloise's."

"The young man I saw with Lester near the garden shed?"

The ladies turned to look at each other, question in their eyes.

"He came to help with the garden," Eula explained. "So did all the ladies."

"All of you?" Miss Adie looked around the room, "For Lester and me?"

"For Doc and you," the ladies said in joyful unison.

"We," Miss Adie paused, her eyes transfixed on the tree and gleaming star. "Lester and I ... Oh, my," she seemed to plead, her voice dropping to a near-whisper. Pressing her thin lips together, she looked up at Eula.

"Are you ready to go to bed?" Eula asked.

"No. Oh, no. What?" she questioned looking at the ladies. "How can . . . thank . . . ?"

Wynene walked toward Miss Adie. Patting a bony shoulder beneath the robe, she reassured her, "You and Doc did so much for this community, for all of us. There is no need for further thanks."

Miss Adie gazed up into her eyes, a hint of a twisted smile on her lips. She placed a palsied hand on Wynene's. "Closer. Please take me. I want to see."

Eula released the chair to Wynene, who rolled Miss Adie up to the tree. The rest of the ladies and Eula gathered around them as Miss Adie's gnarled arthritic fingers reached out for an antique tin Santa.

"Lester and I, our first Christmas, he gave it to me. And this . . . "

She circled the tree with Wynene patiently pushing her wheelchair. Tenderly touching ornaments, she gave a brief history of those she could recall until her voice began to falter with the fading afternoon light. When Eula took Miss Adie back to her room, the ladies retrieved their shoes from the back step.

"What was that?" Norma Mae questioned for all of them. "That burst of light?"

"Perhaps," Wynene mused, "Doc was truly in that room with us."

"We're only part of a greater design," Eloise added.

"It was the one decoration none of us were capable of achieving," Opal agreed.

THIRTY-FOUR

THE LATE AFTERNOON SUN WAS GLIDING the side of tree trunks as Wynene drove home. The sunlit trees, now nearly bare of their leaves, looked as if God had plucked them from the earth, dipped them into a pot of molten gold, and re-rooted them in the ground. It had been a more than satisfying day: Miss Adie's viewing of the garden and then the tree. It seemed suitable that she would think Doc was responsible for the garden's revival, or perhaps her view outside her bedroom window never held a vision of barren earth. Theirs had been such a close and enviable union, an ongoing love affair, working side by side in the office and kneeling in pleasant compatibility on the land they loved. What an amazing relationship. Wynene could recall them as they used to be as if it were just yesterday. She could remember as a small child on medical checkups the looks that passed between them, a sparkle in their eyes that made her feel good being around them. Life was so short, too short.

She felt suddenly maudlin recalling the warmth they exuded in each other's company. Her relationship with Jim was one of deep friendship and duty to the church, community, to each other. Dan awakened in her a sense of all that had been lacking in her marriage. She was approaching middle age, but there was still time, plenty of life left to have all that she ignored missing: true companionship, body and soul; children, part of him, part of her; life ongoing; happiness. By ignoring the truth of her marriage and all it lacked, years of her life had been wasted. She was like the once-barren earth of Miss Adie's garden.

"Hello," Jim called from his study, where he was working on Sunday's sermon, as she stepped into the house. "How was the gardening?" he asked when she walked into the room.

"Eula wheeled Miss Adie out into the yard to see our grand surprise, but it seems it really wasn't. All these years, her mind kept alive a vivid image of the work she and Doc put into the garden. For her, it never stopped blooming. The ladies and I are the ones who benefited the most from restoring it. The tree, however, was a definite surprise. She was like a child delighting in its ornaments and lights. It was a happy day."

"Then why do you look so sad?" he asked, rising from his chair and putting an arm around her shoulder.

"It's my sister, Jim," she lied, looking down at the carpet, studying its floral pattern. "Her health is still not good. She wants me to come help with Christmas, buy gifts and decorate."

"You've made quite a few trips to Montgomery of late, Wynene," he said in an accusatory tone, dropping his arm. "Our congregation misses you; I miss you." Cupping her chin gently he turned her face upward toward his. "You never look into my eyes anymore," he added, a pleading tone in his voice, his blue eyes plaintively studying hers.

"Oh, Jim, you know how busy I've been, and I really do need to go help my sister."

Dropping his hand, he asked in a resigned tone, "When?"

"Tomorrow."

"For how long this time?"

"Just a few days. I'll freeze dinners for you."

"It's not the dinners I miss," he said with a resigned tone in his voice as he sat down at his desk, returning to his work.

A LOG SNAPPED IN THE FIREPLACE, SENDING blue and yellow flickers of flame up the chimney. They sat snuggled side by side on a den sofa in the same house where they always met. They had turned off the lights to further enjoy the hearth's fire. Taking off her shoes, Wynene reclined on the sofa, nestling her head against Dan's shoulder. He held her tightly as if he was afraid she might disappear like the shadows projected across the walls from the dancing flames.

"It's such a cozy home," Wynene said. "I'm surprised it hasn't sold."

"Oh, but it has," he said in a gleeful tone.

"What a lucky couple," she commented wistfully.

"I believe so," he stated, "that is, if she will agree to marry him."

"Dan, you can't mean . . . ?" She sat up, looking at him with astonishment. "You bought it?"

"It comes with a condition, of course," he said, smiling, a slight tick in his left cheek. "She must agree to marry him. There's plenty of yard for your gardening, and it's a wonderful place to raise children, our children." When she stared back at him with an amazed expression, he raised an eyebrow in question. "It's time, past time. You say you want children. I can't go on seeing you infrequently. We have already wasted years apart." When she continued to stare mutely he put his arms around her, embracing her tightly as if he were afraid she would leave. "Say something," he begged.

"I love you," she said in a shaking voice.

"Then damn it, marry me! I know you don't want to hurt Jim, but for once consider your own feelings. If you want me to be with you when you tell him, I will, but don't go on living a lie. You aren't happy. We have wasted too many years with the wrong partners. If you don't want the house, I can sell it. I just want to live with you."

"You bought the house for us?" she asked, still incredulous that he would do such a wonderful thing.

"No," he said, placing his hands on each side of her face, "for *us*."

EULA SAT AT THE TYPEWRITER COMPLETING Miss Adie's book. The garden, setting up the painting of Miss Adie's room, and decorating the tree for Christmas had delayed its completion. It was now almost ready to ship to the publishers. She wondered what the ladies would think about it. They would each get a copy after Miss Adie's passing, a day Eula dreaded facing. Miss Adie was like a mother to her, and this house … this house! She sat back in the chair. Where would she live? The thought never occurred to her. Miss Adie and Doc brought her to their home and nursed her back to health. She became their housekeeper, cook, and in their declining years, their nurse. When Miss Adie passed, Eula would have nowhere to go. She had been too busy to even make friends.

"It's going to be all right," Miss Adie comforted, patting one of Eula's hands. "Don't be frightened. Your wounds will heal with time."

Miss Adie pointed out different parts of the town as they passed them: their church and neighbors' yards, and then she asked, "Do you like to garden?"

"Yes, mum," Eula said. "My mother . . . " She couldn't finish the sentence. Doc's eyes in the rearview mirror registered concern.

"Are you in pain?" he asked.

"Yes." Her voice shook.

"Don't worry," he said comfortingly. "When we get you home . . . "

"Home," he'd said. The word rippled in Eula's heart. The only homes she ever knew were with her mother and Lila Mae. When the car pulled into the driveway beneath a giant oak, Doc opened the door and tenderly took her arm, helping her out.

"Here we are," he said with what sounded like excitement in his voice. "*We* are home."

Eula dropped her head onto her chest as if in prayer.

"There's the garden," Miss Adie pointed, pride in her voice.

Eula turned her face toward the garden, a blur of bright color through her withheld tears. It looked like a slice of heaven to her. "Pretty," she half-whispered.

"We can a lot of the vegetables," Miss Adie said.

Doc laughed. "You mean you do," he corrected humorously, putting an arm around Eula to help her up the steps.

The door opened to a cozy living room with a fireplace and a sofa with what she learned later was one of Miss Adie's quilts thrown over the back. Doc took her down a hallway to a comfy-looking bedroom where another quilt lay across a double bed.

"This is your room," Doc said, leading her to a rocker

where he sat her down while Miss Adie threw back the comforter and pulled down a top sheet. Then he took her by the arm leading her to the bed.

"Rest," he said, tucking her in as if she were a small child. Drawing the comforter over her, he added, "If you need anything, we're here."

"I'll check in on you later," added Miss Adie. "A bathroom is just down the hall. When I finish cooking supper, I'll see if you are up to eating. Would you like anything now?"

"No, thank you," Eula replied, suddenly very sleepy from the shot Doc had given her to fight her pain.

After Miss Adie left, Doc returned to set a glass of water on the nightstand. "It's going to be all right," he reassured, patting her arm. "Get some rest. You have nothing to fear here."

And just like that, Eula found a home. It took her months to recover from the accident. Gradually as she built up her strength, she willingly took on household duties while Doc and Miss Adie saw patients. She knew she was a curiosity to the townsfolk. Many looked startled by the purplish scar on her cheek. But gradually, she became accepted as Doc and Miss Adie's live-in help, although Doc and Miss Adie never referred to her that way. To them, she became simply a member of the household.

"A lucky day," Doc often said of the day they found her, but Eula knew it was not simply luck that led her to the quarters in the town where they lived.

THIRTY- FIVE

CHRISTMAS EVE—THE CHURCH WAS PACKED. Masses of bright-red azaleas flanked the podium. Parents struggled with children eager to get home, excited about the coming day and the toys they would find magically placed under their trees. Wynene envied the parents trying to constrain them. How wonderful it would be to wake on Christmas morning to an atmosphere of joyful expectation that emanated from a child. She had always loved Christmas. As Jim's wife, she sat in the front pew listening to the organ and the choir singing "Oh Come Ye All Faithful." The words filled her with remorse. She had not been faithful to Jim, who sat in front of the choir waiting to deliver his Christmas message. Catching her glance, he smiled down at her. If only he put as much passion into his marriage as he did his congregation and sermons, perhaps . . . No, it was too late for conjecture. She could no more change him than he could her, and she was deeply in love with Dan, with whom she had so much in common—not just their sexual natures but their communication. Being with him felt like home, not just a comfortable relationship, but one of complete harmony. Living with Jim had been like living with a roommate—a friendship. She would always hold him in highest esteem and admire him for his devotion to his congregation.

As he stood up and approached the podium, she was struck as ever by his good looks and his poise. This was where he belonged. As he began his Christmas sermon, she was stirred as ever by his prose, his heartfelt sermon. It was his gift, a God-given one. She restrained an overwhelming feeling of sorrow at what could have been, but she couldn't change him any more than he could her. She knew that she would always have a love for him, and she already regretted the inevitable moment when she would tell him she was leaving. Not now! It would have to wait until after the holidays. She couldn't hurt one of the dearest friends she ever had during this holy and festive season. She hoped he would agree to keep in touch with her, that they could remain friends after all the years spent together. Oh, Dan, she thought, looking down at the program, if only you were here, but there would be next Christmas and all the ones to follow, and hopefully children with whom to share their heartfelt love.

She looked down the row at a young couple sitting closely together. He pulled a pencil from the pew rack and with a shaking hand wrote something on his program, then handed it to the girl. Did she notice a quickening from the young woman? She reached for one of his hands, laced her fingers through his, and whispered in his ear. He sat forward, his hands on his knees and bent over as if in prayer. A ripple of electricity seemed to flow down the aisle toward her. The choir broke into song. She hadn't noticed: Jim had concluded his sermon. As she stood up to leave the pew, the young couple, their hands tightly gripped, followed her exit.

"Merry Christmas," the two young strangers said, their faces exuding joy.

Without hesitation, the words rushed from her: "I couldn't help but notice," she said to the nice-looking young man, "a communication. This must be a special Christmas for you both."

"Oh, yes," he grinned widely, "I just asked her to marry me."

"And from the radiance on both of your faces . . . ?"

The lovely young blonde smiled broadly, tears in her eyes. "I said yes!"

"I didn't mean to pry," she said, feeling a sparkle of sudden joy.

"Oh, no," they said in unison.

"You're the first to hear," the young man said. "I haven't even told my parents yet."

"Then thank you for gifting me. What a wonderful Christmas for you both, and for your parents. Congratulations!"

She hugged them both before they made their way up the aisle. When they reached the corridor, they hugged again before they parted. "You don't know what your sharing means to me," she said in thanks to the two young strangers. "It has made my Christmas more special by your happiness."

EULA SAT IN FRONT OF THE TREE ENJOYING A cup of hot cider, the sparkle of the Christmas tree lights, and the crackle of the fire in the hearth. She could hear church bells ringing. Townsfolk would be attending services. She had attended many in the past with Doc and Miss Adie. Earlier in the day, she walked in the garden snipping flowers—stars of Bethlehem, daylilies, camellias, and winter jasmine—to put in

a vase for Miss Adie, who was now back in her newly painted room. Arranging them in a vase, she admired the bright
yellow jasmine that resembled forsythia. She had to snip off
much of its long stem to arrange it with the rest of the flowers, but it added height to the arrangement.

"Are those from Doc?" Miss Adie, a flush of sudden color
in her otherwise ashen face, asked.

"He always give you flowers from the garden," Eula said.
"This year, the ladies been working, helping."

"Kind, must thank them and that young man."

Eula took a deep breath, surprised as ever at what Miss
Adie's confused mind noticed. This Christmas, for the first
time in a long while, she would cook fresh vegetables from
the garden: peas, beans, and Brussels sprouts. She could smell
the turkey already cooking in the kitchen. Nothing spiced up
the air like the special smell of a turkey. It smelled nearly
as Christmassy as the tree. All afternoon, she worked away
baking pecan and pumpkin pies. It would be only the two
of them for Christmas dinner, but she wanted this to be an
extra-special Christmas for Miss Adie. Even if her taste buds
weren't what they used to be, she might notice. Maybe Doc
would join them, too. Who knew how much or how little one
world was separated from the other? Right now, she could
feel Doc's presence in the room with her. He had always enjoyed her Christmas cider.

"Tastes like Christmas, Eula," he would say. "Like it better than eggnog."

She could see him now, seated in his favorite chair across
from her gazing at the tree, that wonderful smile crinkling his
face. He had been a good-looking man, not fancy-looking,
but manly with a comfortable, warm personality. You felt
you had always known him. Eula smiled at this last thought.

How she missed him jest or nearly jest as much as Miss Adie did. Suddenly, she could hear his warm laugh; hear him joke about the Christmas turkey as she carved it for dinner.

"Don't give me the part that jumped over the fence last." And he would throw his head back, chuckling. The warmth of his annual joke would flood the room. It was a gift in itself.

"Miss you," Eula said to the empty chair across from her.

"HELLO," ELOISE CALLED IN THE PARKING LOT. "Merry Christmas, Wynene."

"Oh, how good to see you," Wynene said, embracing her dear friend. "Are you ready for the big day?"

"Our young man is coming, but not for Christmas Day. He's spending that with his mom, but the day after."

"Wonderful! Is he staying long?"

"No, never long enough, but he wants to check on the garden before he goes back to Atlanta."

"Now, Eloise, you know that's not the only reason. He's become very fond of you."

"And I of him," Eloise said. "Life does deliver surprises, doesn't it?"

Wynene felt a near-chuckle of happiness as she smiled and nodded, thinking about the reaction of the ladies if the surprising news of her leaving her marriage for Dan were to leak out, but it dissipated with the thought of the emotional trauma she would cause Jim. Suddenly, the joy the young couple had handed her like a Christmas present receded.

The ambivalent emotions playing across Wynene's face were not lost on Eloise. She put a hand on her shoulder. "Something is troubling you. Are you well? Is it Jim?"

Wynene looked into the eyes of her friend. How she wanted to tell her, to get some release, but she couldn't spoil her Christmas. She was the one person she would miss most when she left Simpsonville. "You know Christmas. I love it, but it's tiring. Be sure to bring Bobby by, unless we plan to do some more cleaning up in the garden and I see him there."

"Being a pastor's wife has to be hard particularly at this time of year. I've told you that before. You should let me help more."

"Oh, I'm okay, really. Just need some rest."

"Well, Jim's sermon was beautiful, as usual," Eloise said.

"Was it?" Wynene said, hugging her friend and getting into the car.

Eloise shook her head as her friend drove away. 'Was it?' There was something troubling Wynene. Perhaps Christmas was especially poignant to her since she didn't have any children to share the joy. She could relate to that, for Christmas always brought special memories of Jake and also of Walt. They had both loved it. Having Bobby in her life had placed a slave over a large wound in her heart. She loved him like a son. This Christmas would be a brighter one for her. The house was festively decorated for his arrival. She usually had a tree, but not one as special as this year's. It nearly touched the ceiling, and she had added more ornaments and lights. Every room had a touch of Christmas in it, including Jake's. She had bought special needlepoint pillows with Christmas scenes and put scented candles in the room and the adjoining bath. She had learned Bobby's shirt size and bought him several dress shirts for work and also some casual short-sleeved ones, all gaily wrapped and underneath the tree. A special after-Christmas dinner was also planned. As she drove toward home, the thought hit her: If she had not lost Jake, she would probably never have met Bobby, and he wouldn't have been present to help restore Miss Adie's garden. How very strange life was: Her tragedy brought about a happily needed transformation in the ladies' lives, as well as in the lives of Eula and Miss Adie.

{THIRTY-SIX}

"ADIE," A LOW VOICE CALLED. LESTER. THE warmth of his hand was on her shoulder. "Wake up," he whispered. "Christmas, your favorite time of the year, come with me."

"Where?" she asked reaching out for his hand in the dark.

"Into the garden."

"But it's cold."

"I'll warm you. Take my hand."

Finely sculptured surgeon's hands closed around hers, gently lifting her from the bed. Suddenly, she was in the garden. The night sky was brilliantly studded with stars. The aroma of the dewy garden enveloped them with its earthy fragrance. He enfolded her in his arms, bent his face toward hers. She could feel the muscles in his frame envelop her, the bristles of his still-unshaven face brushed lightly across her face, and the smell of him—she had forgotten his scent, uniquely his as is every human's. How she had missed all of it!

"Merry Christmas, my love," he said, placing his lips on hers.

She threw her head back and laughed with joy. "Oh, Lester, we really shouldn't be out here in the cold."

"Why not? This is where we belong. Look at the stars, diamonds in the sky; smell the earth, the flowers. We're part of it all. You and I, Adie, we are stardust. Every particle of our body, every molecule, is formed from those stars, many of them no longer there, but sending their light to earth. We are so carefully structured, conceived. This," he pointed to the sky, "is our universe, and this," he gestured with outspread arms toward the garden, "is also our small portion of it."

He brought her closer to him, touched her face, tracing its outline in the dark. "I've missed you, Adie. Have you forgiven me?"

"Long ago, but I never said, you never said! How did you know?"

"Our minds are so finely tuned. They always have been. Somehow, I felt that instinctively the day I met you."

"Lester."

"Yes?" he asked, dropping her hand and stepping away, taking the warmth of his presence, leaving a vaporous outline floating through the garden.

"Don't go!" she called, fanning the air with her hands, hoping to touch him. "Please stay!"

"Never . . . " he said, from somewhere in the distance, his words receding, " . . . forget . . . not far away."

Darkness enveloped her; the stars gone, Lester gone. She was lying in her bed pulling at the blanket around her.

"Now, now," a voice said as someone patted her arm. "Miss Adie, it going be all right. It jest be a nightmare. Go on back to sleep. I sit right here beside you in this rocker. Soon, it be Christmas morning."

Eula, it was Eula, and Lester was gone, but a promise?

Something he said? The words echoed in the room, silent save for the squeak of the rocker as Eula took a seat. "Not far away," yes, that was it. She turned her face toward the window and the night sky above the garden, twinkling with stars.

OPAL SAT ON THE FLOOR OF THE DEN surrounded by gifts, wrapping paper, ribbon, and tags. Her fingers were beginning to ache from cutting so much paper, but it didn't dull the excitement she always felt at the season. So many presents; as a little girl, there were so few. This time of year was poignant. She wished her mother could be here. What a delight it would have been to finally be able to give her all that her life with Kylie Mae's father denied her. Somehow, she felt that in some mysterious way her mother was with her, delighting in her daughter's joy and that of her family. Mattie and Paul would have loved having her for a grandmother; she would have made a good one. Her mother would have loved Hank and he, her.

What a year it had been: Miss Adie's garden; firmer, finer friendships formed with the ladies; uniting with Susan . . .

"No," she said, laughing, "with Alice. Alice Johnson."

She sighed. How could she reject her now that she had come back into her life? She shook her head. It was too risky. If Hank discovered his wife's true identity, how would he handle it? He would find that he married one woman only to discover that she was someone else without the lofty reputation of Opal St. John. No, Hank was not that kind of man. Pretension never impressed him, but he would be extremely disappointed and hurt that she deceived him all these years. She couldn't do that to him and risk potential damage to their wonderful relationship—and the children! How damaging to find that your mother had lived a lie all of their young lives; not only that she assumed a false identity, but also the terrible fact that she murdered her own father, no matter how horrifically bad he was.

"No, I can't," she said to the colorful Christmas wrapping and ribbon surrounding her.

"No, you can't what?" a voice asked above and behind her.

Hank, she hadn't heard him step into the room.

"Do you often mumble to yourself?" he asked with humor in his voice. "Aren't you through with all the wrapping yet? You should have let me help."

She looked around the room hurriedly to make sure that all of his gifts were wrapped. They were sitting off to one side already ready for the tree.

"You startled me," she said as he knelt on the floor beside her.

"Oh," he said, mischievously, leaning over to kiss her neck. "I would like to startle you a little more. Come here." He reached out to grab her, pushing her gently onto the floor, crinkling paper and ribbons. "Here's a package already carefully and beautifully wrapped," he said lying on top of her and nibbling at her neck.

"Hank, the children!" she said, laughing.

"Already in their beds anticipating all of this," he said with humor in his voice, sweeping one arm to the side toward the packages. "Do we have any money left? Hell, forget the money, I've found my Christmas present, and look how beautifully it's wrapped. Let's do a little . . . " he began to unbutton her blouse, "unwrapping. Perhaps I will find a beautiful jewel, an opal."

EULA STOOD IN THE KITCHEN PUTTING AWAY the leavings from Christmas dinner. Miss Adie ate very little of her carefully prepared and festive meal.

"She getting more frail," she said, shelving the food and closing the refrigerator. "We going to lose her."

The thought of it sent a sudden chill through her body. Miss Adie was like a mother to her.

"I jest tired," she said, "Christmas is emotional anyway."

She was awakened early in the morning to hear Miss Adie mumbling in her sleep and then crying out for Doc. Miss Adie's spirits seemed to lift when she was wheeled into the living room for the tree and all the ladies' presents. Eula was surprised to find that the ladies also gave her gifts, making her eyes mist a little. Then after all the unwrapping, Miss Adie grew silent, staring at the fire in the hearth.

"Wouldn't stay," she finally spoke, turning to look toward the window and the garden.

"What's that?"

"Lester wouldn't stay."

"A visit, then," Eula said, putting another log on the fireplace, "like a Christmas gift."

"Well, yes," Miss Adie agreed, her face lighting up at the thought, "Lester, so thoughtful." Then she grew pensive again, watching the flames lick over the logs. Breaking her silence, she looked over at Eula sitting on the sofa drinking a cup of hot cider. "We talked ... about it."

"What that?" Eula asked.

"About forgiveness . . . wanted me to forgive."

Eula put her cup on the coffee table and sat forward, waiting.

"Told him, knew."

"Knew?"

"Love, didn't stop my love."

Eula waited for more, but Miss Adie grew silent again, looking toward the garden, then she turned toward Eula and said, smiling, "Merry Christmas, Eula, Lester and I have been blessed by you."

THIRTY- SEVEN

EULA WASHED UP THE FEW BREAKFAST DISHES while Dr. Pickens did his regular checkup of Miss Adie. Time did fly, it was already January. She, with the ladies' help, finally finished packing away all the ornaments and storing them in the attic. It had been a good Christmas. On his Christmas visit, Bobby stopped by with Eloise to wish them a happy holiday and to check on the garden.

"The violas will be coming up in the spring," Bobby said, admiring the camellias' roselike petals, the winter jasmine, Lenten rose, and the fragrance of the yellow ribbon like witch hazel. "We'll plant Swiss chard and spinach in February. The ladies have done a good job."

"We couldn't have done it as beautifully without your help," Eloise said, her face beaming up at her young friend. "You took wasted earth and turned it into a thriving garden bursting with color. It's the envy of the town."

"We still have a lot to do," he said, putting an arm around her, his face flushing like a small child's at her admiration.

Eloise smiled up at him. Eula couldn't recall her looking that happy. It wasn't just the garden that had taken bloom.

She didn't know the ladies well until recently, but what she had seen of them in the past, they might have been like the garden, waiting for someone to come along and brighten up their lives. A flash of red at the bird feeder outside the kitchen window caught Eula's eye: a male cardinal, cocking its head and peering in at her. "Flying flowers," Doc had called them. "Like the hummer, only lots bigger." He used to comment on how God made a lot of creatures like male birds brighter than the female to attract them during courtship.

"Evolution, I suppose," he would say. "Designed that way by our maker, but look at us humans, we males are the plainer of the species while the women get all gussied up in bright makeup and colorful clothes." Then he would chuckle. "Not that I'm complaining."

Strange, but it seemed since Bobby's appearance and his experience with turning a lumpy piece of ground into a blanket of color, Eula expected to see Doc kneeling on its earth mulching and weeding.

"What I going to do, Doc," she said, finishing up the dishes and sitting at the table with a second cup of coffee, "after Miss Adie join you? I got no place to go and little money. Most folk won't want to hire me with this ropy, rosy scar. I can't go nowhere in this town after all this time without someone staring at me wondering how come my face got this way. I always been a curiosity."

"Your eyes," Doc used to say, sitting across the table from her enjoying another cup of coffee before he and Miss Adie started seeing patients. "They have your heart. That's what people come to see and if they can't, they don't count anyway."

She could feel his hand on her shoulder squeezing it affectionately.

"And the book," she said, staring into the coffee cup, "it going to be delivered soon; what the ladies going to think with all their secrets revealed?"

Now that she had gotten to know and like them, she worried more about their feelings. Going into the living room to see the tree and the lights Bobby thoughtfully left for her to enjoy after he removed the ornaments, promising to remove the lights and tree later, she sat on the sofa to enjoy the tree's glow. This would be, she knew, her last Christmas in this house. It made for a bittersweet Christmas, but she would hold the memory of its glow in her heart and with it, the love she held for Doc and Miss Adie.

IT WAS A LOVELY CHRISTMAS, BUT THE PART Opal hated the most was taking off the ornaments to pack away. Finally, the tree denuded, it was ready for the Boy Scouts, who took away trees for donations to their troop. Packing up the boxes for storage, her mind kept returning to Susan … Alice; it was difficult to replace the name she associated with the girl who helped her in her first desperate days of escape. She was the first real friend in her life other than her mother. The warmth of their reunion was a gift in itself and one, she realized, that she didn't want to lose, but how to tell Hank? She could tell him that she roomed with her before she located a job and leave it at that. After all, Alice didn't know anything about a girl named Kylie Mae and her tragic past. She would like for her to meet Hank and the children, to see how happily established her life was. She had such a wonderful marriage, and she didn't want to do anything to destroy it and the trust Hank placed in her. When she first met him, she was forced to lie about her past, particularly the fact that she had no family.

"No one?" Hank inquired, raising an eyebrow, an incredulous tone in his voice. "No cousins, aunts, or uncles?"

"My parents didn't have siblings and neither did their parents."

"But there must have been some relatives, Opal."

"No," she retorted, a touch of anguish in her voice.

They were seated at their favorite pizza restaurant. The glass of wine she held was shaking, sloshing onto the tablecloth. The bright stains that flowed over the cloth brought a sharp reminder of her father lying on a blood-stained trailer floor. She excused herself and went to the restroom where she stood against the wall breathing deeply, trying desperately to compose herself. A stall door opened and an older woman appeared.

"Are you all right, dear?" she asked. "Is there anything I can do?"

"No, no, thank you," she replied. "Just you know—that time."

"Oh, yes," she agreed, lowering her gaze apologetically. "I didn't mean to intrude, but you are a bit pale. Are you with anyone?"

"It's all right," Opal said, straightening up, disappearing into a stall, waiting to hear the door to the room close.

She wanted to cry, but restrained herself. She didn't want to lose this man. She realized that she was beginning to fall in love with him, but if he started probing for more information, there would be no option. When she returned timidly to the table, Hank stood up, a look of concern on his face.

"I've paid the bill," he said. "Let's get you some fresh air."

When they got into the car, he took her into his arms.

"I'm sorry. I didn't mean to interrogate you. Family must be a tender subject for you. It's not important. What is, though, is the wonderful young woman I've come to respect and like very much. I hope you feel the same way."

She reached up to touch his cheek.

"Your hands are freezing," he said, taking them and rubbing them between his. Then he wrapped his arms around her.

She smiled at the memory of their first ardent kisses. Hank never raised the subject of her family or ancestry again. If there were doubts, he never voiced them. How could she break that bond of trust now? She took a deep breath. If she did disclose her past, how would he take the fact that his wife murdered her father, regardless of the circumstances? And then there was the matter of the prestigious background. When he found out she was raised in a trailer with an alcoholic, uneducated father and that her mother came from nothing, what then? The thought of her mother renewed the childlike anguish she experienced when losing her. However meager her background, she was a lovely and loving mother. It would have been wonderful to introduce Hank to her. She was the one thing from her past she desired most to share with him.

"ADIE," A VOICE CALLED; LESTER'S! "IT'S TIME."

She tried to focus her eyes in the dimness of the night. She was lying on her side facing the window that overlooked the garden and all she could see was the shadowy outline of trees and shrubbery highlighted by a full moon. Lester wasn't there. A heavy weight was on her chest. She opened her mouth to call Eula seated in a chair nearby, but no sound came out.

Hands were gently turning her. She knew their touch. He stood over her, a whimsical smile on his face. "Let's go into the garden."

"My feet, they're so cold," she said with wonder in her voice as a chill spread though her limbs. "Don't know if I can ..."

She was falling. His hands wrapped strongly about hers lifting her effortlessly. They were in the garden. The weakness fell away like an abandoned cloak as a surge of unexpected energy surged through her veins. She held her hands to the light of the moon. Mottled, blue-veined flesh was replaced by the full smoothness of youth. She looked up into Lester's face. It, too, was changed into the features of the man she first met and grew to love.

She had been on an elevator and the door opened. A young man smiled down at her.

"Lester Seabrook," he said in introduction.

The elevator door closed and they were rising, rising toward their future.

"The stars," he said, holding her snugly in his arms, "have never been so brilliant."

WYNENE AND THE LADIES WERE BUSILY KNEELING on the earth in early morning as they set out Dutch bulbs in the garden and planted more roses. So far, the weather had been mild, which pleased the ladies, eager to continue with their planting. Wynene sat back on her heels and gazed at the winter sky; a new year and she still hadn't found an appropriate time, or the courage, to tell Jim she was leaving.

Her studied gaze was not lost on Eloise. Something was bothering her dear friend. Was she ill, or perhaps it was Jim? His Christmas sermons had been just as eloquent as ever, but there was something about his demeanor that was not typical: a slight slump of the shoulders and a smile that didn't register in his eyes. She set her tools aside.

"Let's take a break," she said, patting Wynene's shoulder and heading toward one of the garden's benches.

"Before we know it, spring will be here," Wynene said, sitting down beside her friend.

Spring; she would be gone by then. How she wished she could bypass the pain of her separation and eventual divorce from Jim. There, of course, would be talk, some of it vicious, surely not from her friends, but how was one to know?

"I'm not being nosy," Eloise said, patting Wynene's hand, "but you haven't been yourself. Let me help."

"I wish you could," Wynene said. "There is nothing, but perhaps . . . "

Her sentence was cut short by Eula's cries as her stolid frame raced across the lawn toward the garden. "Miss Wynene, Miss Eloise, come . . . quick. Oh, Lawdy, it's Miss Adie."

THIRTY-EIGHT

WYNENE, ELOISE, AND TWO MEN FROM Heath's Law Practice were seated at the kitchen table. A pot of tea and cookies were on the table. If anyone walked into the room, Wynene thought, looking at the floral patterns on Miss Adie's teacups, they might think they were having a pleasant afternoon tea. Eula, wearing a black dress, stood beside her chair, a teapot in her hand.

"Would you like some more, Miss Wynene? This pot is fresh off the stove, probably hotter than the table's."

"No, thank you, Eula," she said sympathetically, looking up into Eula's puffy eyes. Pain and grief looked back into hers.

"That was very good," Sam Atkins said, his voice conveying friendliness and concern.

"Yes, thank you, Ms. Eula," Clint Morrison agreed, his tone all business as he put his cup down and leaned over to retrieve a packet of papers from his briefcase set on the floor beside him. "Ladies, let's begin," he stated, spreading the papers on the table. "Miss Eula, please take a seat."

Eula frowned as she took her off her apron and sat down beside Wynene. She always knew the day would come when this house would be empty of the two people who had unselfishly taken her in, saving her life. They were missing at this table and in every room of the house.

She had walked into Miss Adie's room the day of her funeral to tell her it was time to go only to realize again in her state of shock that Miss Adie had already left the body that carried her through life and that it was waiting at the church.

Eula's mind played over the events of the day she carried Miss Adie's breakfast tray into her room only to discover that she wasn't breathing. On that terrible morning, a small child's voice echoed from the past: "Mama, please. Mama, wake up." Her first emotion was instant guilt for not trying to wake Miss Adie earlier. The preceding night had been spent trying to calm her as she snatched at her blanket and sputtered words only she could understand. Her arms and hands seemed to have a life of their own as they curled through the air reaching for something only she could see. Finally, she had fallen to sleep, or so Eula thought looking down at her face, peacefully still. Not certain she wouldn't stir and start up, she sat down in the rocker and fought sleep, but it won. When she woke up, morning light spilled through the window and it was way past breakfast. Miss Adie was still sleeping peacefully, so Eula went back to her room to take a shower and prepare for the day. When she drew the drapes in the living room, she could see the ladies were out early doing their winter gardening. Everything seemed so normal, but it wasn't.

Why was she seated at this table? The lawyers insisted that she be present, but for what purpose? Eula's stomach was one huge knot of grief and fear. She had a little money put aside, but it wouldn't last long. Where would she go; what would she do?

Clint still had his stony face and direct manner, thought

Eloise. It got things done; he had an eye for detail. Sam, his new young partner, added welcome personality and warmth to the firm. When Doc made out his will, Miss Adie was already bedridden but she had been a co-signer. Eloise was surprised when Doc called her requesting that she be present when the will was read.

"Wynene has already agreed," he informed her. "If, God forbid, anything should happen to either you or both of you . . . "

"Now, Doc," Eloise comforted him, knowing how difficult it was to go over one's property as if it were a living thing when all it was was just things, but necessary to provide for ongoing life.

Then, he had added, "And there's the matter of Eula." There was a long pause before he said, "It's provided for," leaving her wondering what Doc meant.

Clint cleared his throat as he picked up the paperwork and shuffled through it. He appeared nervous, clearly not his usual manner. "Ladies," he said, his stony glance sweeping over Eloise, Wynene, and Eula. "Will reading is always a delicate subject. This one is particularly so." His eyes scanned Eula's face. A glance not lost on the receiver.

"Oh, my!" Eula exclaimed, leaning backward as if Clint had slapped her across the face.

Eloise put a hand over Eula's, tightly clenched in her aproned lap.

Sam smiled reassuringly.

"Long before Adie's health began to deteriorate," Clint continued in a narrative not normally taken when reading a will, "Doc came to my office for reassurance that all he stipulated in his original will was still instated. I tried once again to tell him of uncontrollable situations that might arise, but he insisted that the town in which he grew up, and in which he and his father gave their life skills, would honor his wishes. At that point, a codicil was added in order to ensure that his wishes would be carried out to the letter. What I am about to read may carry apprehension for some of you present. Let me comfort all concerned that this will and what it implies has been, as it should be in due process of law, placed in the office of lawyers sworn by law to keep all that their clients place before them secret and sacred, to never be spoken of except in the privacy of a client and his trustees or inheritors. I might add," he further stated, looking across the table at Wynene and Eloise, "that it is hoped, and I believe it will be so, a sacred trust honored by those present." Pushing his chair back a little and looking down at the table and its reams of paperwork, he continued, "I want to reassure you, Miss Eula, that what is laid out in Doc's will is legal and binding. It bears his signature and that of Miss Adie, God rest her soul. Excuse me," he added, getting up. Turning his back, he coughed, before returning to the table. "Doc, in order to ensure that all his wishes and those of Miss Adie's were met, designated," he paused to look at Wynene and Eloise, "the two of you to be the executors. He also requested that the rest of the Ladies Mission Society should help carry out his wishes."

What followed was a legal litany of "I's" and "therefores" before the meat of Doc's and seemingly Miss Adie's will was disclosed. Pushing his glasses back and pressing his lips together, Sam drew a deep breath and addressed Eula.

"I will discard the legal wording to tell you, Eula Simmons, that as the legal daughter of Doc you are the primary inheritor of this house, its furnishings, collectibles, grounds, and all monies in Doc and Miss Adie's account, except for a thousand dollars designated for the church."

Eula, her eyes wide, put a hand to her mouth. "Dear Lawd!"

Wynene and Eloise, their mouths parted, sat forward, then back again as they turned to gaze at Eula in amazement.

Doc's daughter, Eloise thought, turning the words over in her mind. That meant that Doc at some point in his life had been unfaithful to Miss Adie unless Eula was born before they married, but she couldn't have, could she? She didn't seem old enough.

Eula, sat stone still, her back braced against her chair, looked paralyzed. She clasped her hands tightly in her lap. Wynene placed a hand on hers. In response, Eula looked out of the corner of an eye at her as if she was afraid to look into Wynene's eyes for fear of what she might see. Eula was as shocked by Doc's will as she and Eloise, but suddenly it made sense to Wynene. Eula's eyes always making her feel that she had seen them somewhere before; Doc's closeness to her and hers to him. How did Miss Adie find out? Did she suspect or even know that her husband fathered a child, a Negro? No, Wynene reconsidered, Eula was half-white. Miss Adie and Doc always seemed like the perfect couple, working side by side in the office and in the garden. Then the thought occurred to her that perhaps Miss Adie never knew. No, that couldn't be, she had seen the will and signed it.

Eula stared down at her lap: the book, Miss Adie's book! With Christmas and then the passing of Miss Adie, she had forgotten about the book. Its delivery would be this week when the ladies met at their Mission Society. It couldn't have been worse timing. The book would arrive smelling fresh and clean from the printers: engraved in gold, on its bound front each lady's name; their secrets boldly printed on each page. The ladies' secrets would be nothing compared to hers.

She dreamed up the idea of the book to give Miss Adie a purpose to go on living. That was before she made the ladies' acquaintance and saw their true selves come out working the land. Now that Miss Adie was gone, what purpose could that book serve except to make the Society women mad after all their dirt and sweat working to restore Miss Adie's garden? She shook her head: the house hers, the furniture, too? How could she keep what Doc and Miss Adie gave to her? She would have to sell everything, pack her bags, and get out of town, but to what destination? She would once again be a runaway, and this for the third time. What could have been in Doc's mind? He was an intelligent man, a good man who loved her mother.

A mental picture from the past, sunlit and gauzy, danced before Eula's eyes: her father swinging her mother's slender form through the air; her mother's hands tightly clasped behind the neck of Eula's father. She was laughing, her large hazel greenish-brown eyes luminous with joy. Her skin was a creamy light brown like the chocolate milk she made for Eula. Her father, shirt sleeves rolled up over muscular arms, was laughing too. He was tall and slender with prominent cheekbones and dark brown eyes underneath arched eyebrows that made him seem to be always looking at life as something to be questioned. They were so young, amazingly young! As a child, they were simply her mother and father, two adult figures she loved and who loved her. Through the gauge of memory, she visualized them jest as they were, individuals in their very early 20s: two young people who adored each other.

Doc happened upon her mother for the first time when he was going through the countryside giving free medical treatment, something he and Miss Adie would later practice in Simpsonville and nearby towns. Eula learned later in life that Doc was still completing his training when he met the woman who would later give birth to her.

Soon after she came to live with Doc and Miss Adie, he called Eula into his private office. It was a Sunday when the office was officially closed except for emergencies. Miss Adie, welcoming some free time after church, was in the garden. Still stunned by Doc's appearance in her life and her arrival in his and Miss Adie's home, Eula, skeptical and fearful, took the seat Doc gestured her toward near his desk as he shut the door.

Pushing her chair in, Doc put a hand on her shoulder, squeezing it, a sense so familiar she nearly cried. "I'm blessed," he said. "It's perhaps a blessing I don't deserve." Then he took his seat at the desk with an unspoken understanding that he knew the desk between them would make her feel a little more secure, giving her time to process her feelings.

"Tell me," he requested, "everything that has happened since I last saw you."

Without hesitation, her words like caged things set free, spouted out the sorry history of her life.

"So that explains your facial scars," he said with emotion in his voice. "Afraid I can't do anything to improve them, but I can do all in my power to help improve your emotional ones. How did you find me?"

"I wasn't on my way to find you," she informed him, eyes misting. "My troubles brought me to your doorstep without my knowing. You don't need ... "

He got up from his chair to put an arm around her shaking shoulders. "Need," he said, "and want ... I have lived all these years needing to know where you were, how you were, wanting to show my daughter how much she is loved."

They stayed in the office talking, father and daughter, about her mother, agreeing that Miss Adie must never know. It was to be their secret.

"Miss Simmons," Clint said, shuffling papers and putting them away in his briefcase, "all that I have related here has been unspoken since Doc came to our office to write his and Miss Adie's will. It will remain so. You have my assurance."

"Yes, sir," she nodded in thanks as she shook Sam's offered hand, who had sympathy in his eyes.

"When you are ready, come by our office and we will talk," Clint added. "Good day, ladies, thank you for the refreshments."

"Lawd!" Eula exclaimed, collapsing into her chair after they left. "What am I to do?"

"We'll find a way," Eloise said. "Won't we, Wynene?"

"Doc and Miss Adie loved you very much," Wynene said in comfort, patting her shoulder. "You have a home, Eula, a home for the rest of your life."

"But . . . " Eula started to protest.

"Simpsonville," Wynene said in understanding. "will find something else to gossip about."

"Do people even need to know?" spoke up Eloise. "Perhaps we can find a way around the talk. We'll put on our thinking caps. In the meantime, Eula, you rest. Losing Miss Adie and the reading of her and Doc's will is enough exhaustion."

Eula saw them to the door before collapsing on the living room sofa.

"What was you thinking?" she scolded, staring at Doc's favorite chair.

THIRTY-NINE

WYNENE SET OUT CUPS AND SAUCERS FOR the coffee and tea she was brewing to host the Ladies Mission Society. Napkins and plates were placed around a carefully arranged vase of fragrant tea olive, Japanese fatsia, flowering quince, and camellias sitting in the middle of the dining room table. She smiled. Many of the flowers came from Miss Adie's garden. It seemed a suitable tribute to her memory and the subject matter she and Eloise planned for the meeting. Setting silver forks and spoons on the table, she fought to put thoughts of Dan out of mind. Miss Adie's passing and the startling realization of Eula's parentage had put aside her plans to leave Jim.

The doorbell chimed as the front door opened simultaneously. "Hello," Eloise called out, her heels tapping across the hall entrance. "I thought this occasion deserved my family's recipe, a Southern Belle cake."

"What a treat," Wynene said. "Perhaps someday I can pry its secret from you."

"You're family to me," she stated, putting the container on the table and removing the lid to display a carefully frosted cake. "Are you ready?" she asked.

"Ready? Wynene asked, raising an eyebrow. She knew Eloise didn't mean for the recipe.

Her worried glance was not lost on Eloise, but she decided to let it pass. They were all suffering over Miss Adie's passing. What would happen to Eula? She had inherited the money and all the property, but how would she manage, a black woman living in a white community? What was Doc thinking when he wrote his will? Didn't he anticipate problems? Half-white wasn't white. Racial issues were particularly tense now. You couldn't pick up a paper or turn on the TV without seeing the face of an eloquent speaker: Martin Luther King. Integration would probably come soon. It was a process long overdue, one she didn't mind, but there were many who would; many who resided in this town and those nearby. The plans she and Wynene devised to help Eula were tenuous ones.

"Not to worry," she comforted, patting Wynene's shoulder.

Wynene smiled at Eloise's mistaken assumption. Her concern over Dan was only momentarily set aside in favor of Eula's predicament. The doorbell and clopping of heels across the threshold followed a flurry of fluttery voices, the kind of music known only to women. The meeting had begun. Once the ladies were contentedly seated with their refreshments and the meeting called to order, Wynene and Eloise, exchanging a look of encouragement, took a deep breath as they stood side by side to call the meeting to order.

"Wynene and I have decided that since Miss Adie's passing, it would be suitable to dedicate this meeting to her," Eloise announced, pausing as the ladies sounded their agreements in unison.

"I'm grateful," Opal said, her voice catching, "that working her garden brought me closer to a woman who loved its land. She put her heart into its soil and caring for the patients who came to Doc's and her doorstep."

Her statement was met with hearty applause.

"She was a kind lady," added Verabelle, to everyone's agreement. "When I pass her empty house and the garden where we spent so many happy hours, I still imagine her there with Eula. Is the house on the market?"

"No," Wynene said, exchanging a glance with Eloise. "It's not on the market."

"Does she have relatives?" Hattie asked.

Eloise shook her head.

"The garden, the house . . . it can't be common property," Norma Mae protested. "After all our work, it can't be."

"The house and the garden . . . " Wynene breathed deeply, exhaling the words, "have been willed to Eula."

"Eula?" perplexed voices echoed as the women looked at each other questioningly.

"You see . . . " Eloise began, but a voice, a male one, interrupted her.

"Excuse me," he shyly stated, standing in the hall foyer. "I rang the doorbell, but no one answered."

Dressed in khakis, he was wearing a Special Delivery cap and a perplexed, apologetic expression on his face. "I have a box here," he informed, "Delivery, this house."

Wynene, her announcement temporarily left swirling in the air, stepped toward him. "To this address? But I'm not expecting anything."

"Says here," the boy pointed, blushing at his disturbance. "Deliver first Tuesday of month to the Mission Society—Mrs. Wynene Chalmers—this address. It's pretty hefty, but I have a trolley. Just let me know where to put it."

"Well, I wasn't . . . expecting anything, but if it says so, bring it in."

A large box, she thought, as she went into the kitchen to fetch a kitchen knife. Was it something that Jim ordered for the church? No, he said it was addressed to the Mission Society, not to the church, but how did anyone know she would be hosting today? The ladies crowded behind her as she stood at the door watching the boy slide a hefty box down the ramp of his truck onto a trolley. Securing the package, he struggled to wheel it toward the doorway. Pausing at the entry, his body at a tilt, he inquired in a winded tone, "Where do you . . . ?"

Wynene gestured toward the hallway as the ladies made way.

"Shouldn't you put something on your wooden floor to protect it?" Sarah Ellen suggested.

"Oh, yes, stop, please," Wynene requested as the boy stood sweating on her paved brick entranceway. "Let me get some blankets."

The boy frowned. "Sorry, I forgot," he apologized. "I have a drop cloth in the truck, but I can't . . . "

"No," Eloise agreed, "you can't. Blankets should do fine."

Her interest piqued, Wynene rushed into the bedroom to grab her purse off the dresser to tip the delivery boy and to get several blankets from the storage closet. The ladies excitedly spread them over the floor as the boy waited patiently, his delivery still at a tilt. With effort, he managed to roll the trolley over the crumpled blankets to deposit the box.

"Forgot the tablet," he announced, rushing back to the truck.

"Where is he from? " Verabelle asked. "I've never seen him around here, but it's addressed to the Ladies Mission Society?" Then she recalled something Miss Adie had said. "A book?"

"It's the book," Sarah Ellen stated, her face pale. Her

Great-Uncle Barclay's murder of the bank president would no longer be past gossip.

"Sign here, please," the boy pointed to a line on paperwork, his face still flushed from struggling with the large box.

"Where did this come from?" Wynene asked, signing the receipt.

"Montgomery, Mrs. Chalmers. The return address is on the package. Sorry to disturb you. Would you mind giving me directions to the library?"

"How did she . . . how did the person who sent it know to send it to the Mission Society at this address?"

"That I can't answer. Sorry. Is there a problem?"

"No, it's fine, thank you, and the library is on Church Street, two streets over, left, another left, and a right."

Sarah Ellen was right. It had to be the book. Didn't Miss Adie say the library would receive one, too? Busy working in Miss Adie and Doc's garden, the question of the book and its contents had receded into the background. Yet it was the common denominator that brought them together. She looked at the women crowding the hallway. A few short months ago, they looked older, heavier, and yes, far less happy. The work and love they poured into a patch of deserted ground had transformed them. Getting their hands dirty, kneeling on the earth weeding and planting seeds, brought them all closer together. It was as if Doc and Miss Adie had placed their healing hands on all their souls. The mystery of the book and its contents initiated it all.

"Aren't you going to open it?" Hattie asked, her hands clutched so tightly they felt bruised.

"Yes, but in a way, I don't want to. I wish we could all just walk away."

"Walk away?" Verabelle looked mystified.

"I know what you mean," Opal said with a smile. "If it is the book, it's already made a huge difference in our lives."

"A positive one," agreed Eloise. "Without it, we wouldn't have come to know and love the people who lived beside that neglected garden, or get to know each other better. I have seen more than that garden bloom."

"Whoever sent whatever is in that box meant for us to have it," Hattie stated impatiently. "Where do you keep your knives, Wynene?"

Still reluctant to open it, Wynene went to the kitchen for a butcher knife. Kneeling beside the heavily structured cardboard box, she forced the knife into the top edge. It took several cuts to get a handhold to lift the corners. The ladies helped to pry it open. Gold letters on what appeared to be imitation leather appeared. A book; many books, hardcover books stacked neatly side by side and on top of each other. She lifted one: Norma Mae Adkins was engraved in gold letters on the book's cover.

"Ohhh," Norma Mae moaned as Wynene handed it to her. Tentatively, she opened the book: a dedication page:

Dedicated to Simpsonville's Ladies Mission Society
Without Whose Help This Book Could Never Be Written

Miss Adie's signature; inhaling and holding, she turned the page.

"Is it that bad?" asked Sarah Ellen.

Grandmother Lizzie's Applesauce Fruitcake
(A family recipe from Charleston generously donated
By Mrs. Norma Mae Adkins)

Yield: one cake. 325 degrees
Two cups brown sugar
Two cups lukewarm . . .”

Norma Mae read out loud: Applesauce, two and a half cups flour, two teaspoons baking soda.” Her hands whipped through the pages. “Why, it seems to be recipes from all of us, nothing but recipes!”

“Recipes?” Eloise repeated incredulously. Her brow crinkled as a slow smile inched its way across her lips. “Not just recipes,” she announced, chuckling. “THE recipe, the Family Secret!”

Wynene lifted another book and handed it to Opal, whose hands shook as she opened it. She noted Wynene’s Royal Legend cake on the second page; her Deep Dark Secret on the third; Sarah Ellen’s Dream Pie on the fourth. “Unbelievable,” she exclaimed, turning the pages to every name in the Ladies Mission Society and their carefully guarded heritage. She exhaled a sigh of relief: a book of recipes, the family secret, nothing but recipes. “How did Miss Adie get them?” she asked of the ladies who were grabbing their books from the cardboard box.

“We gave them to Eula,” Eloise informed her, looking at the page carefully listing the ingredients for her Southern Belle cake. “At least I did when Eula cajoled me with the tale of how Miss Adie enjoyed it and she wasn’t eating much of anything else.” She laughed. “How did the rest of you give up your family recipes?”

“She looked and was so immensely frail. I thought what harm would it do?” Hattie stated. “And really, what harm has it done? Wynene is right. We have seen more than Doc and Miss Adie’s garden grow. However, my ancestors may be turning over in their graves."

The ladies chuckled over her comment and their relief at the book's contents.

"There's a history of the town in the back of the book after the recipes," Verabelle revealed. "That had to have come from Miss Adie in her more lucid moments. After all, look at all the years she lived here."

A history of the town, Opal thought, taking a deep breath, and a history of family recipes. Hers was not a treasure carefully guarded over a century or more. It was simply her mother's, something she cooked for Kylie Mae to celebrate her grades or to give her a semblance of normalcy. Comfort food, like a salve over a wound, something Miss Adie often applied in her life as Doc's nurse and wife.

"Goodness," Wynene sighed. "Ladies, Miss Adie's gift has almost made us forget about the purpose of this meeting. Let's take a seat and have another cup of tea. Eloise and I have a proposition to present."

The book, The Family Secret: nothing more than recipes and a history of the town, Wynene thought as she poured more tea for the group of ladies convivially chatting, reliving the moment their mothers gave them the family secret. Eula was the person responsible for typing its contents and perhaps also for delving into the history of the town. How on earth did she find the time to dictate what Miss Adie told her and to type it while she was keeping house and nursing Miss Adie? It must have also taken some time to find a printer and ship the manuscript. Were her efforts inspired by a vendetta to get back at a town that had socially shunned Miss Adie, or was it simply a way to keep Miss Adie's mind more alert? She hoped that the plan she and Eloise had to give Eula a home would meet with an equally warm acceptance.

{FORTY}

EULA BUSTLED ABOUT THE KITCHEN PUTTING on tea and coffeepots. She took a fork to check the coffee cakes baking in the oven. She had baked little and eaten not much more since Miss Adie's passing. Her appetite had gone missing. She still got up the same time in the morning—"up with the chickens," Doc used to say, though they didn't have any. She sighed, took a sip of her coffee, and set the cup back on its saucer on the countertop. More than her appetite was missing; this house was full of missing. Every morning, she still went into Miss Adie's room half-expecting to see her looking out the window beside her bed in hopes of seeing Doc in the garden. She felt relief to not see her suffering any more, but her heart ached because she was gone. Late at night, she was often awakened by the sound of footsteps in the hallway. It would be Doc, her sleepy mind would say, home after one of his late-night calls. Once, she awakened in the middle of the night to his voice calling: "Eula, Mrs. Baker's baby is on the way." She sat up in bed, longing to see him as she used to standing in the hallway outside her bedroom door.

"Sorry to wake you," he would say, smiling, his medical bag in his hands, his eyes sleepy looking, his face unshaven. "I'll be back soon."

Soon . . . Eula sat down heavily at the kitchen table. "Doc, what am I going to do? You left me a house I can't keep and if I sell, I got no place to go."

As if he were sitting there with her as he often did early in the morning before he and Miss Adie started seeing patients, the words she never heard came: "Eula, Adie and I left you the house to keep."

How did that come about, she wondered? The will; it was in the will, his signature and Miss Adie's. How much did Miss Adie know? The will said "my daughter." Miss Adie and Doc's signatures . . . When did he tell Miss Adie? What did he tell her? All this time while she was nursing him, then Miss Adie, Miss Adie never let on that she knew she was Doc's daughter. Had she always known or suspected? This is what Doc meant when he told her all that time ago sitting on the porch watching firefly flicker like fairy lanterns. "I have made provisions for you—legal and binding."

"Acceptance, Eula," she could hear Doc say. He would be sitting across from her stirring sugar, half a teaspoon in his coffee, pouring in a little cream. "Life should come down to a matter of acceptance."

"And forgiveness, Doc?" she questioned out loud to his empty chair.

"That, too," she could hear him say, "is a matter of acceptance."

"Oh, Doc," she half-moaned, "don't you realize what you have done? Most folk don't think the way you or Miss Adie do. They don't know I'm your daughter, and if they did, they won't see me as half-white. What they will see is a half-black woman living in an all-white neighborhood. Your good heart and Miss Adie's don't beat in most peoples' hearts."

And the Mission Society ladies . . . for all the goodness she found in them as they knelt in the garden or decorated the tree for Miss Adie, what must they think of her now that Miss Adie's book had been delivered; delivered jest the other day according to the notice in the mailbox addressed to her from that Montgomery publisher? What must they think of her getting out of them their family secret? Miss Wynene sounded all friendly and sweet like always when she called about coming over with Miss Eloise, but the book went to her for a reason. How did the other ladies take it? Some, like Miss Opal, were most likely more forgiving, but though she had grown fond of the others, what would be their reaction? Their family recipe, secrets kept, she understood, from Miss Verabelle, from all except close family, printed and published. Lawd, even the library got one for the town to read. She might just as well pack up and head out for nowhere.

"Doc," she said to his empty chair, "I be one crazy woman to expect that kind of acceptance or forgiveness."

The *ding-dong* of the front doorbell made her jump.

"Lawd, they's here," she said pushing her chair back. Its scraping on the kitchen floor sounded nearly like a laugh.

"One on me," she said, hustling to answer the door and whatever anger lay behind it.

What she saw when she answered it took her breath away, as if someone had kicked her in the stomach. All the ladies gathered together as if they had come to work in the garden. More like came to work me over, Eula thought, nearly choking as she tried to swallow her astonishment.

"Eula, how are you?" Wynene said, an eyebrow lifted in concern.

Licking suddenly dry lips and swallowing hard, Eula managed to gulp out, "Getting by, Miss Wynene."

"Can we, all of us," Eloise asked, gesturing to the rest of
the ladies, "come in?"

"Course, didn't exactly expect all of you." Eula stood
aside to hold open the door. "There's fresh coffee and cakes
in the kitchen," she added, gathering her composure, "but
now all of you . . . would you like to sit in the living room?"

"The kitchen's just fine," Opal replied, "or any place that
suits you, Eula."

Spoken, Eula thought, as if the house was truly hers to
pick where her guests sat. "The kitchen then, the pots there
and the cakes, too," Eula said. "I jest has to put out a few
more plates."

"We can help," several of the ladies said in unison.

Candy coating, Eula thought, as she followed the Mission
Society ladies into the kitchen. She didn't know what was
worse, their pity or their anger. Miss Wynene and Miss Eloise
must feel so remorseful they brought in extra recruits.

With the ladies settled in with their coffee or tea, Eula
sliced up the coffee cakes into thin wedges.

"Come join us," Norma Mae said, as Eula set the plate
on the table.

That bad then, Eula thought, taking the only chair left
vacant, the one at the head of the table where Doc usually sat.

"Eula," Wynene said softly, "we all know how much you
are suffering over Miss Adie's passing. She and Doc loved you
very much."

Eula grimaced and nodded.

"The ladies and I, aware of how difficult your situation is,
have come up with a solution that we think . . . "

Eula shook her head. "Don't trouble yourself, Miss Wynene, I'll pack my bag and be gone soon as I get the lawyers help me sell."

"Sell!" Hattie seemed surprised. "Why would you want to do that? I mean, we know the house is, after all, yours."

"We don't want you to sell," Eloise said, while the rest of the ladies nodded in agreement. "Don't you like it here?"

"Course, since Doc and Miss Adie took me in, well, this the only house, home, I've known since I was way young."

"Then why sell?" Hattie asked. "Doc and Miss Adie wouldn't want you to give your home up."

"I don't understand." Eula stared into the faces of the ladies turned to her in equal puzzlement.

"These are delicate times, we know," Verabelle acknowledged. "We can understand how perplexed you must be."

Eula nodded, thinking, Miss Verabelle don't begin to imagine.

"The simple fact, Eula," Eloise stated, "is Doc and Miss Adie wanted, no, want you to have this house, and the ladies have come up with a plan to help make certain that their wishes are carried out."

"How can that be?" Eula asked in exasperation. "They so good; lots aren't."

"That's so," Sarah Ellen agreed as the rest of the ladies nodded in agreement.

"Don't want no trouble," Eula stated, "or to cause you any." She looked around the table.

"We don't believe there should be any," Wynene said. "Not with this plan."

"We're all behind you, Eula." Opal reached over to pat her hand. "You're as much a part of this community as the rest of us. In fact, you've been here longer than most of us."

"Lots won't see it that way, Miss Opal."

"No, they won't," Verabelle agreed. "That's where we come in."

"By the way, Eula, we, all of us, are delighted with our cookbook and the history of the town," Norma Mae informed her.

Eula's cheeks felt as hot as if she had been standing over a stove all day. "Don't go blaming Miss Adie. I to blame for that, thought it might help her, have something keep her mind . . ." She paused. "Delighted?"

A chorus of voices: "Been wanting that Strawberry Souffle," "Never would have guessed secret to Southern Belle," "Finally got Birds of Paradise," followed by smiles and laughter.

Eula sat back in her chair. Look at this, Doc, she said to herself, here I be sitting at this table with the ladies from the Mission Society watching them enjoy a good laugh 'cause of a trick I pulled on them. "Acceptance," she could hear him say. If this was acceptance, she couldn't find the understanding behind it.

"Always thought that tradition too old-fashioned," Sarah Ellen stated as the rest of the ladies nodded.

"You aren't here about the book?" Eula asked, astonished.

"The book? Goodness, no, we came about the house and you," Eloise comforted, reaching for Eula's hand. "All of us understand the strong bond built between you, Doc, and Miss Adie. A childless couple, they took you in and considered you part of their family. No one could have taken better care of them than you."

Eloise squeezed Eula's hand and winked. "Childless couple," she'd said. Was she letting her know that the rest of the ladies didn't know that Doc was her father? Miss Eloise and

Miss Wynene hadn't told the other ladies? Then why had they all appeared at the door?

"There will have to be some changes made to the house," Sarah Ellen announced. "That is, if you agree to our plan."

"Changes?" Eula asked, thinking here it comes, the axe is about to drop.

"We know what a great cook you are, Eula, and this house is plenty big enough to accommodate extra tables and chairs," Norma Mae said.

"Why extra? I got more than enough."

"You jumped the rope too soon," Verabelle said good-naturedly, turning to Sarah Ellen. "We haven't set out the plan yet."

"What plan?" Eula looked down the table at the animated faces of the ladies of the Mission Society.

"Your book with our recipes couldn't have come at a better time," Wynene said, smiling. "Eloise and I were just getting ready to present the plan to the Mission Society when they were delivered. You see, Eula, we feel it's important that you continue feeling comfortable living in a house you have served for a long time; a house that has and will continue to be your home. Of course, we need your approval."

Eloise squeezed Eula's hand again. "You are an excellent cook, Eula, and all of us try to be. There will have to be modifications made to the house, but we are all willing to aid financially and to help run the restaurant."

"Restaurant?" Eula asked with widened eyes.

"Yes," Verabelle's eyes shone with excitement, "serving the family recipes."

"You mean turn Doc and Miss Adie's house into a restaurant? But how? I don't know nothing about running a restaurant and cooking for lots of folk."

"We'll all help and serve tables, too," Hattie said. "It doesn't have to be open all the time; maybe just on the weekends or whenever you like."

"We'll help with the shopping, too," Opal added. "Of course, there will be fresh produce from the garden."

The garden: Eula had forgotten about the gardening and all its upkeep.

"How does The Family Secret sound for a name?" Sarah Ellen suggested. "Even though the library received a book, too, there are plenty of women who would enjoy a break from their daily cooking with a trip to a nearby restaurant. How much closer can you get than your own hometown?"

Eula frowned. Everything was happening so fast. First, the reading of the will; Miss Adie's signature along with Doc's, putting on paper she was his daughter; wondering how she could stay put in this, an all-white neighborhood; and now the ladies.

"Don't you see, Eula?" Wynene asked. "You can go on living here, cooking and gardening."

"What happens when I gits too old?"

"We've thought of that, too," Verabelle said. "By that time, with all the changes going on . . ."

"And although you live in a residential area, just a few doors down there's my husband's hardware store," Hattie added. "No one will dispute your license to run a part-time restaurant."

"And," Norma Mae said, "there aren't any other restaurants nearby. You won't have competition."

Eula sat back in her chair and sighed. Lawd, she thought, I has a home, my very own home. It was the first time these four walls felt like her very own.

"Have we overwhelmed you?" Eloise asked.

Eula shook her head, afraid to speak with all the emotions rippling up her throat. Months ago, she didn't know the women who sat at the kitchen table, their faces flushed with excitement like little children. Most she hadn't cared for 'cause of their thinking they were better than Miss Adie, leaving her out of their fancy doings. It was the garden. Out of a piece of barren, stony ground, more had blossomed than just flowers and vegetables.

FORTY-ONE

EULA STOOD ON THE DOORSTEP, A SMILE OF gratitude on her face as Wynene backed the car out of the driveway.

"You handled that well," Wynene congratulated Eloise, who was riding with her. "Eula knows we are still the only ones besides the lawyers to know her parentage. The rest don't suspect."

"Poor soul. Who knows what trauma she endured in the past before she came to Doc and Miss Adie? Your idea about the restaurant is an excellent idea. However, we have our work cut out for us. Hattie's husband Roy has already offered to discount anything bought from his hardware store. In fact, he's going to donate as much as possible. That will help immensely."

"And there's still plenty of work to do in the garden," Wynene added, a wistful note in her voice.

What is it?" Eloise asked. "Something is bothering you and has been for some time. Can I help?" she asked as they pulled up to Eloise's house.

Wynene sighed. "Can I have a cup of coffee? "There's something you need—no deserve—to know, and I'm afraid it will ruin our friendship."

"Nothing you do can destroy that," Eloise reassured her as they entered her house.

"Just let me get the kettle going."

"AND I WANT YOU TO MEET HIM," WYNENE concluded, setting her cup back on the coffee table. "He's a wonderful man, but then so is Jim, or I wouldn't have stayed with him as long as I have, hoping. If only . . . well, he isn't and there's nothing I can do to change that. Miss Adie's closeness to Doc and now her passing have made me realize even more how short life is. I want to be happy. Dan makes me happy. He should have been the man I chose long ago." She turned to look at her dear friend. "Now, I have ruined your day completely by shocking you."

"No, not shock or even totally surprise," Eloise said, patting her friend's hand. "I have known for some time that you weren't completely content. I thought it was because you didn't have children, something I know you have wanted for some time."

"Dan wants them. Jim never brought up the subject until recently, probably just to satisfy me. He's too bright not to suspect that more than my sister's health keeps me returning to Montgomery." The cup of coffee in her hand began to shake. "Oh, Eloise." She began to cry.

"My dear," Eloise said, taking the cup from her friend's hand, setting it on the coffee table, and putting her arms around her, "I wish you'd confided in me long ago. No need to punish yourself so. You have been unhappy for a long time.

If Dan is as wonderful a man as you are a woman, then you are both blessed, but I also feel sorrow for Jim. Sometimes, couples are simply mismatched."

"He's still a good man," Wynene said, "and very attractive. I hope he'll marry again. I didn't want to hurt him. You know that, don't you?"

"You wouldn't intentionally hurt anyone," Eloise affirmed. "This decision will obviously be hard for you as well."

"There will be talk, some of it vicious. I don't care so much for myself as I do for Jim. I don't think it will affect his position. Do you?"

"You will get the brunt of it, I suspect, something I hate for you. It's a good thing you will make a life for yourself away from here, although I already miss you."

"Dan and I will welcome your visits," Wynene said, dabbing at her face with a handkerchief. "I want you to meet each other. He has heard so much about my wonderful friend. This is so difficult particularly with Miss Adie's passing and the two of us named executors, something I can't carry out, except infrequently, under the circumstances."

"We'll call the lawyers. Perhaps someone else can be designated to take your place. When are you telling Jim?"

"I won't leave until we get the restaurant up and running for Eula."

"Then we have plenty of time to consider someone else," Eloise reassured her. "I already can think of an excellent possibility."

"WHAT IS IT?" HANK ASKED, AS OPAL STOOD staring into her bath mirror, brushing out her hair before retiring for the evening. He wrapped his arms around her gowned waist. "Still grieving over Doc?"

She buried her face into his chest.

"You're shaking." Tightening his arms around her, he led her to the bed. "Sit down and rest."

"Come sit beside me," she said, wiping at her eyes. "There's something I have to tell you."

"Sounds pretty serious," he said, sitting beside her. "Something happen with the children? They seemed pretty happy at dinner."

Inhaling deeply, she began, "I've been living a lie. My name isn't Opal St. John; it's Kylie Mae Applegate, and it doesn't come with the St. John pedigree. I grew up in a trailer with a wonderful mother who took in washing and did odd jobs for rich people while my alcoholic father squandered what little we had to support his habit, which also included periodic beatings of my mother."

Hank's eyes widened. His arm around her shoulder dropped. He opened his mouth to speak, but no sound came out.

Opal reached for his hand, but he clutched both in his lap, finally asking in an incredulous tone, "Where are your parents? Are they alive?"

"My mother died during childbirth. Miss Adie was there."

"Miss Adie?!"

"She was in nursing training. A doctor sent her into the countryside to assist with what should have been a normal birth. I was a little girl when my mother died. When we first moved here, I know Miss Adie recognized or thought she recognized me, but I put her off with the same lie I told you when we first met. I've been living with that lie ever since."

"But why didn't you tell me?" He stood up and started pacing, then stopped in front of her where she was still seated on the edge of the bed. Putting his hands on her shoulders, he stared into her eyes. "My God, Opal, or whatever, whoever you are, do you think me that shallow? I don't care about your damn pedigree; I love you, not a lot of begets and begots."

"Oh, Hank." She struggled against tears. "There's more. Please sit down."

He sat down heavily. "More? What more?"

"When I was in my teens, my father sent me to get groceries. He was drunk when I returned, more drunk than usual, which was a lot. One of the things he had me get was a knife. I was . . . " her voice quavered as she remembered the scene.

Her father was behind her. She was putting away the groceries. The knife he ordered was on the sink. A blast of his beer-laden breath fell across her neck. His thick hands grabbed her around her waist.

"No, Daddy," she screamed, "no!"

They were struggling. His mouth was on her neck as he bent her backward. A calloused hand slithered up her jean leg, reaching for the zipper.

"Somethin' yummy," he said, pushing his bulging belly against her. "Time you larned."

She closed her eyes as he shoved her against the kitchen sink. Her mother's face appeared before her. It was Christmas Eve. A small child cowered in her bed, trying not to hear the pommeling blows and tortured pleas, 'No, please . . . Oh, Hal, please . . . don't. God, please!' and the demanding, drunken cursing slurs of her father as he slammed her around the room, forcing himself on her. Kylie Mae slid deeper into the shelter of her cover, but she could still hear his frantic pants like a wild beast and the painful cries of her mother. Instead of going into the next room to somehow save her, she shivered in fear beneath the shelter of a thin blanket, her hands covering her ears.

Rough hands clutched at her panties. She opened her eyes. His flabby face pressed hard against her cheek. Yellowed eyeballs stared back at her. Rancid breath blew across her skin. Her mother's once-pretty face appeared before her. Over the years, Kylie Mae watched that wasted beauty turn into deep wrinkles, chasms of disappointment and abject fatigue. Even before her death during childbirth, her mother's hope and loveliness was long buried by an abusive, ignorant alcoholic Kylie Mae couldn't bring herself to think of as father. Murderer, she wanted to shout, but the scream that tasted of bile was captured in her throat.

"Goin' to like . . . " he mumbled, his massive body bending her further backwards.

The knife, his hunting knife, it was behind her somewhere on the counter. Desperately groping, she touched its handle. Pursing her lips rigidly, teeth bared like a wild animal, her hand closed around it firmly.

"Hate!" she yelled, the muscles in her face taut, as she forced the knife with a strength she didn't think she was capable of deeper and deeper into fatty folds of flesh "I hate you! Hate you! You destroyed my mother! You won't destroy me!"

His eyes widened in pained surprise. A large paw flapped back at her, sending her head against the sink. When she came to, he lay crumpled on a blood-slick floor, the knife embedded in his chest.

Kylie Mae sat on the edge of the bed, shaking like the child she had been, spilling out the tale of her escape and eventual haven of safety in a boardinghouse with a girl also escaping a dysfunctional past.

"Her name, the name she gave me, was Susan Wade. I ran into her Christmas shopping in Montgomery. Her real name is Alice Johnson. She doesn't know mine or what I was running from when I roomed with her, but I know now that the friendship we shared was special and I don't want to lose it. After my mother died, the only true friend I ever had was Susan—I mean Alice."

"And I don't count as a friend?"

"Oh, Hank, of course you do. I didn't mean that."

"My God, Opal, or whoever you call yourself, why in hell didn't you tell me all this before now? We made a life together, children together . . . what happened to trust?"

"You only knew Opal St. John. I was afraid you wouldn't accept Kylie Mae Applegate. Hank, I murdered my father. Doesn't that change the way you feel about me?"

"The story you just related sounds like self-defense. Why do you think you purposely did it? You said you were putting things away. He came behind you, grabbed you, was trying ... In the struggle, you said you hit your head. Your father's death could have been a tragic accident. If intentional, any jury in their right mind would consider it self-defense."

"I despised him."

"Of course you did. Any normal human being would: beating your mother, constantly putting you down. He was a drunk. Have you ever considered that he was going to rape you; perhaps even kill you?"

"You think I was wrong to run, that I should have gone to the police?"

He shook his head, stared into the distance. All these years of love and seeming trust, his wife had lived a lie. He thought he knew her, the mother of his children, the only woman he ever truly loved in his life. Placing his head in his hands, he announced, "I need some time to think." Getting up, he walked to the closed door of their bedroom. Opening it and keeping his back to her, he said drily, "I will sleep in the guest room tonight."

The door closed behind him. Kylie Mae sat staring at it. What had she done? All these years of living a lie, but they had been happy years. For the sake of renewing Susan's—Alice's—friendship, she destroyed her marriage.

FORTY-TWO

BOBBY STOOD WITH A BEMUSED GRIN IN EULA'S kitchen admiring the paint job on the chairs from Hattie's husband's hardware store. The room smelled pungently of fresh paint on the chairs stacked randomly around the room. Instead of sticking to a single color, the ladies decided to paint some green, others red, and the rest blue. The windows and screen door leading into the backyard were open to release the smell of fresh paint. The ladies cleverly divided their chores. While some chose to paint, others were busy weeding and planting in the garden. The ones in the kitchen knelt or sat on drop cloths covering the kitchen floor, their paintbrushes deftly sweeping color onto the bare wooden chairs. Bobby smiled. Their hair pulled back or covered with scarves for protection from paint, they looked as delighted as little children.

"What you think, Mr. Bobby?" Eula, her voice laced with excitement, asked.

"You'll need a shingle to hang outside to advertise the restaurant," Bobby advised. "Have you thought of a name?"

"Oh," Verabelle, a dab of green paint on her left cheek, smiled up at him, "that's been settled. "How does The Family Secret sound?"

He laughed. "Why did I even bother to ask? You ladies are always a jump ahead. Perfect! Eloise has already informed me about your cookbook and judging from her cooking, if you ladies, and I'm certain you do, dish up similar food, your restaurant will be an immediate success."

"And you get a free meal anytime you are in town," Sarah Ellen offered, turning the leg of a chair to stroke on paint. She smiled widely. "Lord, I can't recall having this much fun in a long time."

"Speaking of food, how are you faring, Eula, with no place to cook for a while?" Bobby asked.

Eula grinned. "The ladies done thought of that. Every night, one of them bring in dinner and in the morning, another comes with a big mug of coffee and cakes. I still manages for lunch."

"And you will oversee everything, I understand," Bobby said, "and stay here to maintain the house and restaurant."

"Yes, sir, that be the plan," Eula replied, adding, proudly, affection in her voice, "The ladies and I will run the restaurant together."

"Then they're in good company and capable hands, but have you thought of hiring extra help?"

"I has given it some thought, Mr. Bobby, but not until we see how successful the restaurant is. There is someone who helped me before Doc and Miss Adie took me in. She might be interested."

"Better give her a heads-up. Even with you and the ladies, there will be plenty to do and probably not enough hands. You do have a bank account?"

"Oh, yes, sir. Doc took care of all that long time ago when his health started going. The ladies has all kinds of plans. The tables will be painted in different shades to match the chairs. Miss Eloise and Miss Opal are sewing special tablecloths and napkins to match."

"Plastic not good enough? He asked with a chortle in his voice. "Sounds like a lot of extra laundry. What about a logo for the sign?"

"Hadn't thought of that," Sarah Ellen said, sitting back on her heels. "We'll have to come up with something special, and for the menus, too. We'll all take turns cooking, serving, washing up, and working in the garden. Eula will sleep in her old room to maintain the house."

"Clever minds with clever ideas," Bobby declared with admiration.

"Oh, we couldn't have done it without you," Verabelle said.

"It's a team effort," Bobby said, his cheeks flushed with her admiration. "Eula, it's clear you and the ladies are in each other's capable hands. Time to check on the garden. Let me know if there's anything I can bring you from Atlanta."

As he pulled open the kitchen's screen door and stepped out into the bright spring day, he thought of the varieties of life. If he hadn't come back to Simpsonville to meet Mrs. Parsons, *Eloise,* he wouldn't have met Eula, the Mission Society ladies, or made the exceptional friendship he shared with Eloise. He didn't realize how deeply he desired acceptance until he met her. She was like another mother, and in many ways closer to him than his own, who he felt still disdained his genetic make-up. All the ladies filled a void in his life and made him realize what a difference one life, his life, could make in another's—or in this case, in many. Also on their hands and knees in the garden were the rest of the Mission Society ladies, spading, planting, and weeding. The lushly green vegetation and colorful flora and fauna he looked upon were nothing like the neglected, wasted earth of this past year. At the time, he wasn't even certain the nutrients, hard labor, seed, and plants the ladies introduced in the garden's abandoned soil would survive from one season to another, but they more than succeeded in doing so. A labor of love: Perhaps that is what all life came down to. Even if the earth hadn't produced its bounty, it built a common bond in the lives of these women. He felt blessed to have been a part of it.

"Bobby," Eloise called, putting her gardening tools aside and standing up.

Her face was suffused with delight, the same pleasure he grew to love and expect whenever he visited, but for all its expectation it still filled him with immense warmth.

"What do you think?" she asked, spreading her gardening gloved hands toward the garden.

"It's amazing, and due to the hard work of people who poured their souls into it."

"It has given back more, much more," she said, smiling.

"I know," he agreed, wrapping his arms around her. "There will be a bounty of produce for the restaurant. Nothing tastes better than the freshest fresh. You may have to think about keeping the restaurant open for a lot longer than Fridays and Saturdays."

"How are they coming in the kitchen?"

"All happily splashed with paint."

She laughed. "Are you staying for supper?"

"I'm afraid I can't," he complained, further complimented by the regret he saw on her face. "There's lots of work waiting in Atlanta, but I promise—next visit."

"Make it soon. Perhaps the restaurant will be up and running."

"Oh, I plan to be present for that; would be hurt if you didn't ask."

"We, all of us," Opal said, still kneeling on the earth nearby, exclaimed, "want you there." A wan smile rippled across her face as she continued adding bonemeal to the crocuses that had faded.

There is definitely something wrong, Eloise thought. That's the first hint of a smile I have seen on her face all day.

Leaving her garden work temporarily, Eloise walked with Bobby to his car. Reaching up with a gloved hand, she affectionately touched his cheek. "Come back soon, son. I find myself missing you terribly when you aren't here."

Placing a hand over hers, he held it there as he looked down into her teary eyes. Son. She called him son! Even his own mother's face never displayed the emotions he saw playing across her face. Wrapping his arms around her, he said, a tremor in his voice, "And I always miss you, too."

"Call me when you get home," she said, returning his embrace, "and try to come back as soon as possible. *We* are family!"

As he drove off, he looked into his rearview mirror. Eloise was still standing there, one gloved hand waving. It felt like a blessing.

OPAL WAS SURPRISED TO FIND HANK'S CAR IN THE driveway when she arrived home. Taking a deep breath, she closed the car's door and headed toward the house. He was seated on the living room sofa.

"How's the garden?" he asked, his tone neither unfriendly nor warm.

"Full of bloom. Bobby was there. We couldn't have done it without him." She hesitated, then gathering her nerve, asked, "Why home so early?"

"Told the staff I felt ill."

"And are you?"

"Of course I am! What man wouldn't be when he finds out the woman he loves is not the person he thinks she is? I couldn't sleep last night thinking about this other woman, the one who knifed her father. Then, at work ... come sit beside me." He patted the sofa.

Taking a seat near but not too close to him on the sofa, Kylie Mae sat down, her chin tilted, spine rigid, prepared for the worst. Hank didn't look at her. He seemed focused on something ahead of him. What? she thought, waiting. Her hands, tightly clenched in her lap, felt cold. Slightly rubbing her palms together, she felt a callus beginning on her palm from working the garden.

Hank cleared his throat. He turned to look at her. "You look the same," he said.

Was he trying to be sarcastic? She raised an eyebrow.

"That's what I decided today. Whatever horrors your life held in the past, you survived. Your mother must have been a pretty amazing woman to have suffered what she did and raise someone as lovely as you." He reached across the sofa and put one hand over her still-clenched fists.

"Hank . . ." she managed to whisper, her throat still tight from fear of what she thought he was going to say.

"Come here," he said, sliding her close to him. Placing his hands on each side of her face, he looked into her eyes. "I knew long ago that you were running away from something terrible in your life, but every night I slept with a good woman and every morning I woke up to the same woman. Whatever lay in the past was past. I suppose that was naïve, but I have always loved you and I believe you. You didn't have to tell me anything about your past, but you did, and that took a great deal of courage."

"Then you aren't . . . ?"

"What? Going to leave you? I would be a fool to leave a woman with the fortitude it took as a teenager, with no resources and no family, to go out into the world and work to make a life of her own. If our children have half your courage, their lives will be blessed. My anger last night was ego-laden. I couldn't understand why you didn't trust me enough to tell me long ago, but I started thinking about the fact that you never had a man in your life you could depend on. God, you are strong!"

She placed her hands over his. "Was I wrong, Hank . . . to leave him? Should I have called the police?"

"Stop," he said, wiping away her tears. "He tried to rape you. There was a knife on the counter. You fell, hit your head."

"But, Hank, I was in a rage. I wanted him gone."

"However he died doesn't matter now. In his drunken state, you're lucky you survived. He could have killed you. You made a life for yourself, for a husband who adores you, and you brought two wonderful young people into the world who feel the same way."

"But it doesn't change what happened."

"No, but you didn't cause what happened, either. What you did was in self-defense. Now, what about this friend of yours? Does she know what happened to your father or your real name?"

"No."

"You must never tell her, but if you trust her enough to allow her into your life, then I would be happy to meet her."

"Someday, Hank, I want the children . . . I need for the children to know about their grandmother and what a wonderful woman she was."

"Let's save that discussion for some other day," he said, standing up and lifting her with him. "Right now, I want to be with the woman I love regardless of the name she calls herself."

{FORTY-THREE}

EULA STOOD IN THE FRONT YARD LOOKING UP at the colorful shingle advertising the restaurant. The men Mr. Bobby hired picked the perfect spot for the shingle to hang: at the left of the yard where it would be clearly visible to any passersby.

THE FAMILY SECRET: EULA'S KITCHEN
Garden Fresh Dining
Fresh and Fragrant
Friday-Saturday: 6 P.M. to 9 P.M.

"My, my," she said, still not quite believing she now had an excuse to remain in the home Miss Adie and Doc willed to her. She had traveled down some mighty hard roads to get here. How she wished her mama and Lila Mae could be here to share in her excitement, but who was to say they didn't know? Of course, she knew all the cooking and cleaning would be hard work, but she was used to doing both for Doc and Miss Adie plus all her nursing, and she would have plenty of help, with the ladies planning on taking turns helping in the kitchen and serving.

"Lawd," she said aloud, "I has jumped the gun."

What if the restaurant wasn't successful? She brushed aside her apprehension. Somehow she knew it would be, with all the ladies backing it and the garden in full bloom with vegetables and flowers. The living room would serve as a seating parlor in case there was a wait for the many tables placed around the dining room and in Miss Adie's former bedroom. Many of the room's windows looked out on the garden. It was difficult at first to watch as Mr. Bobby and the men he hired moved Miss Adie's bed, dresser, and nightstands up into the attic for storage. Although Miss Adie had no use for them anymore, it felt like one last goodbye, but Eula knew somehow that Doc and Miss Adie would approve. She turned to look at the garden. Its once-stark earth full of stumps of decaying plants now looked jest as it had when Miss Adie and Doc had worked the fertile earth—and in many ways, due to Mr. Bobby's planning, even better. Though Doc and Miss Adie were gone, every room held their presence. Many times, when Eula looked out on the garden, she could see them seeding, planting, and weeding as they knelt side by side.

"Finally," Eula said, looking up at the sign, "I has come home."

THE TABLES WERE DRAPED IN CALICO TO MATCH the brightly painted chairs. They were placed strategically around the rooms with just enough distance for private conversation and close enough to talk to those seated nearby. A vase of fresh flowers from the garden graced each table. Bobby donated the china and flatware, simple enough, beige with a band of light green, to add some color, but not enough to conflict with the colorful tables and chairs. The kitchen was full of the wonderful aroma of the ladies' cooking. Busy all afternoon, they tried not to bump into each other as they helped Eula bake cakes and cook garden-fresh vegetables ready to be reheated when the guests arrived. The ladies decided to prepare two main meat dishes, meatloaf, "'cause most men want beef," and a chicken casserole, "for women who prefer to eat lighter."

"We might have to start offering another dish," Opal said, an apron tied around her waist, an oven mitt on her right hand.

"Goodness, dear," Verabelle turned to smile at her as she shredded lettuce for salads. "You're being optimistic. I'm just hoping we get one room full."

"Word spreads in a small town," Eloise added. "If the cooking's good, they'll come."

"Lawd, do you think . . . ?" Eula raised an eyebrow.

"That it's going to be successful? Yes, I do," Eloise said, bending over, fork in hand, to check the tenderness of the chicken cooking in the oven. "It's about ready to come out and be diced for the casserole," she informed. "Give it a few minutes, more or less. Now, Eula, take that worried look off your face," she advised, smiling.

"I agree with Eloise," Opal said. "All morning, working in the garden, I noticed cars slowing down to look at the sign. Most of them were women. In this nearly summer heat, they will want a reprieve from daily cooking."

"I'm getting hungry," Hattie added, "just smelling this good cooking."

"You mean The Family Secret," Norma Mae corrected, chuckling with a contagious laugh that spread through the kitchen, with the wonderful aroma of food extracting even a somewhat nervous giggle from Eula.

Who would have thought, Eula grinned, that Miss Adie's book would have brought the Mission Society ladies together cooking in the kitchen and laughing good-naturedly over their carefully guarded family recipes.

"It's really going to be all right," Wynene said, patting Eula on the back.

"I do believe, Miss Wynene," Eula agreed, "it already is."

"Let's have a taste test," Opal suggested.

"We have plenty of time before the guests arrive," Sarah Ellen added, hopeful there would be guests.

It didn't take much encouragement. The ladies grabbed plates to dish up small portions of the hot food when it came out of the oven to sit down in warm compatibility and sample their carefully prepared food. They had just enough time to clean their dishes and straighten up the kitchen as they nervously checked the kitchen clock. With the last dish put away, they changed into fresh clothing and aprons. Eula kept pacing back and forth to peek out the living room windows, checking for parked cars. She was soon joined by Opal, Eloise, and Wynene as the rest of the ladies checked on the table settings.

"It's going to be all right," Opal reassured Eula, giving her arm a pat.

A car cruising down the street made them catch their breath. It slowed, but then drove on. Eloise let out a long sigh. Wynene checked her watch. The ladies in the kitchen were huddled near the kitchen door waiting for a signal to fill the glasses with iced tea, sweetened with just the right amount of sugar and lemon. Another car coming from the opposite direction on the street brought a silent prayer from Opal. The car slowed and then parked at the curb. It was joined by three other cars.

"Well now," Eloise said, letting out a long sigh. "I'll tell the kitchen *we have guests.*"

Soon both sides of the street were packed with cars and the noise level in the living room sounded like a family reunion as townspeople greeted each other. The ladies waiting on the seated tables hustled back and forth taking orders while Opal and Wynene stood at the front door welcoming the guests.

"What a pretty view," several ladies admired, gazing out the window at the garden. "It looks like an Eden."

"Thank you," Wynene replied, smiling with pride. "It's a project of the Mission Society, but its original plan was that of the town doctor and his wife, Miss Adie. Now that they have passed away, the restaurant's main cook is Eula, who nursed them. She still keeps up the house while the Mission Society ladies plan, help cook, and wait tables. I hope you enjoy the food and come back bringing your friends."

The house hummed with laughter and conversation.

"This meatloaf is the best I have ever eaten," commented one husband to Hattie as she refilled his iced tea. "Not that I don't like yours, dear," he added quickly, giving his wife an apologetic glance, to which she replied, "It's a treat not to be cooking and I agree it's wonderful. Since you like it so much, let's make this a regular outing."

"Do you recommend the Strawberry Souffle or the Dream Pie?" a couple asked Sarah Ellen as she lifted their licked-clean plates.

"They're both delicious, but the Dream Pie is a favorite of mine," Sarah Ellen boasted of her recipe. "However, you can't go wrong with either. Why don't you order the Dream Pie," she suggested to the gentleman, "and you the other," she addressed the lady. "That way, you can sample each other's."

"Sounds like bees building a hive out there," Eula said, busily dishing up food as several of the ladies washed dishes, trying not to trip each other up in the crowded kitchen.

"The living room and screened porch are packed with guests waiting for an empty table," Norma Mae said. "Eula, you may have to build on if this keeps up. You have a success."

"*We* have a success," she said, a broad smile lighting up her face.

FORTY-FOUR

THE LADIES, FEET SMARTING, WERE STILL IN THE kitchen washing up at nearly eleven o'clock. Though fatigued, their emotions soared. The restaurant so far was a success. Many of the clients left happy, saying they were bringing friends and more family on the next visit. Many, particularly the women, and most of the men stated that they wanted to make it a weekly outing.

"You ladies go on home," Eula protested as they kept bringing in tablecloths, napkins, and glassware for cleaning. "You has to be tired."

"But happy," they said in unison.

"Did you see Jeannette Blight's face?" Verabelle asked, giggling. "She looked like an old rooster with its feathers ruffled, jealous as hell. Wanted to know why she didn't have forewarning; said she would have run an article in the town paper."

"Then play on that," advised Sarah Ellen, "although I think the folks who ate here tonight will do plenty of advertising, and if she wants to help serve or whatever, let her. We could certainly use more hands."

"Eula, if this keeps up, we might have to tack on another night during the week."

"Lawd," Eula exclaimed, "if your feet ache like mine, Miss Sarah Ellen, all you want right now is to hit the sack, not think about tacking on anything." She put a hand over her mouth to cover a yawn, then grinned widely. "It turned out right good, didn't it?"

"Better than good," Opal agreed.

Finally with all the dishes, pots, and pans cleaned and put away, the ladies packed up the extra clothes they'd brought, embracing Eula at the front door and informing her they would be working their garden shifts in the following week.

"I won't be able to assist as much in the future," Wynene said as she and Eloise pulled away from the curb in Wynene's car.

"You're ready to tell?" Eloise asked. "I'm sorry, my dear. Is there anything I can do? Have you thought about the will and your duties as an executor?"

"I haven't talked to Opal yet, but I will have her act on my behalf except where it requires my attendance. Oh, Eloise ..."

"Are you certain this is what you really want?"

"Absolutely, although I dread hurting Jim. But I can't go on living a lie pretending I'm happy when I'm not."

"If you need a place to stay before you leave, call me."

"I will. Of all the people I'll miss, I'll miss you more than anyone."

"Promise me," Eloise said sympathetically, when they reached her house, "that you'll call and let me know how it went and when you plan to leave. If you want to come over, regardless of the time of night or day, then just come."

"I promise."

When she pulled up in front of her house, Wynene sat

in the driveway looking at the home that had been hers for years. She would miss it and the friends she had made, but no one more than Eloise. Although her marriage was unsatisfactory, she would also miss Jim and always have tender feelings for him and respect for his devotion to his congregation. She dreaded hurting him, but she knew she couldn't go on living a lie. The lights were on in Jim's study when she entered the house.

"Hello," he called.

He was per usual seated at his desk even though the hour was late. "Must have been a success; you're home so late."

"We hadn't anticipated that many for a first night. Couples were waiting in the living room and on the porch for a vacant table. Even the men want to make it a weekly night out."

Cocking his head, he looked up into her eyes with such an astute and grievous expression, she lowered her eyes. A lamentable silence spread between them. "What is it, Wynene?"

"It's been a long day, Jim," she replied.

"If it was that much of a success, your face isn't registering it. Is there something we should talk about?"

"Yes," she sighed with a note of regret.

He closed his eyes and grimacing, nodded. Pushing his chair back and standing up, but not approaching her, he asked blandly, "Who is he?"

She hadn't anticipated the question. Jim knew, had probably always suspected.

"Someone I dated long before we met."

"And you," he paused, took a deep breath and continued, "love him?"

"Yes, I do. I'm sorry, but I do."

"I see." He sat down heavily at his desk. "There will be a

divorce," he said, anger in his voice, "and much gossip ... the town . . . my congregation."

"The church, the town, they won't let you go. They," she paused, "love you so."

"What?" he looked up at her, one eyebrow lifted. "Do you honestly believe I am considering what they think of me?" Placing his elbows on his knees, he put his face in his hands, an action that hurt her more than if he had struck her. "Do you really think so little of me? I'm worried about you, your reputation!"

Kneeling beside his chair, she placed a hand on top one of his.

"Did you ever love me?" he asked, placing his other hand on top of hers.

"Yes," she answered honestly, "or I wouldn't have stayed as long as I have, but our agendas are not the same."

"Where are you going?"

"To Montgomery."

"He must be a good man to deserve you," he stated so sincerely the words hurt more than any anger could.

"And so are you, Jim."

"Will I see you again? Is there some remote possibility we can at least be friends?"

"Of course, that's what we have always been."

"I wish it were enough," he said sadly.

"So do I," she replied honestly.

"IT WON'T BE THE SAME WITHOUT YOU AROUND," Opal said after listening to Wynene's story."

"Then do you mind taking on the responsibility of being an executor when I'm not here? There will be, of course, some legality, paperwork, to process through the lawyers."

"No, the only matters that concern me are yours and, of course, Jim's welfare."

"We're parting as friends, but it's still more painful than I thought. I was a very young woman when we married."

"If there is one thing I have learned from life," Opal said, looking at her friend with sympathy, "it's always try to remember the best of what is past. Don't worry about Eula or the restaurant."

"I'll check in on her whenever I can and, of course, on Jim. He doesn't think he will ever remarry, but he will and I pray to someone who deserves him."

"You mean more compatible; you have always been very deserving."

"Thank you for that," Wynene said, managing a smile. "You know, before we became involved in Miss Adie and Eula's life and the garden, I didn't really know you, Opal, or most of the other ladies. Our relationships were matters of surface. It took a barren piece of earth to bring us together. Kneeling side by side, getting our hands dirty, uprooting weeds, taking pleasure in transforming a forgotten piece of ground into a fertile Eden of greenery and color has brought all of us closer."

"Sometimes," Opal said with a chuckle, "I felt like a little girl again making mud pies. You're right, working side by side has produced more than fruit and flower. Maybe we were all like that piece of land waiting for someone or something to bring some greater design into our lives."

{FORTY-FIVE}

EULA FINISHED PUTTING AWAY THE DISHES from another successful evening. As word of the restaurant spread through the town and surrounding areas, the living room and porch continued to overflow with guests willing to wait for a table.

"We'll *have* to build on that extension to the house if this continues," Hattie commented earlier that evening as she carried a tray of empty plates into the kitchen for washing.

"Miss Hattie," Eula, her eyes wide, exclaimed, "I don't have that kind of money!"

"Not to worry, Roy will be happy to donate supplies and the carpenters."

"We can all divvy up enough to get it done," Sarah Ellen said, adding, "Don't forget my husband is bank president. Goodness, for what we know, folk in these parts might want to invest in a share if it continues to be this successful."

"Who would have known, Doc," Eula said putting away clean dishes, "that thanks to you, Miss Adie, and the ladies, I not only has a home, I has a restaurant and a successful business. It took a lot of hard roads to get here, but here I be."

She thought of Miss Wynene and what she told her earlier that evening about her leaving and how Miss Opal would be executor when she wasn't there. She was surprised and flattered that Miss Wynene confided in her. She prayed Miss Wynene would be happy. She knew from experience that happiness was a hard thing to come by. Every life, Eula said to herself, has a secret hidden away in that person's soul. Look at her life. Who would have dreamed she would find her father, Miss Adie, and have this home, a secure place? When had Doc told Miss Adie? Miss Adie never spoke of it to her and never gave her a wayward glance. She simply took her in and accepted her as if she were her own.

Sitting down at the table to get off her aching feet and have an evening cup of tea, she could feel Doc's presence.

"Happy?" he would ask, as he did so often right after he first found her.

Then he would reach across the table and take her hand in his, squeezing it, affection in his eyes. Instinctively, she lay her hand on the table and looked across it to where he used to sit. He was *there,* would always be there, and everywhere she looked for him. He had loved her mother and he had loved Miss Adie. She no longer blamed him for that. He had also loved her deeply. She was the one responsible for cutting off their relationship. She often wondered what would have happened if her mother had lived. Would he continue their relationship, keeping it secret?

"Don't go back there," Doc's familiar words floated in silence across the table. "Just know that I treasured her."

Eula had never asked him if he loved Miss Adie in the same way he loved her mother. She loved a man once who wasn't worth the trouble it took to throw out the trash. What would her life have been like if she hadn't run away with him? Taking a sip of tea, she shook her head. That part of her life was a mistake. She knew her father never felt that way about her mother. She thought of the night she and Doc sat on the front porch in their rockers watching firefly flicker and listening to cricket strum—the night he first told her about plans for her future. "Summer lanterns," he called the fireflies. What else did he say, something about an Indian chief and the meaning of life?

"Eula," his voice called to her across the years.

She closed her eyes. The sound of their rockers creaking on the old porch floorboards joined cricket chitter-chatter.

"What is life?" Doc said in his mellow voice. "It is the flash of a firefly in the night, the breath of a buffalo in the wintertime, the little shadow that runs across the grass and loses itself in the sunset."

On that night, she felt like a little girl again in the embrace of her father.

"Who would have thought, Doc," she said to his empty kitchen chair, "that rumors of Miss Adie's book would lead to the ladies getting to know and love her, and then Miss Eloise, her young friend, and the ladies bringing back your and Miss Adie's garden? All those years ago, I took a sorry road with a no-account man, but it brought me home to you and Miss Adie after lots of shadows and sunsets in between."

Through the open kitchen windows came the sweet scent of honeysuckle like a perfumed promise. Time seemed to pass more quickly. April had slipped silently into May. Soon it would be June. Jest yesterday, she spied the rapid flitter-flutter of a hummer checking out an empty feeder left from the preceding summer. Starting up the restaurant, she clean forgot it was past time to boil water and get out the sugar canister to mix the nectar they were seeking, although the garden flowers would draw many. Mr. Bobby and the ladies, knowing that the hummers preferred the colors, red, orange, and pink, had planted in addition to the honeysuckle already growing profusely about the house, other bell-shaped blossoms, fuchsia and red salvia. Earlier, she spied a swallowtail butterfly flitting through the yard toward the brilliant orange blossoms on the backyard's butterfly weed. This was the time of year Doc and Miss Adie enjoyed most, jest warm enough but not too hot to work the garden early in the morning. On the early evening air came the nightly calls of finches and Carolina wrens, or was it the haunting melody of mockingbirds copying the other birds? *I'm here*, they seemed to say.

"I'm, here, too," she called back, thinking: "Here" is called home.

Birdsong and perfumed air drew her to the garden. Slipping off her apron and hanging it over a kitchen chair, she opened the kitchen door onto the downy pastel green of late spring. Wave after wave of deep blue flowers, vinca, covered the shady roll of the backyard like a carpet. A barn swallow skimmed the hazy air looking for flies and other insects. Startled by her presence, a wren nesting in an eave of the house flew over her head and past banks of azaleas, hibiscus, and spotted geraniums.

Carried before her on the early evening air was the garden's heady perfume. The herb garden smelled deliciously fragrant of chives, basil, rosemary, and lavender. She would make lavender sachets to surprise the ladies, who were busy earlier setting up a cold frame where they were starting cauliflower, Brussels sprouts, and celery for a fall garden. More butterfly favorites, cosmos, dwarf marigold, lantana, zinnia, and glove amaranth, were in full bloom. Orange and yellow tulips were ruffled-skirted. Peach trees full of beautiful pink flowers were the same color as the blush splashed on the early evening sky. The dewy earth gave rise to the fresh scent of corn ripening on its stalks and green beans, new potatoes, snow peas and snap beans, eggplant, spinach, and zucchini. She would have blossoms of fruit and vegetables plucked fresh from the earth to cook and can. Multihued roses added to the bouquet of scents. Fireflies like fairy lanterns were rising from the ground, drifting through the cooling of the evening, flickering their play of passion as they looked for mates.

It all still seemed like a miracle. All these years, the earth lay barren with nothing to show for Miss Adie and Doc's hard work but dead stalks. It took a bunch of strangers who had never set foot on the land to bring it back to life, and all because of Miss Adie's book. She shook her head. Life did have its strange twists and turns. Town ladies she never met standing on the doorstep with all those casseroles and Miss Eloise's young friend, Mr. Bobby, led to this fertile garden and a restaurant. And all 'cause she came up with some far-flung idea of a book about the town to give Miss Adie something to do 'sides grieving away, staring out the window at a piece of stubby earth.

"Lawd," she said, looking up at the star-flooded sky, "you has a fine sense of humor."

All those years of wandering, she lost her sense of self. Being in this house was like being at home, not the one she left long ago when she was still jest a child, but one found, a miracle waiting for her broken spirit and battered body. She sat down on a garden bench the ladies bought to listen to the quiet. Beneath that star-studded sky lay a piece of earth, once barren and wasted, waiting jest as she had for the touch of human kindness as healing as Doc's touch on the injured and the ill. An image of Doc as a young man twirling her mother in his arms on an early summer evening appeared in the shadows of the night. She could hear their laughter echoing from the past. Her father's life had been blessed with two fine women. However great her disappointment, Miss Adie forgave him and took her in, accepting her as if she was her own. A shadow flickered in the early evening, bringing an image of her kneeling in the garden, her basket of garden tools beside her. Her handprints and Doc's were on this earth.

Eula stood up and walked past bushes of blue indigo and candytuft, stepping carefully between rows of flowers and vegetables into the center of the garden, where she could view the beginnings of a nearly full moon. The air was perfumed with the dewy scent of flowers, vegetables, and the richness of the earth. The last of the birds had gone to nest. Firefly flicker twinkled. A breeze blew over her. In the softness of the early evening as she looked up into the heavens, she heard the soft footfall of Doc, Miss Adie, and her mother as they stepped beside her. The earth remembered, and she would never forget.

TRUSSVILLE PUBLIC LIBRARY
201 PARKWAY DRIVE
TRUSSVILLE, AL 35173
(205) 655-2022
4

CPSIA information can be obtained at www.ICGtesting.com
Printed in the USA
LVOW10s2005080415

433775LV00007B/992/P

9 781630 264963